GW00469767

A River of Retribution

By

Clive Ridgway

ISBN:
ISBN: 9798446812042

DEDICATION

For Fiona

ACKNOWLEDGEMENTS

My thanks go to all those who helped me and put up with me not doing what I should have been doing when I was doing this. Also thanks go to those that read and gave me advice, suggestions and encouragement, namely Rémy, Lesley, Katy, Dave, Suzi, John and Mark.

Not forgetting my long-suffering wife and my son — they've had to put up with me.

FORWARD

At the back of this book, there is a short dictionary of St Giles' canting language as used by some of the characters.

In the meantime, travel back in time to:

London, 1741.

CHAPTER 1

Just as the last ebb of light slipped away, I entered the narrow alleyway, leading from Monmouth Street to a large court of decaying buildings. The harsh aroma of excrement, urine and decomposing offal rose up from where my boots disturbed the slick surface of slime, assaulting my nostrils and catching in my throat. I traversed the alley and came to the unused doorway, the entrance deep in impenetrable gloom.

The new Church of St Giles in the Fields loomed ahead as if keeping watch, whilst around me, rickety tenements grew, their facades crumbling, their timbers distressed, covered in grime and soot. Rats scampered, their scratchy claws scoring the cobbles beneath the slime as they hurried away.

Scuffling footsteps and voices approached from Monmouth Street, so I eased into the doorway and observed, as three men, senseless in alcohol, lurched by just a few inches from me, a bottle passing between them, their voices loud and belligerent, bemoaning their lack of funds and the injustice of it all. A few steps later they were out of the alley and disappearing into the crowd ahead.

There were perhaps seventy or eighty people gathering, of both sexes and all ages, most in a state of inebriation. The whores and their pimps, the thieves and the murderers, as well as the innocents, all assembling for the gin-fuelled entertainment. I could see a brewhouse full of customers who would undoubtedly pour out as soon as things began, adding their numbers to the throng.

I leant my shoulder against the wall, wincing a little as I sensed the cold slime penetrating the sleeve of my jacket. I then watched the bare-footed urchins playing in the mire of the yard in their threadbare clothes, the men and women yelling their protests as they waited impatiently, though admittedly, I too was eager for things to begin.

Pitch-dipped rushlights illuminated the yard as the dusk turned to night, the flames spitting embers with the dark acrid smoke rising above, the eerie flickering glow casting a sombre light on the gathering. Noise rose as shadows danced on the faces of the crowd, some angry, some bemused, most expectant with anticipation.

A heightened murmur spread amongst those present as I watched the men begin to form the crowd so that an open circle appeared in the middle, they shouted and waved sticks and cudgels to encourage those too drunk to comply quickly enough. Then on the far side, a path formed as one of the combatants pushed through to the accompaniment of raucous cheers from the crowd. After a few seconds, the other arrived, this time to little enthusiasm, only a few doughty individuals calling encouragement.

The first to enter the ring turned and regarded the opponent with a sneer of contempt, a squeezing of the fists and then spitting a gob of phlegm into the muck on the ground.

Money changed hands in quick order as the crowd weighed up the odds: who would win and how long it would take.

I had more than a passing interest in the outcome; having largely instigated the fight in the first place, I wanted to make sure that no serious injury occurred — at least concerning one of the fighters.

At nineteen years old, Kitty Marham already had more than

her fair share of strife. A slender but curvy girl of medium height she had long light-auburn hair, presently coiled and fixed beneath her cap. Straight white teeth were behind soft sensual lips, her skin clear, smooth and unmarked, her eyes green as if polished emeralds. A pretty girl, attempting to take a stance to rid herself of the smear of accusation. She took quick breaths and licked her dry lips as she looked around.

In opposition, Poll Gordon, a squat, obese woman in her thirties. Poll wore life's woes as part of her being; she had lousy brown hair, lank and unkempt beneath her greasy cap, a few brown stubs for teeth and a pudgy pockmarked face, her eyes just two thin slits of dark malice.

Poll snarled at Kitty, who just stared back in silence, until the men with the sticks signalled that the time to begin had arrived.

I felt my heart begin to beat just a little faster as Kitty removed her cap and then slipped off her jacket, leaving her standing in just her shift and stomacher, with a ragged green fustian skirt. Poll Gordon took off her coat and I could see she wore just a tired leather stay, with a skirt of indeterminable colour, the fat of her arms billowing like sails. Shorter than Kitty, Poll certainly made up for it in girth.

The two women held out their hands for the pennies, their fists closing around the coins and holding them firm; the fight would continue until one of them either dropped a penny, received a knockout blow or simply relented and gave up. The penny there to prevent them scratching and clawing or gouging at the eyes and mouth.

Kitty stared at the circle of onlookers, her head turning as she took them all in; whether she searched for me or not, I did not know but then her face set in grim determination. Poll Gordon must have weighed twice her weight but that would make her slow and cumbersome, so Kitty should have the advantage in speed and agility. I took a deep breath as Poll bobbed forward in a semi-crouch; her fists held out before her.

The crowd gave a raucous cheer, which seemed to spur Poll into action and she launched herself across the divide towards Kitty, who just reacted in time, raising her arms protectively and bracing for the assault.

Punches rained down on Kitty's arms as she sunk her head into her shoulders and I winced at the speed and strength of the attack. Poll Gordon surprised even me but then Kitty managed to take a step sideways and twisted on her heels and Poll carried on past with the momentum. I saw Kitty eye her warily as she stopped and slowly turned around, breathing heavily. I surmised that Poll had spent much of her energy in that first assault, hoping that Kitty would be overwhelmed and it would all be over quickly, resistance all but gone but she assumed wrongly. Kitty raised her fists then took up a guarding stance as she had seen the men do and waited for Poll to try again. I had to admire the girl, as she tried to think, conserve her energy, wait for an opportunity and not rush into things as Poll had done. Poll readied herself again by taking a ragged gasp and narrowing her eyes, her enormous chest heaving.

The crowd then pressed closer together and my view became blocked. Uttering an oath, I raised myself onto my toes to see over the heads but that did not work and I could not just wait for the outcome, I had to see, I had to witness it myself. Leaving my place of concealment, I walked forward into the yard; fortunately, my clothes fitted in and the smell from the doorway had seeped into them, lending them authenticity. Lurching drunkenly, I joined the crowd at the back, pushing a little, straining to see.

'Steady friend,' warned a man to my left as I bumped into him.

I gave an apology and grinned. 'Couldn't see,' I explained, which seemed sufficient as he turned back to the fight, ignoring me.

The woman to my right dug her elbow into my ribs and handed me a bottle; the folk of the slums may be poor but they are generous to a fault when a crowd gathers for a spectacle. The bottle may have only cost a few pennies but it passed from hand to hand around the crowd and it would be churlish of me not to indulge, so I upended it, letting most of the gin dribble down my chin and onto my coat and then passed it on to my friend on the left. I thanked the lady profusely and continued to watch as a small gap had opened up in front. At least I had a better view than from the doorway and the air had improved too, but only slightly.

Poll had not yet launched her second attack as I settled into my place but I did not have to wait long before she did. Fists flying, Poll went for Kitty again but Kitty had anticipated this and sidestepped before the punches landed, snaking out a fist herself, straight onto Poll's unprotected nose. Poll bellowed in anger and renewed her windmilling, rushing towards Kitty and forcing her to step back. A blow caught Kitty high on the cheekbone and then a second smacked down on the top of her head as Poll pushed forward again, sensing a victory as her weight began to count. She forced Kitty to retreat until she came up against the first rank of the people, who stood their ground, preventing the women from going further, shoving them back into the ring, back into combat.

I could see Kitty breathing hard as she contended with the onslaught but being young and lithe, she had nimble feet, so managed to dance away from Poll who now needed a rest, her hands bracing on her thick thighs as she bent to draw ragged gasps of breath. She looked as if she had had enough already.

Kitty saw her opportunity and quickly closed the gap, rapidly throwing two quick punches, catching Poll on the eye and one on her chest.

Poll yelled again and stormed forward, the crowd urging her on, the drunken comments lewd and brash; even the children joining in.

Kitty defended the next attack easily and swung a well-aimed punch into Poll's mouth, loosening one of her few remaining teeth. The woman grunted as her chest heaved up and down and she spat out a few drops of blood as she eyed her more nimble adversary, who now skipped agilely away.

Poll took a deep breath, which had the unfortunate effect of putting too much pressure on her tired stays; they gave, ripping along the sweat-soaked rotting seams. She did not even consider her modesty, just wriggled out of them and cast them aside.

'You gonna smuvver 'er wiv yer heavers now, Poll?' cried a voice from the crowd, which resulted in a wave of laughter.

Poll ignored it all, still struggling to catch her breath. She eased from side to side, hands on hips, the rolls of fat undulating as if a sea-swell, her enormously heavy blue-veined breasts swinging in a double pendulum.

'Coz when you done wiv 'er, I'll give a few pennies to get me head between 'em.'

Another bout of laughter greeted this, which, I am sad to relate, I joined in.

'Wot's going on?' asked a latecomer to my right.

I turned my head but fortunately, someone else answered.

'You means yer don't know?'

A shake of the head indicated that he did not.

'Well, Poll's man, Abe, wanted a bit of Kitty there.'

'Abe? I 'eard 'e got taken.'

'Too right 'e did. Poll's blaming that there Kitty. She reckons 'e wouldn't have got pulled if 'e hadn't gone after 'er. By all accounts, she got the chink but he got nuffing, now she wants the chink back. Kitty denies it all, so we got this,' he added, pointing a finger.

'Reckon that's true?'

I watched the man shrug his shoulders. 'Kitty or Poll?'

'Poll.'

'Nah, Kitty wouldn't suffer a touch from the likes of Abe, nor take 'is chink neither.'

Both men turned their attention back to the fight and I felt pleased that the word had got about.

'Bitch,' screamed Poll.

I too then turned my attention back to the fight, just as Poll launched yet another frenzied attack on Kitty.

The fists rained in and Kitty raised her arms again, trying to block the blows and protect her face but I could tell the attack had lost the impetus of before; Kitty seemed to realise this too as she took a step forward to cramp Poll, giving her no room to swing her arms. Kitty grimaced and heaved the massive weight of the woman away from her, allowing a space to develop. Poll seemed glad for the opportunity of another rest and bent forward, taking great lungfuls of air as she eyed her opponent menacingly.

Kitty decided to go on the offensive now, she would not allow Poll to catch her breath so took a few paces forward and swung a fast right hand straight into Poll's face, right on the nose again and heard a grunt of pain as a reward. The big woman stepped back trying to get away from the stinging fists but backed into the crowd of men who took advantage of the opportunity to paw at her chest. Poll screamed blue murder at them and swung her elbows back in indignation, catching one with a sharp blow. She then stared hard at Kitty again before rushing forward but I was pleased to see Kitty go into a crouch to make herself smaller, keeping her steady eyes on Poll.

I watched and my apprehension rose as Poll came in but I should have known that Kitty had a plan; she exploded out of her crouch with a snap of her legs, her head arrowing in to the jaws of the big woman and then came a sickening crunch as the head hit home.

Poll grunted and then collapsed as if a sack of grain, unconscious before hitting the ground, the pennies tumbling from her fists.

The crowd moaned and inadvertently a whoop of delight came to my lips. I looked around at the faces then clamped my lips tight, realising that most had lost their money, but there were also nods of appreciation at the way Kitty had won.

I watched Kitty rub her head as she gazed down at Poll, a satisfied expression on her face but not one of gloating triumph. A man approached and pressed a half-crown into her hand: the winners' purse. Another man returned her jacket and cap and then the ring suddenly filled with people, most gathering around Poll and shaking their heads ruefully at the recumbent woman who lay on her back, her arms loose by her sides, part-deflated bladders hanging down her ribs. The men continued to stare at the groaning half-naked woman as consciousness returned.

The few people who bet on the winner collected their money and hurried off wearing broad grins, presumably to spend their new-found wealth on gin and ale, the others beginning to melt away into the dark alleys and ramshackle streets to drown their sorrows.

Swaying unsteadily, I began to push my way through, pulling my battered hat low down over my eyes. My drunken gait caught Kitty's eye and she looked up towards me. I stumbled over to her and fished about in my pocket for a few loose coins. 'Wot'll it take?' I asked, slurring my speech. 'Fer a little time wiv the winner?'

Kitty studied me for a few seconds. 'More than you can afford,' she said, dismissively.

'I might surprise you, girl. Half-a-crown's the going rate fer a street-girl like you, I'll give three shillings and it would've been more if it weren't fer that bruise on yer eye.'

Kitty's hand went up to her face, touching the swelling around her eye where Poll's punch caught her. She thought for a moment and then nodded her agreement at the proposed transaction.

'Good. You'd better be worth it,' I said, leering at her.

'I'm sure I can give satisfaction, sir.'

Kitty slipped her arms into her jacket and placed her cap back on her head, her hair dishevelled from the fight and gave a contemptible last look at Poll who attempted to roll over in order to get up. Her arm slipped into mine as we began to head across the yard, the folk watching us with interest and trying to eavesdrop on our conversation.

'You got a libken close by?' I asked, taking a stumble.

Kitty nodded and flashed me a knowing look from her good eye, a hint of a smile touching the corners of her mouth.

We headed down the alley towards Monmouth Street, the men following giving me suggestions as to what they would be doing to Kitty if they had thought quickly enough and made her an offer. I surmised that a little bit of jealousy fuelled their comments.

Kitty clung tightly to me as we progressed, me still keeping up my drunken lurching, her doing her best to keep me upright. We crossed Broad Street, somehow avoiding a speeding carriage, the driver of which hurled a string of offensive expletives at us, then we headed up the noisy and bustling Dyot Street, to her lodging house. She led me up the stairs, holding my hand to guide me in the darkness, then up another set of stairs to her room.

She opened the door and let out a great long sigh of relief as she stepped inside. I followed in and waited by the door until she had lit the candle, giving us a little weak light. I pushed the door closed and then quickly studied her home: I could see a sparsely furnished room; a crude bed with just a thin straw mattress upon it, a neatly folded blanket which had seen better days; a small table with a single chair next to the fire grate, a few cooking implements alongside; a set of shelves lay against the wall, having at some time fallen down, a few personal bits adorning it together with a plate and bowl. An old chest completed the furniture. Apart from the damp, the mildew and the newssheets and rags stuffed into the broken panes of the window, it was a clean tidy room. She turned around and sat on the edge of the bed, took off her cap and regarded me as she shook out her hair.

'How are you?' I asked, taking off my hat and moving over to the chair to sit down. I tried to keep the concern out of my voice as I looked at her battered face, which must have been painful.

'I'll live. I ache a little but I suppose that's to be expected. She turned out to be a bit quicker than I thought.'

'I said that you would be taking a risk.'

'You did but we both know I had to do it.'

I acknowledged the wisdom of that. 'It will mean no recriminations; it's all done now so you do not need to look over your shoulder anymore. She challenged you, you fought, she lost.'

She nodded and then pulled a face as her hand went up to her head and found the bump that resulted from the connection with Poll's chin. 'Ouch,' she said, wincing.

I stood up and took a step over to examine her head and found a lump, just above the hairline. 'It's not too bad but will be a bit tender for a day or so.'

'Yes, but this will take a little longer, I think,' she said, pointing to her eye.

'It will, but not by much.'

'Maybe, but I have to work.'

I shook my head. 'Not for a while at least. '

'I don't work, I don't eat,' she protested. 'You know what it's like for a girl like me.'

I felt myself sigh. I still had my hand on her head and I let it slide down so that my palm rested on her cheek and I felt her press into it. She looked up at me with a soft eye, the other now closed and puffy. Kitty acted as a lure to catch a murderer: Abe Gordon, Poll's husband. He had killed Peggy, a young street-girl, knifed her when she threatened to go to the magistrate. At thirteen years of age, Peggy had only just begun to learn the trade.

'I'll stay away from Covent Garden; I still can't face working there at the moment.'

'Then don't work there, you have no need and you need to recover.'

Kitty smiled at me. 'Thank you but men rarely look at my face; they're more interested in other parts of me.'

'More fool them,' I said, looking at her. 'It's all done now; Poll will not be after you for the money Abe supposedly paid you.'

She laughed without humour. 'That scared me, enticing him away like that. It did cross my mind that you might not be there; that I might end up like Peggy with a knife in my ribs.'

'I wouldn't let you down; maybe you should learn to trust a little.'

'It's hard, trusting, especially in my game. Peggy trusted Abe Gordon and look what happened to her.'

'Think on the man who saw Abe knife Peggy. He said he would speak and he did. We are not all bad, Kitty.'

'I know, I'm just feeling a little down, is all. I trust *you*,' she said, with a true smile.

'I'm glad for that, at least.'

'If I hadn't found you in The Brown Bear, Peggy wouldn't have got justice. That watchman said that they wouldn't look too hard for the murderer of a street-girl, they're two a penny and another dead jade didn't mean that much.'

'The sad thing is, he is right. The magistrates don't as a rule but you found out his name in that tavern in Seven Dials, and when I took him in, they had to act. You got him away from his friends and I did the easy bit.'

Abe Gordon soon found himself in the roundhouse, shortly after that he visited Bow Street, and then he discovered the joys of Newgate, awaiting the sessions at the Old Bailey.

Kitty had seen the murder from the shadows but did not need to tell her story to the court, the man who saw it all did and Abe Gordon received a guilty verdict; but Poll searched for the whore who led Abe away, blaming her for everything, eventually finding out her name. She said she just wanted the money back that Abe had paid her and intended to make Kitty's life hell until she did. I suggested the fight to end it all as I had heard that she just wanted revenge; the money did not in fact matter to her.

'He will still swing, won't he?' Kitty asked, referring to Abe.

'Soon, the next hanging session, if he doesn't die of gaol fever first.'

'Good, it's what he deserves; I owe that to Peggy.'

A brief moment of silence occurred as Kitty looked at me and then she stood up and placed her hand in my hair, brushing out the tangles with her fingers, then she gently touched my nose, my cheek and then my lips, her fingers warm.

'You are a handsome man and you promised me three shillings,' she said, nearly in a whisper.

I knew women generally found me a man of pleasing looks, with my long dark hair, dark brooding eyes - their description, not mine - with a pleasing figure of proportion and just thirty-two years of age

'I did,' I replied. 'Only you do not have to earn it.'

'Oh,' she said and I detected a little bit of disappointment.

I shook my head. 'No,' I said, touching her face again. 'You have already earned your three shillings, and more besides.'

I found some coins in my pocket, counted out the three shillings, and put them on the table. I reached into my inside pocket and pulled out a pouch and put that next to the shillings. 'Twenty guineas,' I said. 'Some of your wages, for helping to catch a murderer.'

'What?' She exclaimed, astonished.

'Twenty guineas,' I repeated. 'We worked well together; perhaps we'll do it again.'

She stared at me, shocked. 'Twenty guineas?'

I nodded. 'There is a bounty for catching felons, paid for by the government,' I explained. 'For a murderer like Abe Gordon, that amounts to one hundred guineas. This is just part payment, I'll give you half for what you did, after all, you took most of the risks.'

Kitty just stared at me. 'Twenty guineas?' she repeated, shocked at the amount of money that had just appeared in her damp-infested room. 'Twenty guineas,' she muttered, trying out the words. 'Never seen that amount in one go, not in my hands anyway.' She looked back up at me. 'Twenty guinea's, three shillings and two pennies; not bad for a day's work. You sure you don't want me to earn the three shillings?'

I laughed. 'No, Kitty. Though I think you're undercharging.'

She smiled, her good eye wide, open and honest. 'Tell me; who *are* you, Richard Hopgood?'

I grinned back. 'Good question. When I find out, I will let you know.'

CHAPTER 2

I left Kitty still beaming in gratitude at her windfall, promising that the rest of the money would come soon. Out on the street, the people were still going about their business: the hawkers were selling; the children playing; the idlers gossiping; the musicians piping; the taverns and gin-shops full; a cacophony of noise and bustle amidst the reek of smoke and ordure. I joined the crowded pavement and walked down, trying to avoid the girls plying for trade, the hands clawing with promises of passion and delights; these coming from slips of girls with tired hollow eyes, pale starving faces, forcing smiles that they did not want to give.

Turning left at Broad Street, I walked towards Holborn, the slum disappearing quickly behind me. I headed towards the Courts at Lincoln's Inn, to visit my friend there.

Bartholomew Cruikshank and I had studied law together and he had chambers at the Inn. I had become disillusioned with law at an early stage, though Barty found he had a natural ability for dealing with the minutiae involved with the laws of contracts and commerce. A junior partner, he thus spent most of his waking hours imprisoned in his chambers, bent over various documents, living a life that I did not wish to lead. Criminal law and the criminal interested me more, but opportunities were few and hard to come by in that field. I found the law staid and unrewarding so I left it to those more suited to the boredom, like Barty. Fortunately, for me, I have a private income, allowing me to occupy my time by catching criminals. So far, it has been very rewarding, in both a financial way and giving me a sense of satisfaction. I also found that I have a talent in that direction which serves me well.

'You'll do your eyes no good, Barty, working all these hours by candlelight,' I said, as I walked in through the door.

Barty looked up from his work and recoiled at the smell of gin and muck on me as I went over to the chest containing my good clothes. 'Maybe but Mr Jipson is old and I do not believe he'll be long in this world. Once I get to senior then I can leave all this behind, let some other junior have the pleasure.'

I pulled my clothes out and lay them on the chair besides. My old hat went in first, followed by my jacket and old shirt; battered shoes, torn stockings and breeches went in last. Barty had left a bowl, jug and towel there for me to wash and I rubbed myself down, getting rid of most of the grime. 'If you need someone to help him on his way, then you only have to ask. I am sure I can find a willing helper for a small charge.'

'Richard,' said Barty, aghast. 'What are you suggesting?'

Sometimes Barty does not see the joke. 'I meant it as a quip, Barty my friend. However...' I grinned and gave him a wink, though he could hardly see it in this light.

He shook his head and a smile broke out on his face. 'I sometimes wonder at the people you have become acquainted with, Richard. You'll come to a bad end one of these days.'

'Maybe, but conformity has never sat right with me.'

I began to dress in the attire I first arrived in, having come straight from a formal reception: clean linen shirt, silk breeches and stockings, embroidered waistcoat, my blue silk jacket with gold threading, hand-made bespoke black leather buckle shoes; thankfully the fashion for high heels had ebbed away as I already stood just over six feet and I did not want any more height. A lace jabot set the coat and waistcoat off perfectly.

'Wig,' said Barty, knowing how much I loathed the embellishment.

I pulled my own hair back, tying it at the nape of my neck then fished out the hated peruke from the chest, just a small affair, merely a nod to convention, and placed it on my head. A tricorne went on top and then I buckled my sword and picked up my cane, I was ready to go out into the world once again.

'Approve, Barty?' I asked, as I stood posing in front of him.

'I do not suppose you are returning to St Giles as you wouldn't last a moment dressed like that?'

'No, but an equally insalubrious establishment infested with crime and debauchery.'

He raised an eyebrow and grinned, knowing full well my next place of call. 'Then good luck there, you'll need it.'

'Ah, the good colonel's reputation is spread far and wide.'

'Sometimes I think you actually like him.'

'I do not dislike him,' I answered truthfully.

'No, you get too much from him for that.'

'Nothing I do not deserve.' I grinned and tapped my hat with my cane. 'Good evening to you, Barty. I owe you a good meal at least, for allowing me to use your chambers.'

'I will look forward to that; but I'll not hold my breath,' he added, wryly.

I made my way down the stairs and over to the gate at Chancery Lane. I roused the gatekeeper and set him to finding me a chair. He found a lad outside to go and fetch the conveyance then engaged me in conversation as I waited but I did not learn anything that was not common knowledge: Walpole still had serious issues to resolve.

I dispensed the obligatory gratuities to the boy and the gateman as the chair arrived and I stepped in, giving my destination: Bow Street. The link-boy set off before I had settled and I bumped down into my seat as the chairmen lifted the contraption and hurried after, shouting at the pedestrians in front of them to make way. Fortunately, the journey did not take long but I felt my teeth rattle at all the bumps and shudders as those worthy men negotiated the narrow, slippery and congested back streets and alleyways.

I paid my shilling as I stepped out and pressed a penny into the hand of the boy, reflecting that it was becoming an expensive evening, though I did not object to paying anyone their rightful dues, unlike many of my class. I knew the struggles that the average workingman had to put bread on their families' table.

I brushed myself down and adjusted my hat before knocking at the door. A servant allowed me entrance and then left me waiting in the hall. I began to pace as I waited, my footsteps echoing on the bare wooden floor and after several moments found myself walking down the corridor towards a door. I opened it and then stood and perused: a few hours ago this room would have been a hive of activity, the colonel presiding as all and sundry were ushered in before him. I had brought Abe Gordon here, to be arraigned for trial at the Old Bailey. This was Bow Street Magistrates Court, with the Chief Magistrate being Colonel Thomas De Veil.

The colonel had a reputation of being hard but generally fair. He took the law seriously but was aware of its shortcomings. Many people did not like him, others, like me, were ambivalent. Everyone though, had to admit, that he displayed tenacity when investigating a crime.

I heard footsteps behind and I turned to see Digby coming towards me.

'Good evening, sir,' he said, in greeting.

I inclined my head and returned the salutation.

'The colonel is, er... indisposed at present, I'm afraid,' said Digby, glancing at the ceiling.

'Is he now?' I replied, following his gaze.

'Er... Yes, sir, though he has given me instructions, should you happen to call.'

'So, Digby, here I am,' I said, holding out my arms expectantly.

'Yes, Mr Hopgood, I have noticed. If you would care to come with me,' he said, turning on his heels and heading back to the hall.

I liked Digby; he suffered the whims and fancies of the colonel without complaint, just quietly getting on with his work. I knew some of his history: though born a pauper, he had somehow learnt his letters, a talent that lifted him out of poverty. A diligent and capable man, he assisted the less fortunate where he could, especially those who crossed the threshold of Bow Street.

We entered the office and crossed over to the desk. He lit the candles, allowing a little light to illuminate the room.

'So, Digby,' I said, as he shuffled some papers on the desk. 'This indisposition of the colonel?'

A grin flashed on his face and I knew straight away that I had made the correct assumption.

'Er...Mrs Quiller,' he admitted after a few moments pause. 'She appeared before him earlier today.'

I nodded my approval. Mrs Quiller ran a house not far from Bow Street. Expensive, but she catered for the more discerning client. Though ostensibly retired from active participation, for a select few she sometimes came out of retirement. A beautiful woman still, in her forties, she could outshine girls half her age.

'She and the colonel are coming to a sort of agreement, I

believe,' he continued. 'The fine is to be paid in instalments.'

'Ah,' I said, understanding. 'So, you expect to see a lot of her over the coming weeks.'

'I expect so,' he replied, not altogether approving.

The colonel had a weakness where women were concerned, especially attractive women, and in some circumstances, non-fiscal arrangements were sometimes made. Who profited more from those arrangements was hard to tell, because both sides had a hold over the other. A widower now, in his late fifties, the colonel had been several times married and had many children, round of face and fond of his clothes, especially his wig which hid his receding grey hair. He lacked my height by a good few inches and did not need to worry about what others thought of these arrangements; both sides kept their counsel, so that nothing could be proved.

He found the document and pushed it over towards me and as I picked up the quill to sign, he rummaged in a drawer, pulling out a pouch and putting it by the document. I signed my name and took the pouch, weighing it in my hand.

'Are we to be seeing you again soon?' he asked, as I pocketed the pouch.

I shook my head. 'Not at the moment but I'm sure something will garner my interest at some point.'

'I will inform the colonel, sir. I'm sure he'll contact you should he hear of something that suits your abilities.'

'Thank you, Digby,' I said as I turned to leave.

There were times when De Veil would contact me, normally when the pressure of his office prevented him from giving a crime the time it deserved, sometimes a serious crime but mostly to do with stolen property and the more expensive the property, the better. It could prove quite lucrative to both of us as the state gave a reward for catching the criminal and the victim often gave a reward for the property recovered. The colonel made sure that he had a slice of whatever came my way.

I bid Digby a good evening and left the Court, walking around to Drury Lane to find a hackney carriage to take me to my house in Jermyn Street, close to St James' Park.

Grateful to be home at last, I paid my fare and entered, leaving the noise and the bustle of the London streets behind me, revelling in the peace and tranquillity, a short-lived peace and tranquillity, as I could hear an argument break out at the back of the house. I sighed, took a deep breath then decided not to get involved and let them continue to argue. I deposited my cane and sword by the door and climbed the stairs, my staff oblivious to my presence, to the bedroom so that I could rid myself of the peacock dress and return to normal. I found my banyan robe laid out on the bed and my silk slippers were on the floor beside the dressing table. I stripped to my shirt and breeches and put on my robe and slippers and made my way back downstairs to my drawing room, the argument still proceeding and now seemingly becoming a little more heated. Someone had lit the fire and even though spring had arrived, the evening air still had a chill to it. I warmed my hands briefly then held a candle to the flames and lit the others. With a warming fire and plenty of light, I sat down in my comfortable chair and picked up the latest Gentleman's Magazine and began to read about Walpole's woes: the Election had been called and I cannot say I had much sympathy for the incumbent; the time had come for him to find something else to occupy his intellect.

I had asked Mary, my housekeeper, to decant a bottle of Burgundy for my return and I was pleased to see that she had followed my instructions. I poured a glass, then picked up my pipe and pressed a little tobacco into the bowl, using a taper to get it going and after a few attempts managed to do so. I sat back luxuriating, drawing the cleansing smoke deep into my lungs and then I again picked up my newspaper and continued to read.

The argument at the back of the house had stopped and it took several moments before I realised that peace had broken out. I cocked an ear, hearing some light footsteps coming down the hall, then I heard them stop, another few moments and then I heard a sudden increase in pace. I could not help but smile as someone must have spied my sword and cane on the floor where I discarded them.

'Oh, sir,' exclaimed Mary, as she stood aghast at the door. 'We never heard you come in.'

'No matter, Mary,' I returned. 'You seemed to be occupied, judging by the sounds of the discourse I could not but help overhearing.'

She rung her hands and looked down apologetically. 'I'm sorry, sir, but it was that man again. When you left, he followed soon after. I didn't see hide nor hair of him from that moment until just half an hour since. I was just letting him know of my displeasure.'

'Drunk?' I asked, mildly.

She nodded. 'I hope you have no need of him as he'll be no good to anyone for a while.'

Mary sounded exasperated but I knew from long ago that her bark was worse than her bite. I inherited her from my father's house when I moved to London where she had worked directly beneath the Housekeeper, the exacting Mrs Strang, who ruled with strict discipline, which Mary, thankfully, had not tried to emulate. She stood at the door wearing a little lace cap that topped chestnut brown hair with a few strands turning to grey, a pleasing face that had begun to show some lines of worry, which I admit, might be down to me and my vocation. She neared forty years of age, wore a practical brown dress and, though slim and petite, she towered over us all in regards to her presence. The man in question happened to be Ned, employed as my footman but mostly as my assistant. I had allowed him some time for himself, so I was not surprised to learn he had returned full of alcohol; being fond of ale and gambling, he had obviously found a tavern or two to his liking.

'No matter, Mary,' I consoled. 'I allowed him to be loose from the tether, so the fault is mine.'

'Begging your pardon, sir, but he should know to present himself back here in a suitable condition.'

I could not help but smile at her umbrage, which would certainly mean an early start for Ned in the morning.

'Now, sir, I will get Jane to sort out your things. I assume that your clothes upstairs need to be put away?'

'Indeed they do, Mary, thank you.'

I'll just see to those things by the door,' she said, turning. 'Jane,' she yelled as she closed the door.

I sat back in my chair, drained my glass and refilled it, then continued to read and smoke my pipe. Bliss.

*

The worst time to be awoken is when your slumber is deep and dreamless, the room as dark as pitch and your bed as warm and comfortable as a cocoon. I vaguely heard a banging noise, as if distant and muffled, which only momentarily awakened my senses. I turned in my bed, ignoring the sound and dived deep back into the abyss. It must have been only moments later when I heard a gentle knocking on my bedroom door, increasing in volume and urgency the more I ignored it. Eventually the door creaked open and the flame of a candle flickered in the aperture.

I closed my eyes against the intrusion until enough light had penetrated through the skin of my eyelids to risk opening them, only to see Jane holding a candle and creeping towards me.

I raised myself on my elbow sharply, giving her quite the start.

'Oh, sir,' she exclaimed, holding one hand to her mouth. 'It's only me, Jane.'

'Jane? What are you doing?' I replied, not quite yet back in the land of the living.

Mary and I had found her some months ago as an innocent, fresh off the carriage that had brought her from Northampton, orphaned, penniless and hoping to find her fortune in the city. Just sixteen years old, we witnessed a bawd trying to entice her into a line of business which would ultimately lead her to a dissolute life. Small, pretty, with hair the colour of ripened straw, she was easy prey for the huntress tailing her.

'There's a gentleman downstairs wishing to speak to you and he's not prepared to wait until morning.'

'Who?' I asked, sitting up now and rubbing my eyes.

'A Mr Digby, sir. He asks to see you this very minute.'

'All right, Jane. Bid him wait and I'll be down presently,' I replied, needing a few moments to get myself together.

Digby's presence indicated that my person might be required at some street in the city and so I dressed accordingly in plain apparel. I also pulled out my greatcoat as I could still discern the chill of last night and hastened downstairs to find what my immediate future beheld.

I found him in the kitchen, sat at the table with a pot of restorative in his hands, a small beer warmed by immersion of a poker. Mary had got up too and both of them looked up as I entered. Digby gave a tired smile and it seemed as if he had been up all night as he was still dressed as I had seen him last evening.

'Ah, sir,' he said in greeting. 'I've been sent by the colonel and he has graciously asked that you accompany me down to the river. There...er... a body has been found.'

'A body in the Thames?' I asked, raising my eyebrow. 'Just one?'

'Er...yes, sir. Not a vagrant, apparently.'

'Murdered?'

'The colonel believes so. He thinks you may be interested in exploring the circumstances as he is very busy at the moment and doesn't believe he can devote the time required.'

'He normally likes the difficult ones.'

'That's true but he really can't devote the time at the moment.'

I nodded, thinking that I too relished the challenges a murder could bring. Robbery could be lucrative but sometimes the intellect needs stimulating and nothing could do that so well as a good murder with the assailants unknown.

'Do we know the identity of the victim?' I asked.

Digby shook his head. 'Not as far as I know. I rather think the colonel is hoping you might find the answer to that conundrum.'

'Let us hope he's right and that I can. Mary,' I said turning to my housekeeper. 'Could you rouse Ned; and might I suggest you stand well back when you wake him.'

'Yes, sir,' replied Mary, not too happy about having to waken a drunkard, destined to spend the next few hours on the banks' of the Thames.

CHAPTER 3

The carriage drew to a halt at Queenhithe stairs next to the Queenhithe Dock, where barges off-loaded their cargo from the towns and villages upriver of the city.

Digby caught my eye and then turned to look at Ned, slumped in the corner with his head against the side of the carriage, snoring loudly.

'He has his uses,' I answered, knowing the question going through Digby's mind.

Ned did indeed have his uses, helping me to apprehend Abe Gordon and many others. I can send him to lodge in tenements and slums, inveigle himself into low brewhouses and various dens of iniquity. His low birth enables him to mix with the worst of society, whereas I could do so for short periods, I could not sustain it for a long period of time, which Ned could do easily. He rested there, his wig askew, beneath which he kept his brown hair cropped short, his normally dark pallor, wan, after his exploits of last night. We were of the same age, though he lacked an inch or so of my height but made up for that with his solid build and usefulness with his fists. I nudged him awake and received a groan of complaint as a reward.

Digby did not know anything more than that a man had been found dead. De Veil had sent his carriage to Bow Street to collect Digby who then had to proceed to my home, which meant that the colonel had arrived early at the scene of the crime. I could not help but be intrigued as to the reason why.

The tide was out and clustered on the reeking mud by the stairs I could see a little huddle of people, two of them holding lanterns.

'Ah, Hopgood,' I heard from behind.

'Colonel,' I acknowledged, as De Veil walked up to me.

We both made our way to the edge of the wharf and looked down. 'A corpse lying on a bed of muck and mud, Hopgood, beaten, from what I've been told.'

'You have not been down there?' I asked, with a whimsy.

'Indeed not; I have no intention of dirtying my shoes and stockings. Those men will bring the corpse to us,' he replied, without a trace of irony.

I regarded the colonel as the men below began to haul the body from the sucking muck. He wore his best clothes and wig and I could detect the slight aroma of a woman's perfume about his person as well as a taint of alcohol from his breath.

'How come you're here, Colonel? It is not as if you're routinely appraised of deaths on the river.' I asked, curious.

'No, Hopgood.' He coughed. 'I just happened to be returning from a visit and came across men calling in the street. I decided to stop to find out the reason why.'

I turned to look at him but he turned away, clearing his throat yet again. I felt a grin appear on my face. Mrs Quiller as his first course and I reasoned he had gone elsewhere for his main. I had to admire his stamina; I just hoped I would have the same energy when I got to his age.

The bang of the carriage door behind me indicated that Digby had just helped Ned alight. Digby went over to De Veil, while Ned, belching loudly and rubbing his head, dislodging his wig even more, came over to me.

De Veil sighed. 'I believe the corpse was deposited there as the tide ebbed. The watchman has been on the wharf all night and states that he has seen nothing untoward until he spied the body down there.'

Ned sniffed, yawned, then manfully cast off the effects of his inebriation. 'In that case, sir, he either went in just a little while ago up that way,' and he pointed up river. 'Or he went in on a rising tide from down there,' and he pointed towards London Bridge.

'He could have been in the water for days, man,' snapped De Veil, looking at the men bringing up the body on an old tarpaulin.

'Doubt that, sir. I reckon the body is in good condition, judging by how they're handling it.'

'We'll see soon enough,' I said, interjecting. The colonel had never taken to Ned and took every opportunity to remind him of his situation in life, that being of the lowest of births who should not argue with his betters.

The men brought the body onto the wharf, huffing and puffing and gasping as they dragged the weight engulfed in the tarpaulin. They dropped their burden and stepped back, wiping the sweat from their eyes. The two holding the lanterns directed the light to fall on the unfortunate corpse.

Digby held back but De Veil, Ned and I leant forward to look closely. The body was that of a young man with light-brown hair. He had pleasing features, even allowing for the fact that the face had been battered and bruised. He had a slim build, not emaciated but not gone to fat. There did not seem to be any putrefaction yet, making Ned correct in his assumption that the body had only recently entered the river. His clothes appeared to be of good quality, which indicated that this could be a man of means, possibly a man of quality. I cast a quick glance at De Veil who pursed his lips in thought. Ned lowered himself and tried to raise an arm.

'Stiff,' observed Ned, stating the obvious.

I knew from experience that a body went rigid a short time after death and then later relaxed and became malleable again, which confirmed that this body had not been that long in the river.

'Been fair battered,' continued Ned, pointing at the face. 'Eye and lips swollen; nose could be broken too.'

'So it would appear,' I answered. 'Could it be that someone tipped him in unconscious? Press his chest, Ned. See if we get water or air.'

Ned leant on the chest and I heard the cracking of the ribs but a series of small bubbles arose from his lips, not the torrent of water that I expected. A puff of air followed the bubbles, much like that of a bellows.

'He didn't drown then,' I said, turning to De Veil.

The colonel nodded. 'So it would seem. Then he must have been dead when he went in.'

Ned began to unbutton the clothes to look beneath for a wound but found nothing on his chest but he did find some items in his pockets. He handed them up to me and then turned the body over to look at the back.

'A rosary,' I said, looking at the string of beads. 'A pouch of money and this soggy piece of paper.'

De Veil took the rosary and looked at it, running the beads through his fingers. 'A Catholic then, more fool him for carrying it.'

'Sir,' said Ned, as he pushed the loose clothes up. 'A wound.'

De Veil and I bent our heads to look, as did those who had dragged the body up from the river. I could see a slit of a wound, just over an inch wide, just below the heart. Ned pulled the clothes back into position and found a corresponding tear in the material of the jacket, waistcoat and shirt. De Veil crouched down and inserted his finger into the wound.

'Deep,' he announced as his finger penetrated right to the knuckle. 'This is what killed him,' he continued as he withdrew his finger, emitting a sucking sound.

He wiped his finger on the clothes of the corpse and stood up. 'Now we know how he died, I will leave it to you to find out who he is and how he came to be in the river, Hopgood,' he said, as he turned and began to walk back to his carriage. 'I have a busy day ahead of me and I wish to get an hour or two of sleep before it all begins. Let me know how you're progressing. Good evening to you. Digby,' he said, beckoning his clerk. 'Come now or you can walk back.'

'Yes, sir,' said Digby. 'I'm just taking names for the inquest.'

'Be quick about it, I'll not delay.'

Digby raised his eyebrows at me and then hurried to get the names, lest he be left behind.

'Well, Ned,' I said, as the carriage rattled away. 'It's down to just you and me and our wits.'

'Yes, sir; but perhaps you'll allow me to sleep off this headache before we start.'

I grinned and slapped him heavily on his back, which elicited a satisfying groan of discomfort. 'No time to lose, Ned. We've a knotty problem to unravel.'

'Yes, sir,' said Ned, the disappointment evident in his response.

I relented in the end and allowed him to return home, but he would have to find his own way there and at his own expense. I watched him trudge off and then returned my attention to the corpse; I needed to get it somewhere where I could examine it further.

The Church of St Mary Somerset was just around the corner and I supposed De Veil would wish me to take it there to keep it in the parish. I knew a small stone barn sat in the grounds of the graveyard, useful for the storing of corpses; being close to the river, rarely was it without an occupant.

By now, dawn had arrived and the buildings around the dock began to get busy with people coming to work. I sent one of the men still with me to get a cart and he quickly returned with an old handcart, used for off-loading grain from the dock. We loaded the corpse, still within the tarpaulin, and two of us trundled the cart along to the church.

Fortunately, I found the rector in the church and he unlocked the door of the little house of the dead, which contained one other incumbent, an unknown vagrant who died in the street. We placed the body on a bench and I gave my helper a shilling for his aid before he returned to the dock.

I unwrapped the body, and with the light coming in from the door, began to examine it. The rector stood by my side, watching me closely as I set to the task.

I untied the victim's clothes with little effort and then ruffled them up so that I could regard the body properly for the first time. A well-nourished and fit young man, he appeared to be in his early twenties with light-brown curly hair down to the nape of his neck; in life, he would have caught the eye of many a girl, if not for the damage to his face. I checked his hands for signs of bruising around the knuckles but there were none, though the fingers of the right hand had stains, which were not the stains associated with death, probably ink, which raised the possibility that he could be a clerk. The torso had some bruises around the abdomen and chest and the face had received a lot of punishment. I turned the body and looked at the wound: I did not follow De Veil's example and test it with my finger but looked on the floor for something that would suffice, finding a discarded long nail in the corner. I put the nail into the wound, which entered some five inches by my reckoning, presumably penetrating the heart. I turned the body over again and stood back a little, fixing the look of the man in my mind.

'What are you doing?' asked the rector.

'Looking,' I replied. 'I need to be able to describe him to people.'

'Ah, I may be of some help there,' he said with a smile.

He hurried out and returned a few minutes later with a sheet of paper and a little stick of graphite.

'I will take a drawing for you; I do it quite regularly so that relatives have a memento of their loved ones.'

'Could you do it without the damage to the face?' I asked, interested to see what he would produce.

He nodded. 'Yes, but prop his head up a bit and hold his jaw closed.'

'I am afraid he's too stiff for that.'

'Ah, never mind. In that case, I will do my best for you.'

He chatted as he drew, talking about his dwindling congregation and how the parish had become poorer over the years; the river trade might be growing but the wealth did not pass down to those that lived there. I could see with the few deft strokes he made that he had depicted the likeness quite well. Within a few minutes, he had finished and handed me the sheet.

'You have a rare talent there, Rector,' I said, as I regarded it against the body before me. 'He could be alive and walking out of here.'

'Thank you, it is one of my interests and I enjoy doing it.'

I washed my hands at the nearby pump then left the rector with the drawing in my pocket and a few shillings lighter; I felt I had to give a donation to the church as he had provided me with the means to identify the unknown man. I came out onto Thames Street and then headed up the hill towards Cheapside. I felt hungry, so I purchased a part-loaf of bread and some cheese from a vendor and chewed as I walked. The bread and cheese filled the hole in my stomach but I felt I needed something to wake me up and get my mind working. Coffee should provide enough of a stimulus and I could smell that heady aroma in the air. I entered the coffee house and sat down, there were only three customers and I gave greeting to each of them, then picked hold of a newssheet, as I did not wish to engage in conversation; I could appear to be reading instead of doing the thinking that I intended to do. I ordered my coffee and then noticed some little pastries that the owner had just baked, so I ordered two of them too. I could smell the intense aroma of the coffee though it seemed a trifle burnt; even so, I waited with anticipation as the noxious black liquid poured from the long-spouted pot into my bowl.

I took a few sips, chewed my pastries and then remembered the soggy piece of paper that Ned had taken from the corpse. I pulled it out and laid it on the table, stared at it for a few seconds then began to open it out delicately from its folded state.

The ink had run, which I expected, but there were blotches and smudges and just about discernible were four words. "Ship" "olb" "unda" "Ten."

I sat back and wondered which ship and what it contained and what might be the significance, if any. I took another sip and then signalled for a refill. The door opened and two men walked in, talking loudly and enthusiastically about their morning's business. They sat at the table next to me and began to call out to the other patrons, with whom they were obviously acquainted. I regretted my decision to have a second bowl as the noise intruded into my thoughts. I hastily finished my coffee and then left.

Deciding that I had no cause to be wandering around the

streets without a plan, I hurried up to Cheapside and found a hackney to take me home, at least then I could sit in the comfort of my own house whilst I contemplated a plan of action in order to identify the man in the river.

*

By the time I returned, Ned had restored some of his equilibrium and helped Jane prepare some vegetables for the evening's meal, which entailed a fair bit of leg-pulling as far as I could tell. We were without a cook as she had left to go home to look after her ailing mother, so to produce some food for us all, everyone pitched in. It seemed to be working so well that I considered not hiring another; I did not eat regularly at home, though, if needs be, I could always bring one in for an evening of entertaining.

Jane looked relieved as I drew Ned away from the kitchen. I gave her a quick grin and a wink and she blessed me with a shy smile of gratitude.

'Well,' I said, as we sat down in my study. 'Any thoughts on our corpse of last night?'

Ned shook his head. 'No, sir, only that he was fresh in the water. I had hoped that you might have found out a little more.'

This time, I shook my head. 'Not much, only that bit of paper he had on him; some of the words are still legible, though the paper is still damp.' I opened it out for him carefully and passed it over. 'What do you make of it?' His thick finger spun the paper around and he considered it for a few moments. 'It is a shame it does not tell us which ship it alludes to,' I continued. 'It would go some way to help us identify him.'

He shrugged. 'If it is a ship.'

'Does it not say?'

'No, it don't. If it referred to a ship, then it would say the name of the ship. This just says "Ship."'

'Meaning?'

'Not sure.'

'That is not a lot of help, Ned.'

'That's because letters are missing, you can see where they should be but not what they were.'

'Yes, I know.' I grabbed a sheet of paper and copied out what I could see. 'Look, there are smudges after the "olb" and that could have been a mark before the "o". The same kind of smudge is before the "u" and after the "a."'

We stared at the sheet for several minutes, both of us deep in thought, hoping for inspiration, passing it back and forward.

In the end, Ned sighed and took my sheet and looked, frustrated. 'Ship, olb...er, unda, Ten,' he said, speaking aloud.

I nodded as the words went around in my mind and then his hesitation, his "er", made me look up. 'Say that again, Ned.'

He did but without the hesitation.

'No, you hesitated before, after the "olb". Try again.'

'Er... "Ship, olb...erm, unda, Ten.'

I looked at him as I focused on the words; the corpse was a Catholic after all. 'Ship, 'olberm.' I repeated. 'Could it mean The Ship, Holborn?'

Ned shrugged his shoulders. 'It could, sir, though you might be jumping there, it could also mean something else.'

'I don't know. Let me have a look again.' I pulled the sheet back, sighed and stared at it again, wishing that the letters would somehow reveal themselves.

'Could it be that we are looking at something that has nothing to do with him?' asked Ned.

'All is possible,' I replied. 'But it came from his pocket, so he had to put it there.'

'But it doesn't mean it's important.'

'No, but we have nothing else, so we work on what we have.' I lit my pipe, hoping that the action would aid my thinking. 'You can always go back to helping Jane, you know,' I added, as I could see his enthusiasm waning.

'No, no,' he said, a little too quickly perhaps. 'I'm just thinking, is all.'

'It's a shame it was not dry,' I said, tapping my pipe stem against my lips.

'Why?'

'Because we may be able to see the marks of writing, the scratches as the nib made the letters. The paper has absorbed moisture, thus swelling it and obscuring any indentation.'

'Then allow it to dry out.'

'I doubt there would be anything left but you never know. Get us something to eat, Ned, and I will put it in the sunlight for a while.'

The note dried out quickly in the sun and by the time we had finished eating it was easier to handle. I sat in my chair and held it at all angles, trying to see if any scratches were discernible. Ned watched me as I held it up to cast the light upon it.

'Er, sir,' he said, leaning forward. 'Hold it there a moment.'

'What?'

'No, not there. Up a bit. Angle it, there. Stop now.'

'Why? What can you see?'

'The back; the ink has come through and there are faint lines.'

'Where?' I quickly turned it over and began to study the reverse.

'Wait a moment, sir.' Ned scraped back his chair and came around my desk to stand, leaning over my shoulder. 'Move it slowly so that the light glances off it...There, see?'

I did and I felt an inrush of blood, a sensation rippling up my neck. 'Write what you see, Ned. I'll hold it still.'

The ink had soaked into the paper and through to the back, though most had been washed away, it left an imprint of ink where the nib had pressed, compressing the fibres of the paper. The letters were reversed as if seen in a mirror but the general shape of the missing ones were there. It did not take long before we had our answer.

'You owe me an apology, Ned. "Ship, Holborn, Sunday, Ten,"' I finished triumphantly, sitting up straight. 'Why did we not see that earlier?'

'Because we didn't look at the back, sir. Anyway, it's dry now, easier to see.'

'How long has it taken us?'

'Couple of hours; one dinner and two small beers each, sir.'

I knew The Ship Inn; I had drunk there a few times. Many Catholics frequented it, sometimes even holding their religious Mass there; although the authorities largely turned a blind eye, occasionally the blind eye opened and a raid commenced to catch the worshippers. They rarely found anything except an Inn full of drinkers, the priest conspicuous by his absence. Personally, I did not care who worshipped what, my faith had gone missing a long time ago.

'I think we may have to visit the Inn,' I said, showing him the drawing that the rector had made and he nodded approval.

'Good likeness,' he opined, studying the lines.

'Apparently, he regularly utilises his talent for the relatives of the departed, so that the family can have something to remember their loved ones by.'

He leant forward. 'How do you intend to use this drawing?'

'By showing it, of course. I'm hoping that someone can put a name to him.'

'Folk are wary; they may not want to help or get involved,

especially there, in The Ship. A man comes in showing a drawing of a Catholic to other Catholics and they may think he's to be arrested for heresy or something.'

'He is dead and I'll make that plain.'

'Even so; they're going to be suspicious.'

He had a point. To lead a Catholic life meant leading a secret life: although there was an element of tolerance nowadays, few would openly admit their faith. Still, I could not use that as a reason not to try.

'It still needs to be done,' I said, after thinking a while. 'We need to find out this man's identity. You can go in before me and settle yourself. I will come in later and make enquiries. We, of course, will not be acquainted. If someone tells me something, then all well and good, if no, then they may talk once I have left and you'll be there to hear the gossip.'

'Yes, sir,' replied Ned, brightening at the prospect of an hour or two indulging in his favourite pastime, even though he had only just recovered from his exploits of yesterday.

'We will meet up again at The Black Bull near Holborn Hill.'

*

The Ship Inn nestled on the corner of Little Princes Street and Little Turnstile, just a stone's throw from Lincoln's Inn Field, a low-beamed establishment, restricted in light by the nearby buildings. The few times I had supped ale there I found it convivial and lacking in threat, the fare being quite palatable too.

Ned had been inside for an hour now and I hoped he had begun to win the trust of the locals. I took a deep breath, opened the door and entered.

I walked into a smoky atmosphere with a great fog seemingly suspended from the ceiling and I could smell beer, tobacco and the obligatory stale sweat. A fire blazed in the hearth. The Inn had many customers and all eyes turned to watch me enter. With nowhere to sit, I approached the counter, threading my way through the crush. I spied Ned sitting with his back up against the window to my right and laughing with a companion. A pot-girl hurried about with her jug.

I ordered a twopenny ale at the counter then leant with my shoulder against the wall, just enjoying the feeling of the ale as it slid down my throat. I looked around and saw that the customers had now returned to their own business again, largely ignoring me. Then I took out the drawing.

The landlord returned from the cellar, so I caught his eye. 'Cast yer glaziers on this phyz, will yer. Trying to put a name to the cove,' I said, affecting the local dialect. 'Washed up from the river last night. Had a rosary on him.'

'Dead, I presume?'

I nodded. 'Hushed. Anyone you know?'

He shot me a look and then studied it for a few moments. I watched as he pursed his lips and then shake his head. 'No,' he answered simply, looking at me.

'You sure? It's a good likeness.'

'I said no, didn't I?'

'You did; shame, was hoping to get him back to his family. Mind if I ask around?'

'Can't stop you doing that,' he said, dismissing me with a curt nod.

'Appreciate it,' I replied, with a feeling that I would be getting the self-same answer from everyone there.

I was correct in my assumption. No one owned up to recognising him as I walked around and Ned diligently shook his head as I approached him and proffered the drawing beneath his nose. Once or twice, I saw a twitch in an eye, a slight hesitancy

41

here and there, a guarded look but the answers did not change. No one admitted knowing him.

I drained the dregs of my tankard and felt myself sighing. Placing the empty pot on a table, I left the Inn, turned up towards Holborn and then walked down to The Black Bull to await Ned, hoping that someone had said something after I had gone.

Ned appeared some thirty minutes later and as he joined me at my table, I signalled for the girl to replenish my pot and to bring another.

'Well?' I enquired as he settled himself down.

His face broke into a grin. 'We have a name, Thomas Sorley. What's more, I know where he worked.'

'Good work, Ned. Well done.' I breathed a sigh of relief. 'What happened?'

'It all happened just as the door closed behind you. Everyone started talking at once. They thought that you were after this Thomas because of his Catholic faith. I then said that I'd heard that a body had turned up down at Queenhithe and that made them think. I asked if they knew him and my fellow drinkers told me all about him. That note pertained to last Sunday. They had a Mass, with the priest standing behind the counter in all his get-up as if he were about to start pouring ale. Anyways, this Thomas was there as he helps the priest, which is how they all knew him. Worked down a warehouse in Thames Street near the bridge.'

'I think we can say that you achieved a good result: which warehouse?'

'Thompson and Gutteridge. Worked as a clerk in the office there. Importers mainly, bring loads of different stuff into the country.'

CHAPTER 4

The hackney dropped us off on the corner of Fish Street and Thames Street as he had no wish to negotiate the one-way route that had carts coming into it from the east and leaving to the west; he had suffered in the past for the officious way the rules and fines were enforced, so we were left to walk the last few yards to our destination. The warehouses were enormous, some of brick and some of timber but all rose up three or four storeys high: great cavernous buildings stacked full of goods from all parts of the world.

The noise deafened our ears as carters and porters screamed and yelled to each other in a most raucous manner, both Ned and I grinned at the course language used as we dodged both the traffic and workers hurrying about their business. Just a short distance further up, the fish-market at Billingsgate traded and the smell of fish permeated the air with the cries of gulls competing with the cries of those men toiling.

We found the warehouse we sought but, being curious, we turned down a little lane that ran down to the river by the side of Thompson and Gutteridge, the frontage of which sat directly on the wharf, in prime position. As we walked, we could see a veritable forest of masts and spars come into view and as we stepped onto the wharf, I could not help but stop and stare as I had done many a time before and I still could only marvel at the sight. There were ships of all sizes crammed into the Pool, too many to count, with lighters ferrying goods from ships to the wharf. Gangs of men were unloading the lighters, some by hand and some with cranes, putting the goods on carts or carrying the crates, suspended from poles between the shoulders of two men. Workers were pushing wheeled barrows along the wharf, scurrying like ants, everyone in a rush. Gang leaders were shouting, calling and gesticulating but there was an orderliness about it all, everyone seemed to know what everyone else should be doing.

Ned and I kept out of the way as we viewed the Pool of London. To our right, London Bridge crossed the river, the edifice a town within a city, such were the buildings crammed along its span. To our left, a little further down on the far side of the fish-market, just near the Tower, the Customs House stood, where importers paid the taxes on the goods unloaded; customs men with tally-sheets were keeping a beady eye on the whole proceedings.

We turned and watched a hook descend from a beam protruding from the warehouse towards a cart positioned below it, containing what looked to be a large bale of cloth. A worker attached the hook to a rope surrounding the bale and then at a signal, the winch took the strain and the bale rose to a hatch higher up. The cart moved away to collect some more goods, so Ned and I took advantage of the lull to enter the warehouse.

I could see a central aisle devoid of goods with large numbers of crates and barrels stacked to the sides. Stout wooden posts positioned regularly around the interior supported the floor above. A man wearing a sword with a pistol in his belt and carrying a nasty looking cudgel halted our progress; of a size with Ned, he had a face that appeared hard-used.

'You gentlemen lost?' he enquired, stepping in front of us.

'Ah, good day to you,' I said, giving him my best smile. 'Not in the least. This is the warehouse of Thompson and Gutteridge, is it not?'

'That it is,' he replied, not unpleasantly.

'Good. We wish to speak to someone of authority. We have an enquiry regarding someone who is employed here.'

'An' who might that be?'

'I believe it is someone from the office.'

'The office, eh? You'll be wanting Mr Cummings then, 'e deals with all that kind of stuff.'

I smiled again. 'And where will I find Mr Cummings?'

'In the office.'

I could feel Ned tensing up beside me. 'Could you take us to see him, in that case?' I asked, giving him another smile.

The man shook his head. 'Can't leave the floor.'

'Then could you point us in the direction?'

He shook his head again. 'Can't do that neither. Can't have folk just wandering about.' He had a look around and spotted a young lad. 'Wallace,' he called, waving a beckoning hand. 'Gentlemen here want to see Mr Cummings, be obliged and show them up.'

Wallace appeared to be a callow youth of about fourteen years, thin, undernourished and poorly dressed. 'This way, sirs, if you please,' he said, conducting us over to the stairs that led to the floor above.

'Good place to work?' I asked, as we ascended.

'Same as all the rest,' replied Wallace, with a shrug. 'Work 'ard, get paid. Don't work 'ard, don't get paid. I always work 'ard as I got me ma and sister to look after.'

From that, I presumed his father was no longer around but I did not press him on that.

'This is the office,' he said, as we stepped onto the floor.

Several small rooms were constructed in a sectioned off part of the floor. Wallace knocked on the door and waited until a curt response came from inside.

'Gentlemen to see Mr Cummings,' he called, as he turned the handle and opened the door. He stood grinning at me for a few moments and eventually I sighed and then fished out a penny. 'Ver' kind o' you, sir,' he said, as he gave a knuckle to his forehead before running off back down.

We entered the office to see a dark-haired man of around forty years sitting at a desk with a mound of papers in front of him. He had dark eyes and a sharp nose with a small plump mouth. He had placed his wig on the chair next to him, looking very much like a cat asleep. His clothes were of good quality but he looked a little flushed of face. He looked up as we entered and regarded us.

'Mr Cummings?' I enquired.

He gave a nod. 'Yes, Nicholas Cummings,' and he waited for me to state my business.

'My name is Richard Hopgood and this is Mr Edward Tripp. We believe you have a clerk working here, a Thomas Sorley?'

Cummings looked at me and then at Ned and then he shook his head. 'Not any more. He didn't turn up for work this morning and not a word has come to me of his whereabouts. As such, he has forfeited his position. As you can see, I am having to do his work as well as my own.' He cast his hand at the mound of papers to indicate his workload. 'It is not good enough, sirs, not good enough.'

I exchanged a quick look with Ned; it would seem the information from The Ship was correct. I pulled out the drawing the rector had done and placed it in front of Cummings on the desk. 'Is this a good likeness of Thomas Sorley?' I asked, stepping back.

Cummings continued to look at me for a moment and then turned his attention to the drawing. After a few seconds, he nodded and swallowed a gulp. 'That looks like Sorley. What is this all about? Who are you?'

'I apologise,' I replied. 'I should have made it clear in the beginning. I am working under the direction of Thomas De Veil, Chief Magistrate of Bow Street, and I am afraid we believe we know the whereabouts of your Mr Sorley. A body has been found in the Thames and we believe this to be your missing clerk.'

Cummings stared opened eyed; his pallor changed and he gulped again. 'You are sure?' he asked, a slight hesitancy.

'As much as we can be, sir. It only needs someone who knew him to view the body to make certain we have identified him correctly.'

'Oh God above, poor Thomas,' he said, immediately placing his head in his hands. There were a few moments of silence as he digested the news. 'He was a good worker,' he said in the end. 'Taught him myself; had hoped he would one day take my position.'

'Yet you just said he had forfeited his position by not turning up for work this morning,' said Ned, regarding him sternly.

'I did but my sour temper had got the better of me,' said Cummings, raising his head. 'I would welcome him back with open arms should he walk through that door now.'

The news had clearly affected him, so I gave him a few moments to come to terms with it and recover his composure. 'As I say, we need someone to identify him; do you think you would be able to do that?' I asked, gently.

'Yes...yes, of course, though I am not sure how I will be.'

'I am sure you will be fine, Mr Cummings. The deceased cannot hurt you.'

He paused a moment as if contemplating my reply. 'You are right, Mr Hopgood,' he said, straightening his back. 'God has his reasons and it is not for us to question them.'

I ventured that we should take a hackney but Cummings insisted on using the company's carriage, which they kept close by in the yard of The Salutation Tavern. The journey would not take long, just along Thames Street to the church but time enough to get a little information out of him: Thomas Sorley had no family locally; he had come up from Devon just two years ago, his mother still in residence there. He had few friends that he knew about apart from one co-worker, Joseph, who had been sent to Newgate to await trial after being caught stealing from the company. He lodged in Botolph Lane, not far from the warehouse but he knew nothing of his interests outside of work.

'When did you last see Thomas?' I asked, as the carriage rattled and bumped along.

'Oh, yesterday. I left him at dusk; he had some work to finish before he too could go. As you have seen, we had cargo come in today. He had to complete the formalities on the manifest before the customs would allow us to unload.'

'Who else was there?'

'Mr Gutteridge of course, as well as the men keeping watch on the warehouse.'

'Then I wish to have a list of the names of those men and should you see Mr Gutteridge, please inform him that I wish to speak to him. So, Mr Cummings, you cannot think of any reason for poor Thomas to be found in the Thames?'

Cummings shook his head. 'No, none.'

'No reason for someone to batter him and then stab him to death?'

'I beg your pardon?' said Cummings, sharply. 'You did not inform me of that.'

'Did I not?' I replied. 'Then I apologise. Indeed, Thomas has been in a fight and then someone stabbed him. We are talking of a murder here, Mr Cummings.'

Cummings's face drained of colour as he digested the information, plainly shocked at the manner of Thomas's death.

I got nothing more from Cummings as he lapsed into silence, with the next two or three minutes spent staring out of the window. We pulled up at the church and when we alighted, Ned took Cummings around to the graveyard and the little stone house, while I went into the church to find the rector so he could unlock the door. The original church had been destroyed in the great fire, this newer one, they had built smaller and more compact with whitewashed walls and a low tower gracing the far end. I found the rector in the lower room of the tower in his small vestry. He smiled at me in greeting and when I explained my presence he picked up the keys from a hook behind the door and led me outside.

'Well, at least you will be able to put a name to him, unlike that other man, poor soul: the inquest allowed his remains to go to St Bartholomew's hospital, to be used for purposes of study. Your young man will at least have the benefit of a Christian burial.'

'That is true, Rector, though I suppose he wouldn't have wished it to come so early.'

'God has his designs, Mr Hopgood. He gives us life and then He takes it away, there is a purpose to everything.'

The rector greeted Cummings and Ned with a nod of welcome and then proceeded to unlock the door to the stone house. 'The cart hasn't long gone, so I'm afraid your young man will be lacking company.'

He pulled the door open and Ned went inside, followed by Cummings and then myself. We all stood there staring.

'There is no one here,' I exclaimed, turning to the rector.

'What!'

'The body, both bodies have gone.'

The rector pushed his way inside. 'Oh God! The hospital. They have taken both!'

Cummings, Ned, the rector and I just stared at each other; Cummings, having girded himself for the unpleasant task, now just looked confused.

'How?' I asked.

'I left the men to their own devices as a parishioner came to see me; I knew them as they had been here before. They locked up after and gave me the key. I did not know they had taken both.'

'When did they leave?'

'Not an hour since. Mr Hopgood, I am dreadfully sorry.'

I did not know what to think, I felt angry but that would get me nowhere at the moment; however, if we were quick, there might still be time to wrest Thomas from the anatomists.

'Mr Cummings, I believe we may have to impose on you once more. Could you convey us to St Bartholomew's with all haste?'

'By all means, Mr Hopgood,' said Cummings, understanding the situation now.

We regained the carriage at a run and gave instructions to the driver. The rector watched us go, still wringing his hands and professing his great apologies at the circumstances.

Quickly we traversed the streets; very soon we were passing St Paul's and then turned right up St Martin Le Grand hoping that Aldersgate would be free of traffic. We intended to come to the hospital from the rear of the buildings, avoiding Newgate and the market at Smithfield, which would be extremely busy. Thankfully, we made good progress and it did not take too long before we pulled up in Well Yard at the rear of the hospital.

I led the way, as I knew the route to the Dead-Room, in the coolest part of the hospital, in the basement, hoping that they would have taken Sorley there.

Once there, I explained to the orderlies what had occurred; a circumstance, which I am afraid to relate, they found extremely amusing but they did admit that two men had arrived only a few minutes ago, which they were now preparing for the surgeons.

With reluctance, after having to suggest that the wrath of the courts might fall down upon them, they showed me in to identify the corpse we required.

Thankfully, one of them was Thomas Sorley, now divested of his clothing and lying upon a wheeled conveyance with a linen sheet covering him.

'The clothing will be required for the inquest,' I said, knowing that they would be sold otherwise. 'I will inform the Magistrate that you have been most accommodating.'

The man who seemed to be in charge agreed that this would be so and proceeded to wheel Sorley through to another room, promising that he would be kept away from the surgeons' attention.

Cummings viewed the body tentatively but confirmed that this indeed was the mortal remains of Thomas Sorley and that he had no doubt that Thompson and Gutteridge would fund the removal and burial of Thomas and he hoped that it would be a small comfort to his mother. He then made a hurried exit, not wishing to stay in the proximity of so many dead bodies, declining our assistance to guide him back to his carriage saying that he had taken note of the way we came. I called after him, saying that I would make a return call in the morning, but I did not know if he heard me. We watched his retreating back as his little steps took him down the corridor.

'Where to now?' asked Ned, once we had made our way outside to the Smithfield side.

'We still have an hour or two of daylight left, so I think we should pay a visit to Sorley's lodgings in Botolph Lane.'

'What?' said Ned, quickly twisting his head to me. 'We could have got a lift with Cummings.'

'We could have,' I agreed. 'But I sensed that any more of our company would be too much for him. We can walk, it's only about a mile away and it is a pleasant evening, after all.'

The market had reached the end of the day, the pens almost empty apart from a few skinny cattle and unruly sheep. Blood and the deposits of the animals littered the ground and the stench still hung in the air. Butchers were still hard at work, selling the poor cuts at cheap prices in order to clear everything before the day's end. The noise had now become bearable but earlier it would have dulled the senses as the cattle, sheep and swine called out as their lives ended at the swipe of a knife.

We walked down to Newgate and through the gate of the prison that spanned the road, the edifice looming large and imposing above us as we passed under. The Newgate market was still open and the street-traders and stallholders were many and I again wondered how the area could sustain the butchers' trade with Smithfield just around the corner, but it did, selling mainly cheap cuts like offal and tripe. The smell of blood rose thickly adding to the smell coming from the prison where the poorer inmates could only dream of partaking of the food sold just a few yards from them. The juices had leaked from the carts and stalls making it slippery underfoot, so we hurried on towards firmer ground, passing the shops and taverns towards the bottom of the street where it joined Cheapside, and there the area transformed. A plethora of shops and businesses, their gently swinging signs creaking in the breeze, indicating the commodities they were selling. Even now, at this hour, ladies of quality were perusing the goods, with maids or aunts or with gentlemen looking bored and restless. Parked up next to the posts that protected the pedestrians from the roadway, carriages waited for their masters and mistresses to finish their shopping. Then onto the Poulterers, where all manner of birds were sold for consumption, then down past the Lord Mayor's mansion to Lombard Street, again with its myriad shops and stalls but also an area concerned with money and lending houses, we turned right onto Gracechurch Street then left into Little Eastcheap and then we arrived at Botolph Lane.

Botolph Lane had been rebuilt after the Great Fire, but like so many streets devastated by the conflagration, many of the buildings and tenements were rebuilt hastily, using cheap materials. The area was poor but not in the deep poverty of the more insalubrious slum areas: most of its inhabitants were not destitute but lived in the grey area between.

Sorley's lodgings were just south of the Church of St George, a three-storey building showing signs of neglect with its peeling paint and cracked timbers, windows appearing dull and lifeless. Outside the door stood two women gossiping while they watched some young children playing in the street.

'Good evening, ladies,' I said, with a smile to put them at their ease.

Both looked us up and down and then frowned when they had our measure.

'You've the wrong place. Down there a bit, 'ouse on yer left,' said one, tiredly, pointing further down the lane.

Ah, you misunderstand me,' I replied. 'We are not after a dose of the french pox, we are looking for the lodgings of Thomas Sorley. I believe he resides here?'

'Young Tom? What do you want wiv 'im?' said the other lady.

'You know him? Then I am afraid I have some bad news for you. My name is Hopgood and I am working with the Magistrates; and you are?'

The two women looked at me distrustfully and then they exchanged glances.

'I'm Grace and this is Ella,' said the first lady, hesitantly. 'Wot about Tom?'

'I am sorry to tell you that he was found in the river last night and will not be coming back.'

Both women stared at me for a few moments as if not comprehending what I had said, then their mouths opened at the news and then one grabbed the other as if to steady herself.

'There, ladies,' said Ned, stepping forward. 'There's never an easy way of telling these things. Do you need to sit yourselves down?'

'No, no,' said Grace, holding on to her friend. 'It were a bit of a shock, is all. Poor Tom, 'e were a nice young lad too, same as 'is friend.'

'His friend? Is he here?' I asked, surprised. Perhaps this friend could shed some light on the death.

Grace shook her head. 'Not no more, shared the room they did. Wondered if summat were wrong as Tom didn't come back last night.'

So, the friend had left; that might be relevant. 'You knew Tom well?'

She shook her head. 'No, not well, but 'e weren't one fer drinking and whoring. Both 'im and Joseph, they kept themselves to themselves mainly. Few drinks 'ere and there but they were always polite and gentlemanly; they would bring both of us a few treats now an' again, for the littluns there.'

'You said Joseph?'

'Yeah, Joseph Morton. Got dun fer thieving which I never would've believed, had he not now be sitting in Newgate.'

'This is the Joseph whom Tom worked with?'

'Yeah, that one. Poor Tom, this news 'as quite wrenched me

heart, it 'as.'

'I can only say I am sorry to be the one to break the news.' I said, my hope disappearing as the friend could not murder Sorley from inside Newgate. 'We are looking into the reason for Thomas's death for Magistrate De Veil. May we look at their room?'

She sighed and then thought for a moment. 'De Veil?'

'Yes, De Veil.'

'Oh, do we 'ave the option?'

'Not really,' I replied, as kindly as I could. 'We hope you will help us, rather than hinder us.'

'Very well, then,' she said, seeking confirmation from Ella.

She led us upstairs to the garret where she pointed to the door on the left. As with most of these types of lodgings, the door had no lock, so I opened it. I saw a spacious room with two beds, separated by a large piece of cloth hanging from hooks in the ceiling, presumably to give a degree of privacy. A small stove on the far wall gave heat and somewhere to cook food and beneath the window, a table and two chairs. A small dresser contained a pot, a pan, some plates and cups, together with some other cooking utensils. I could see a small looking-glass, a jug and washbowl too. Two small wooden trunks contained clothes and beneath the beds were locked boxes and piss-pots.

Grace looked on in alarm as Ned removed the boxes from beneath the beds and in turn, began to use his expertise in releasing the locks.

'Do you know which one belonged to Thomas?' I asked, as Ned worked.

'That one,' she said, pointing at the box Ned worked upon. 'I keep the room clean fer 'em. Er...kept.'

I nodded my thanks just as the lock sprung open and Ned lifted the lid.

All three of us looked inside, Grace's curiosity getting the better of her.

We found five pounds, ten shillings and thruppence in money, a small locket with nothing inside, a man's gold ring and various letters in a woman's hand, presumably from his mother. Then there were some newssheets relating to the riots and rebellion of seventeen fifteen, and others relating to the uprising of seventeen nineteen. Other pamphlets referred to both those times and beneath them, more documents and pamphlets supporting the restoration of the Stuart's.

'Was Thomas Scottish?' I asked Grace, appalled at what I just read.

She shook her head. 'I don't know; he seemed as English as you and me.'

'Then perhaps he came from Scottish stock. Possession of these indicates that he may have been a Jacobite sympathiser and involved in sedition.'

Ned finished rummaging and came up with another rosary and a small prayer book.

'Did you know Thomas was a Catholic?' I asked Grace, as I showed her the items.

She shook her head. 'No, no idea at all. As I said, they kept themselves to themselves.'

I had no reason to disbelieve her and pondered a moment on the contents until Ned gave a grunt, indicating triumph as he worked on the other box.

'Well?' I asked, as he peered inside. 'A second Jacobite?'

Ned shook his head. 'No, none of that in 'ere. A few letters, a bit of money. Nothing else, nothing like that one,' he added, pointing appropriately.

I took a look and saw very few items except for the letters, tied with a red silk ribbon.

'A lady's hand,' I said, as I opened one up, 'and certainly not from his mother. "My dearest Joseph, I can still feel your presence when you last took me in your arms."'

Ned grinned. 'Definitely not his mother, then.'

'No,' I agreed. 'She goes on about a yearning deep within her.'

Grace intervened at that point. 'Them's private, I reckon. Personal, like.'

'Yes, they are,' I agreed. 'But they may be pertinent. They are all signed with the letter "E". I wonder who "E" is?' I said, tapping the bunch of letters against my palm.

CHAPTER 5

As we rattled along in the hackney, my mind dwelt on what we found in the boxes, which were on the floor between us, clamped by our feet to stop them sliding around.

'So, Ned,' I said, turning my head from the window. 'What do you know of Jacobites?'

'Jacobites, sir? Well, not all that much. I know they don't like our King, want their own one, a Catholic one.'

'James Stuart, who is in exile in Rome. What else?'

He thought for a moment. 'Tories,' he said. 'Something about the Tories; they want rid of the Whigs.'

I nodded. 'Yes, they prefer the High Church with all the rituals instead of the simple one we have now. Anything else?'

'There were those battles twenty odd years ago.'

'There were, in fifteen, some disaffected Tories were ousted by the Whigs from Parliament so there was unrest in the country. The Scots took advantage and joined in, supporting James Stuart, hence the battles.' I tapped the box with my toe. 'The pamphlets in here refer to it. The battle of Sheriffmuir in Scotland and the battle of Preston in England put an end to it in fifteen but they had another attempt in nineteen, a smaller one, which was dealt with quickly.'

'Seems as if they're fond of these risings, I can't be doing with it all myself. I keep as far away from politics as I can.'

'That's the trouble with politics; you can't get away from it. It's everywhere. This Jacobite thing has been around since the

58

last century, and, I dare say, it will carry on to the next.'

Even now, in our more enlightened times, there is still support for the Jacobite ideals, mainly amongst the Tories and Catholics; around London, dissenters still hand out material pertaining to that cause but I believed all thoughts of a further rebellion was well and truly in the past. However, after having read some of the pamphlets in Thomas Sorley's box, I might have to revise my opinion.

I alighted at Bow Street, bidding Ned to continue home with the boxes where I would look at them at more leisure, while I acquainted De Veil with the name of the deceased and have Digby look at a court record for me.

The footman allowed me in and I requested that I see Digby before meeting with the colonel. The servant hurried away into the building and a short while later Digby came hurrying down the corridor wearing a slightly confused look on his face.

'Good evening, sir. I believe you wished to see me?'

'Yes, Digby. There is something you may do for me, if you please.'

Digby inclined his head as if I should continue.

'Joseph Morton, clerk at Thompson and Gutteridge, came before the Magistrate at the beginning of last month. He's presently in Newgate awaiting trial. I would like the details of the case, if you will.'

Digby nodded. 'Morton, you say? I will look it up for you. Does it concern the body found in the river?'

'Possibly, but at the moment I'm a bit unsure how. The deceased shared lodgings with this Joseph Morton.'

'You found the name of the man?'

'I did indeed, a Thomas Sorley, lived in Botolph Lane.'

'That is fine work, Mr Hopgood, fine work in such a short amount of time.'

'That just leaves me with the task of discovering why he ended up in the river. There is still much to learn, Digby.'

'Yes, sir, but it is a good start.'

'Indeed; now, is the colonel available?'

'He is, just go up, sir. I will have the information you require by the time you come back down.'

However, he did not have it ready, as no sooner as I placed my foot on the staircase, then the colonel began to descend.

'Ah, Hopgood. Good to see you. If you wish to have conversation then you must join me as I step across the road. I believe a mutton stew is being served.'

Across the road meant The Brown Bear, De Veil being a regular patron. Strangely, the magistrate's court had no holding cells but the tavern had rooms that were secure enough to act as cells. For a small consideration, the landlord gave assistance to the holding of felons coming before the magistrates. Friends and relatives of those held also frequented the tavern along with an assortment of men in the same business as myself: thief-takers, which increased his trade enormously.

De Veil preferred to take wine with his sustenance so we ordered a cheap Portugal red with the mutton and attempted to take our seats, but various acquaintances wished for brief conversation with us, so it took some minutes before we finally sat down at a table, close to the fire.

'You have information to impart?' asked De Veil, as he picked up his spoon, ready to attack the stew.

'Yes,' I said, wincing a little as he slurped the meat into his mouth. 'The name of the young man from this morning. A Thomas Sorley of Botolph Lane. Worked at Thompson and Gutteridge, Thames Street.'

'Oh, yes? I know the company, brings spices and the like into the country.' He put down his spoon and took a large mouthful of wine before resuming with the spoon again.

'Yes, that is correct. However, I found out two other things as well,' I said, as I began to eat.

'Go on,' he encouraged, raising his eyes from the bowl.

'The young man he lodged and worked with came before a magistrate. He is in Newgate awaiting trial for theft. I searched their room and found that this Thomas was indeed a Catholic, but...'

'Yes, yes?' he said, interested at my hesitation.

'I found material relating to Jacobites in his locked box; could even be seditious. I have everything at my house and intend to go through it all later.'

'My, my, that is interesting,' he said, looking over the spoon at me. 'I would like to view these items.'

'Of course,' I replied, taking a measure of my wine. 'I am wondering what you know of Jacobites in London?'

He put down his spoon, sat back and regarded me. 'Jacobites,' he spat. 'I just wished they would realise they will not be getting a Stuart for their King. We are done with Catholic monarchs. If this Sorley was involved, then he got his just desserts, sir.'

His passion regarding the subject took me aback a little. 'Be that as it may; however, do you know of any planned insurrection, or anything that's hiding beneath the surface?'

He shook his head. 'I am not privy to that sort of information. You would need to speak to Newcastle about that; that is if you have influence enough to meet with him. If you were providing him with information, I dare say he would find time enough but to get information out of him, well, that is a different game entirely.'

He had a point, also taking into account the parlous state of the government with the Tories exerting pressure. As Secretary of State, His Grace, Thomas Pelham-Holles, Duke of Newcastle, would have his hands full trying to keep Walpole in power and the Tories at bay. It would be unlikely that he would grant me the time, even though his office dealt with the Jacobite threat. My little snippet of information would hardly interest him at all. It is not as if I could claim to know of a rising within the next few years.

I finished my meal, drained my glass then got up to leave, just as De Veil ordered a second bottle. He did not look too disappointed that he need not share it with me. He indicated the meal and then raised his eyebrows in question. I sighed, and then paid the bill.

As I returned to the courthouse, Digby waited for me, with a piece of paper detailing Joseph Morton's crime and remand. I read through quickly, noting name, age, residence, place of employment and the value pertaining to the crime: seventeen pounds, seven shillings. Items stolen were a gold pocket watch and a gold ring.

'Who spoke up for him?'

'No one,' replied Digby. 'Though I can remember the case now, having read the file. Mr Thompson, the partner in the company, did ask me whether he could do so when he came to the court after the arrest of Morton. I told him the magistrate presiding decided, that it was at his discretion. In the end, he obviously decided not to do so.'

'Do you know when it is due to come up at the Old Bailey?'

Digby shook his head. 'Not for some weeks, I believe.'

With nothing else to glean from this, I took my leave. I had much to think on and I needed to go through the contents of the boxes more thoroughly, preferably with a decent wine next to my chair.

By the time I stepped through my door, the evening had

turned to night, though Mary still wanted to get me a late meal but I explained that I had already eaten, so she went to my cellar to rummage out a bottle of Bordeaux, which I hoped would clear my palate of the poor wine at the tavern.

Ned sauntered through from the kitchen wiping his mouth. 'I put those boxes in your study, sir, though Mary complained when I brought them in.'

I smiled as Mary liked to keep things neat and tidy and anything not brought in under her instruction was liable to cause her distress. 'No matter, though I sometimes wonder who is master of this house.' I added, quietly, though not quietly enough.

'You are, sir,' said Mary, returning with the wine. She had a glint in her eye and her lips twitched in a smile. 'But as housekeeper, I have to keep everything in order. Those boxes make the place untidy.'

'Then we will have an untidy house for a time, seeing that you agree that I am master.'

I saw Ned wink at Mary as they both left to go back to the kitchen, no doubt an argument would break out, though I think they both enjoyed baiting each other. I sometimes wonder that I am not less tolerant of the way my household staff conduct themselves in my presence but I strive to foster a happy atmosphere and, in truth, they are efficient and generally considerate of my wants and needs. When I have a formal evening, they deport themselves in a most gracious manner, elevating their efficiency to a degree that would be welcomed in a royal court. I have little to moan about, but neither do they, as I pay more than the going rate; even Jane, newly with us, gets nine pounds per annum instead of the normal five or six.

I picked up my pipe and tobacco and walked through to my study. I sat down, lit my pipe and poured my wine. I gave a long sigh as I got comfortable then got down to work: which box to start with?

Sorley's was first upon my desk. I withdrew the contents and placed the box back down. Apart from the money pouch, rosary, prayer book, locket and gold ring, everything else was loose sheets of paper. Some family letters, signed by his mother, as well as news reports, handbills, leaflets, pamphlets, all printed work with some handwritten notes, similar to the one found on him. All these things related to either Catholicism or the Jacobites. Some of the articles went back to the last century, including items about the Glencoe massacre, the Catholic MacDonald clan murdered by the Scottish government for not pledging an oath to the Protestant William and Mary. All of it centred on the restoration of the Stuart House, the denigration of the House of Hanover and the Whigs. Walpole came in for some heavy criticism too. The hand written notes seemed to pertain to Catholic services and meetings; some in the city, some in the villages' just outside, like Chelsea and Hampstead. St Giles parish featured heavily as well, which did not surprise me, considering the many Irish Catholics living there. The Ship had several mentions, as did the Sardinian Church in Lincoln's Inn.

Did any of this relate in any way to his death? I thought that it probably did, but then I wondered at his entry into the river: how did he end up at Queenhithe? Ned was right about the corpse being fresh which meant that he came up on the flood tide and from what Cummings said, he worked late into the evening. He could have met his end at the warehouse, thrown into the river then carried through the arches of the bridge and ended up at Queenhithe. In that case, why throw him in on a flood tide? If it had been me, I would have put the body in on the ebb tide, taking it downriver towards the marshes and the sea. Could it be that the murderer panicked and just wanted rid of the body with no thought to where it could end up? But if it went in at the warehouse, why did nobody see it? There are dozens and dozens of ships waiting at anchor with crews on board, and the wharf would have been busy too.

I needed to speak to Mr Gutteridge, as he saw him last, as well as those who were keeping watch at the warehouse.

I turned my attention to the second box now, the bundle of letters tied up with the red silk ribbon.

Reading through them one by one, I felt as though I were intruding into something that I perhaps should not do. They were deeply personal, professing love and indicating an intimacy between the two people involved. I hoped to have an indication as to the lady writing them but apart from the signature of "E", I had nothing to go on. They obviously met regularly and privately and there appeared to be an element of secrecy involved. Unfortunately, I could see no indication of when they were written, so surmising that they were not bundled together haphazardly, I reasoned that the latest one was on top and the earliest at the bottom. With this thought in mind, I began to read them again in the order I thought they had been written.

The first four seemed to contain an openness as though they were having a conversation, not as two lovers might write; it seemed as if these two people were getting to know each other. The next few showed that they were getting closer, a tentative intimacy, a stroke here, a touch of hands there, a developing warmth. The latter ones showed that they had undoubtedly entered a more physical phase, though not carnally. Kissing, touching, caressing, indicating a want of desire but showing restraint.

I found it quite depressing as these two people were desperately in love and I felt sullied through reading it all, as if I were peeking through a hole in the wall, watching them, hearing them, with them thinking they were alone. This Joseph Morton and his lady must be heartbroken at the change in circumstances; so why did Morton decide to steal, what drove him to do it?

There were many questions and too few answers. Although the murder of Thomas Sorley must be my priority, I wanted to find out more about Joseph Morton and the author of these letters, and to justify my interest, I wondered if the two situations were somehow connected, after all, they both worked together and lived together.

CHAPTER 6

I had a fitful night's sleep, which left me more tired than if I had never slept at all. The letters were to blame as the contents intruded into my dreams. Rarely do I remember my dreams but these were vivid as I somehow transposed the receiver of those letters to myself alone. The author took on the form of a great beauty, sensitive of nature. To outside eyes she was demure and graceful, considerate and charming but to me she was sensual, adventurous and free of thought with a wicked sense of humour. But a barrier had come between us, a physical barrier and try as I might I just could not get over it, and as I stood there screaming, my heart breaking, her figure just withdrew, not of her own volition, she just got smaller and smaller and smaller until disappearing entirely from view. I felt bereft.

My dream dissipated from my memory as I splashed my face with water from the bowl and then dressed in my plain working clothes. Mary, Jane and Ned were already up and had begun the work for the day as I stepped into the kitchen and sat at the table, eschewing the dining room for a degree of sociability.

Jane obliged with some bread and eggs, a slice of cake and some sweet pastries Mary had made, along with a bowl of tea, which I had recently taken to drinking first thing in the morning.

'We doing a bit more investigating today, sir?' asked Ned, as he sat polishing a pair of my boots under Mary's supervision.

'I will be, but your assistance will not be required at the moment. I'm sure Mary can find a way to keep you occupied in my absence.'

Ned stopped his polishing and looked up. 'You sure about that, sir?' he said, casting a swift look to Mary and then back to me, a bit of hope in his voice.

'Of course he's sure,' said Mary, turning to him. 'He wouldn't have said, otherwise.'

'He might be thinking he don't need me but many a time he says it but then finds he does,' responded Ned.

'Not today, Ned,' I replied. 'I am only going back to Thompson and Gutteridge, so you'll be at Mary's disposal.'

Ned sighed in disappointment then continued with his polishing, but now with a bit more vim, vigour and violence.

I stepped out of my door and looked at the sky; a dull day with a bit of a breeze, a few drops of rain falling as if presaging something more. I found a hackney as I walked up the road and soon I bumped and bounced my way through the streets. As I sat uncomfortably on the hard seat with my boots stirring up the mess on the floor, the dream I had came suddenly back into my mind, it sort of flashed a remembrance, a fleeting episode that I could see clearly, feel intensely and then it vanished, just as suddenly as it arrived. I did not know how I felt at that intrusion because intrusive it was. I blinked my eyes and the memory of the dream washed away. I could not now recall it but I knew it had happened. Strange the tricks the mind can play.

I arrived, paid my fare and thankfully, the rain had abated as I entered the warehouse. Wallace appeared immediately as if waiting for me and guided me up the stairs to the office, grateful to receive my penny in thanks.

As he had been the day before, Cummings sat at his desk as I entered; a quill in hand, marking and checking documents. He looked up and nodded at me, then pointed a finger to a chair.

'You have the names I requested?' I asked, as I sat down.

Cummings sighed as if reluctant before pulling a piece of paper towards him and writing quickly before passing it over. 'Three watchmen, there are their names but I do not know where they reside.'

I thanked him then scattered a little pounce on the sheet in order to aid the ink to dry.

'And Mr Gutteridge?' I asked, as I looked at the ink and considered it sufficiently dry to fold it and put it in my pocket.

'I informed him last evening of events and that you wish to speak to him, but he said it will have to wait as he was repairing to his country house today.'

'Really?' I felt surprised that he had not thought to delay the excursion, considering the circumstances.

Cummings nodded. 'Mr Gutteridge is not one to change his plans once they have been set.'

I rubbed my chin as I thought. 'He did not deem the murder of his clerk important enough?' I asked, fixing him with my gaze.

Cummings shifted uncomfortably in his seat. 'You will have to ask him that, Mr Hopgood. I do not question my employer.'

'And how was he, when you told him of the death of Thomas Sorley?'

Cummings shrugged. 'I couldn't tell; his back was to me. He just told me what I just told you and then left, straight away.'

I wanted to voice my opinion on Mr Gutteridge's actions but decided against it as Cummings only repeated what he had witnessed. Instead, I asked the obvious question. 'Where is Mr Gutteridge's country house?'

'Chiswick,' replied Cummings. 'He has a house that overlooks the river.'

I had been to the village several times in the past and had seen the houses of the wealthy lining the river, that part being upriver from London and still tidal, thus being reasonably clean and without much of the smell.

'And what of Mr Thompson?' I enquired, deciding that a word with the other partner might be worth my while.

'Ah, yes, Mr Thompson. He wishes to speak with you, although he does not believe he could be of any help in the matter.'

At least someone wishes to speak to me, I thought, as he imparted this information.

'He will be here presently, I believe,' continued Cummings, checking his watch. 'He told me he should arrive no later than ten o'clock and that should you arrive before then he would be obliged if you can wait.'

'My pleasure, Mr Cummings.' It lacked just twenty minutes to that hour so I decided to use the time profitably, in learning of the business. 'Tell me, if you will, how did this company come to be?'

He placed his quill in the stand and sat back in his chair, a thoughtful countenance on his face. 'You know this is one of the biggest shipping companies in London?'

'I did not, but I do now. I know very little about the business, so forgive my ignorance.'

A smile almost reached his mouth. 'It's all to do with investment and returns. Years ago, Mr Thompson and Mr Gutteridge were part of a syndicate of investors, speculating in chartered ships. In short, they made money on those investments, so decided to risk a partnership between just the two of them. They succeeded beyond their expectations and so the company of Thompson and Gutteridge came to be. Since then, it has gone from strength to strength, and now instead of chartering ships, they own eighteen of various types and tonnage. Our ships travel the oceans bringing in all the things that this country needs and desires. We are most fortunate that several years ago, Mr Thompson negotiated an agreement with John Company, you know, the vast East India Company, to operate under licence. We are able to use their markets and ports and they take a percentage of the profits. It is quite a lucrative agreement for both sides.'

'You do not do the Africa trade?'

'You mean the trade in human cargo? No, we do not, though we do trade in sugar, rum, cotton and tobacco from the West Indies. Mr Gutteridge has some private interest in that sphere but as a company, we do not. Mr Thompson would not allow that.'

'He is against the trade in slaves?'

'Very much so, he considers it abhorrent.'

'What of you, Mr Cummings, do you find it abhorrent?'

'I, er...am ambivalent regarding it. The trade makes a lot of money and it is a legal business.'

In other words, you agree with Mr Gutteridge then, I thought, which did not surprise me. I too found the trade abhorrent and agreed with the abolitionists. Many think the Negro to be a sub-species without the intellect and reason of the white man. They are wrong; having spoken to many freed slaves in London I know that is not the case and some of the reports of their time in captivity would chill the very marrow of you. I just hoped that we abolish the trade so that we could all live in harmony.

A noise on the stairs outside alerted me to someone's imminent arrival to the office and a few seconds later a well-dressed bewigged gentleman came through the door.

'Good day, Cummings,' he said, slightly breathless from coming up the stairs. 'And is this Mr Hopgood?' he asked, turning to me.

I rose to my feet. 'Yes, sir, it is. You are Mr Thompson?' I asked, just in case Mr Gutteridge had returned, having changed his mind about travelling to his house in Chiswick.

He acknowledged the question with a nod of the head, affirming that I was correct in my assumption. 'Jonathan Thompson; and this is a most distressing circumstance regarding young Mr Sorley. Most distressing. I understand you are from De Veil, the magistrate?'

'Let us say he has tasked me to investigate the matter on his behalf, sir.'

'Well and good, well and good. Come through with me, sir,' he said, indicating the door through to a back office. 'Cummings, see if you can find some refreshment; tea, I believe would be most welcome.' He turned his attention to me. 'I can offer you some wine if you would prefer it?'

'No, no, tea will be most welcome,' I replied, following him through the door.

I entered an office dominated by two big oak desks. As in the other office, a small window offered a little light. Behind the desks were chests of drawers, with cupboards lining two other walls. Mr Thompson seated himself behind the desk with several documents neatly stacked upon it. He offered me the chair opposite and came straight to the point.

'Mr Hopgood, Cummings has explained a little about Thomas Sorley but when he spoke to me last evening he was still distressed from his ordeal at the hospital. I would be grateful if you could indulge an old man and explain the circumstances.' He took his wig off and placed it on a stand next to the desk.

As I recounted events, I regarded him: perhaps middle fifties, short grey hair with side whiskers to match, green inquisitive eyes, a few deep lines carved into his face, a rugged face but not hard. He was of average build and the fingers of his hands toyed nervously with each other as I spoke. I received the impression of an astute man but considerate of others.

Cummings came in with the refreshments just as I finished relating events.

'So, you believe Mr Gutteridge was the last man to see Thomas,' he said, as Cummings withdrew.

'That is my understanding, but I have yet to speak to the three watchmen of yours who were here that night.'

'Then do so at your earliest, sir. Speak to Loxley on the warehouse floor; he may know where to find them.'

'Who is Loxley?' I asked.

'He is the man who finds the gangers and watchmen for us. He used to be a bosun on one of our ships. Reliable man, hard but fair.'

'Thank you, I will. May I also enquire as to where you were two nights ago?'

'You may indeed. I spent the evening at Lloyd's Coffee House; I was there until quite late doing business. William came in at about ten thirty.'

'William?' I asked, not quite understanding the relevance.

'William, William Gutteridge,' answered Mr Thompson. 'My partner in this company.'

'Oh, I see. He did not mention anything untoward happening here at all?'

'No, though he did say that he had dallied in a tavern for a while. Had a bite to eat and some refreshment, but that is normal for him.'

'Which tavern?'

'He did not say but he uses The Salutation more often than not.'

'The one over the way?'

He nodded. 'Yes.'

'Thank you,' I replied, thinking I might need to sample the ale at that establishment. 'Now, Mr Thompson, I understand you had another clerk, a Joseph Morton?'

His eyebrows rose a little. 'Yes, we did, but unfortunately, no longer. He stole some items and is awaiting trial.'

'So I understand. Were you surprised he stole from you?'

'Yes, very much so. Joseph always seemed to be an honest young man. I had even welcomed him into my home a few times. When they caught him with William's watch and ring, we were all shocked.'

'Who caught him?'

'Loxley. Cummings noticed the items were missing and informed William when he came back from checking a consignment; they were taken from that desk,' he said, pointing. 'He called down to Loxley, who began to search for them; they were found on Joseph, in the pocket of his coat.'

'You were here?'

'No, William told me about it later.'

'Was that why you did not speak up for him at the magistrates?'

'Yes. Thomas Sorley came to see me and I hastened to Bow Street. I did speak to a clerk there but then William told me what had happened, so I declined to speak in the end. I felt betrayed.'

'You thought him innocent?'

'At first, yes. I could not believe he would do such a thing, but then...'

He trailed off with the sentence unsaid.

'So, Thomas was here when the theft was discovered?'

'Yes, he was helping William check the consignment.'

'Has anything else gone missing, I mean since Joseph Morton was caught?'

'Not that I know of, but...'

'Yes?' I encouraged.

'It is nothing really, but at the same time I noticed a miniature portrait had gone missing. I probably took it home and forgot where I put it, but we did not find it on Joseph. I am sure it will turn up.'

'Who was the portrait of?'

'My daughter. It will turn up, I am sure.'

I returned to asking about Thomas but Mr Thompson could find no reason why someone would wish to murder him and knew nothing about his religious inclinations.

I finished my tea then took leave of him, giving him my details so that if anything else occurred to him, he could contact me with the information. I still had many unanswered questions but I was beginning to get a better knowledge of both Thomas and Joseph. When I returned to the warehouse floor I found the man Loxley, who happened to be the man who first greeted Ned and me the day before.

I took the opportunity to question him regarding finding the stolen items but he had nothing to add to what Mr Thompson had said and was as surprised as everyone else at Morton's crime. I then read him the names, not wishing to chance embarrassment on his part in case he did not have his letters. 'Henry Griggs, Tom Howard and Jacob Brice. Do you know where I might find them?'

He nodded slowly as if his head weighed heavy, then pointed a finger out over the river.

'Southwark?' I asked, following the route of the finger.

'Southwark?' He repeated, grinning. 'Never meant that. They's out there, on the Jimmy Ross.'

'A ship?'

'Aye, the Sir James Roscoe. It's that big bugger out yonder.'

'What are they doing on that then?'

Loxley sighed. 'Where do you think sailors are meant to be,

sir?'

The "sir" had a definite disrespectful tone to it. 'I apologise, I did not realise they were sailors. If that is the case, why are they working as watchmen?'

'They came in with the Jimmy Ross and they'll go out in it, but while it's here they ain't getting paid. The Master lets them berth there and they earn a bit by working here for the company. It's like keeping it in the family.'

'How do I get out there?' I asked, looking across at the ship out on the edge of the Pool.

'Only one way to do that,' he replied. 'If'n yer up to it.'

Once Mr Thompson gave permission, Loxley rowed me out. I inwardly scoffed when he asked if I was up to it but now I realised what he meant. The Pool stank worse than a cesspit. The close proximity of all the ships prevented everything being washed away, all those ships excreting excrement, urine and food waste, all of it going over the side. Low down, the water was a vile soup of everything unmentionable. I struggled to stop myself gagging as each breath hit my lungs and each odour hit my nostrils. Loxley grinned as he noticed my discomfiture.

'Not too much for you, sir?' he asked, as he manoeuvred between two ships and their cables.

I waved a hand to dismiss the question, not trusting myself to open my mouth.

Loxley grinned again and continued to row, stirring the effluent with the oars. Shortly we came alongside the Sir James Roscoe and he tied up at the entryway. He called up and we waited a few minutes. After an explanation of why we were there, a ladder unfurled and I climbed up, followed more swiftly by Loxley.

A deckhand went to fetch the three men, whilst Loxley conversed with another whom he obviously knew well. I waited on the main deck, pacing with my hands behind my back, trying to envisage what it would be like to sail this vessel on the open seas: the deck heaving, the sails taught as the wind blew hard, carrying the ship forward, riding wave after wave, the spray washing the decks as the bow breached the mountainous seas; the crack of the ropes as they took the strain and the masts flexing with the power. I decided I did not wish to observe the picture first hand and that I would stick to being the occasional passenger, comfortable in my own cabin and not having to be part of the crew.

Griggs, Howard and Brice came up from below and staggered towards me. As they got close, I could smell the reek of alcohol coming from them. I momentarily wondered how they could be drunk at this hour but then realised that they had been working all through the night and this, for them, was time for relaxation.

They fidgeted, sniffed and belched throughout my questioning: they began work at seven and only Mr Gutteridge, Mr Cummings and Thomas Sorley were in the warehouse. Mr Cummings left just after dark. Mr Gutteridge left about nine and Thomas Sorley a little after that, all exiting by the side entrance that led to the little lane that ran alongside the warehouse. Griggs mainly spent the night close to the big door that led to the front of the warehouse whilst Howard stayed by the entrance to the wharf. Brice patrolled the warehouse and occasionally took a turn outside but none of them saw or heard anything amiss.

'Just the normal comings and goings,' slurred Brice. 'A good few coming back drunk to their ships, the lucky bastards, after drinking and whoring, no doubt. Three of them needed a handcart to carry them.'

My ears pricked up at this. 'Is that usual, I mean using a handcart?'

'Oh, aye, it is, many gets so pissed they can't walk, so their mates always looks out fer them. 'Appened to me no end of times, ain't that right, 'Enry?'

'It is, Jacob. You gets so pissed sometimes, you shit yer breeches.'

A picture briefly flashed in my mind, which thankfully rapidly dispersed.

'Yeah, good times, them,' said Jacob. 'I always say, if yer can stand at the end of a night, then you ain't had a night.'

Part of me agreed with that last statement, however, I could not remember the last time I had a night like that.

'So,' I said. 'No one saw Thomas Sorley after he left the warehouse?'

All three shook their heads, so I reasoned that I would learn nothing more. I thanked them for their time and gave a nod to Loxley, indicating that I had finished my questioning.

I breathed a sigh of relief once I had regained dry land, thankfully largely unscathed by my close encounter with the Pool of London, just a few splashes, which I hoped would come out in the wash. The wharf, the warehouses and the traffic on the river was frantic with activity; the noise deafening as everyone called out in their loudest voices, intermingled with the bangs and crashes as the men unloaded the cargo. My task now completed, I hurried away up the lane, swerving to avoid the carters as they hurried down to the wharf. At the top, I forced my way through the crush, eager to be away from the noisy crowded riverfront.

My trip to The Salutation would have to wait; inadvertently, I had headed in the opposite direction and did not wish to fight my way back through the crowd. I decided instead to get a bite to eat at a chophouse before going to the livery stables to hire a horse for a journey to Chiswick, which I thought prudent to undertake in order to speak to William Gutteridge while events were still fresh in his memory.

Above me, the sky had begun to clear and a hazy spring sunshine peeked through the gaps in the clouds. I called in briefly to my home to don my riding gear and Ned immediately assailed me with pleadings to relieve him of the purgatory instigated by Mary; in the end, under undue pressure, I caved in and gave him the task of finding out how Mr Gutteridge had spent his time from leaving the warehouse to appearing at Lloyd's to meet with Mr Thompson on the night of the murder.

Mary stood with her hands on her hips and looked fiercely at me as Ned blew her a kiss and hurried away to dress more appropriately. I smiled ruefully at Mary as she slowly shook her head. I finished pulling on my riding boots, flung my cape over my shoulder and rushed out, feeling her Medusa stare assaulting my back.

I took a deep breath once outside and stood for a few moments, letting the tension drain away. I realised with some surprise that my housekeeper scared me more than some of the hard-nosed roughnecks I had met from out of the stews who attempted to skewer me with three foot of steel. The horse, seemingly to sense my mood, looked sidelong at me, with, I thought, a degree of sympathy.

Giving the mare a pat, I mounted and then set off towards Hyde Park and the green fields beyond. Once there, I headed to the village of Kensington, which I went through at a trot and then turned left, meaning to skirt Hammersmith and so come to Chiswick. All in all, it took me a little more than an hour, but I had a pleasant journey and the fields and meadows and woody copses lifted my spirits. I could have used a wherry but I wished for some solitude: every now and again, I liked to get away from the grime and noise of London and breathe the fresh clean air of the countryside.

I entered Chiswick at a walk and somehow managed to ignore the temptation of partaking of refreshment at The Mawson Arms, instead just asking some patrons as to the whereabouts of William Gutteridge's house. They pointed me in the direction and I reluctantly bid them a good day. It had been a thirsty ride in the sunshine and I would have liked to slake my thirst there and then but business beckoned and I anticipated that I would be offered something at my destination.

Gutteridge's house lay at the eastern side of Chiswick where a few grand houses were on slightly higher ground, affording a view over the river. I turned into the tree-lined drive and rode up to the house. Dismounting, I tied my horse to the post and then knocked at the door. Several minutes elapsed until eventually a footman answered the summons.

'Mr Gutteridge is not in residence, sir,' he replied, once I stated my business.

'Then where is he?' I asked, trying to keep the frustration of a wasted journey out of my voice. 'Mr Cummings informed me that he had removed here from the city.'

'You are correct, sir, but Mr Gutteridge only paid a brief visit here. He left to see an acquaintance.'

'May I ask who and where?'

'You may ask, sir, but I am not at liberty to discuss Mr Gutteridge's business. Good day, sir,' he said, dismissing me and shutting the door in my face.

I stared at the door for several seconds, the curt dismissal instigating a brief rage inside me. I let out a slow breath, which dissipated my anger; I should have dressed as a gentleman, which would have at least got me inside the house. I wondered why William Gutteridge was being so elusive, whether he was deliberately trying to avoid answering my questions.

I could do nothing more now but return to London, a sense

of frustration still lingering but I hoped that Ned had found out something of interest at The Salutation. As I passed The Mawson Arms, this time I decided to take advantage and stop for a drink before heading back.

CHAPTER 7

It was now late in the day, so with the horse deposited back at the livery stables, I decided that I had no further relevant information to relay to De Veil. I hailed a hackney, which carried me swiftly home; so fast, it led me to suspect that he intended me to be his last fare of the day.

I arrived breathless at my home and went inside, happy that my travels for the day had ended, albeit a frustrating one. Ned had not yet returned and I found the house quite tranquil; probably owing to his absence with Mary having no one to gripe at. I got Jane to pour me a tankard and I stepped into the garden to sit upon the bench, enjoying the late afternoon sunshine. I let my mind clear for a few moments and then called Jane to bring me my pipe, preferably with a means to light it. Having obliged me, she left and I drew the smoke deep into my lungs and began to order the day's events in my mind.

William Gutteridge appeared to be trying to avoid me, even though he knew that I requested to speak with him. Why? In doing so, he must know he would raise suspicion; or could he be that arrogant that it would not occur to him? Mr Thompson, in contrast, appeared to be most concerned, genuine in his replies to my questions and prepared to offer any help required. The three watchmen seemed to be truthful in their answers; I detected no awkwardness or signs of dissembling: no shifty eyes, hesitancy or tension in their bodies. Mr Cummings seemed to have largely recovered from his ordeal of the day before, though he did show a little residual angst, which I could understand, considering his lack of experience in that area.

All in all, I had moved no further forward in discovering why Thomas Sorley ended up in the Thames with his face punched to a pulp and a knife wound in his back. It was a conundrum that I hoped would be nearer solving once I had spoken to William Gutteridge, he could be the missing part of the puzzle and until I knew differently, I had to wonder at his motive.

Out of the corner of my eye, I detected movement in the kitchen, followed shortly after by the door opening and then Ned came into the garden, slightly flushed of face but wearing a grin.

'Well?' I asked in enquiry as he approached me.

'As you were informed, sir,' he said as he came to stand in front of me. 'He went to the tavern just after nine, stayed there for an hour or so, then left.'

I indicated the bench so that he could sit down next to me. 'I detect by that grin on your face that there might be a little more to add.'

He nodded as he took the seat. 'They know him quite well in there. I began by just taking my ease, as it were, but then I started passing the time of day with a few of the regulars. As luck would have it, one of them mentioned the clerk what got killed; word didn't take long to filter through, so I began to ask some questions, all innocent like. Apparently, there were nothing amiss about Gutteridge, he came in as normal and were talking to a couple of ship Masters, not his own, but those that do the Africa trade.'

'Slaving?' I asked, a little startled.

Ned nodded again. 'Aye, slave ships. They take goods down to Africa, then they takes those slaves across the sea to the Carabee and the America's, then comes back home loaded with sugar, rum and the like. Gutteridge does a bit of dabbling in it, from what they says.'

'Thompson mentioned something about sugar and tobacco, but he seemed to indicate that he does not touch the slave ships.'

'Maybe he don't like to admit it,' answered Ned. 'Buggered if I would; wouldn't want to be associated with that type of thing.'

'You may be right, though I understand it is quite lucrative; anything else?'

Ned grinned again. 'Yeah. Gutteridge can be a bastard. They says that your man has roughed up a few people, a bit fond of using his fists, is Gutteridge.'

'Is he? Now that is interesting.'

'Got a short temper apparently, don't take much to set him off, they say; got a long memory too. They say if you cross him, he'll always find a way to repay you, even if it takes years.'

'Sounds a nice man; do you reckon it possible he could have had a hand in Thomas Sorley's demise?'

'They said he were acting normal, but when he's used the rough stuff before he's been agitated for a while after, as though he were still living the experience.'

'So, you think no.'

'I think it's possible: maybe Sorley crossed him, maybe he ended up in the river because so.'

'Something tells me I will not find Gutteridge agreeable company when I finally catch up with him. Thank you, Ned. A fine day's work and I trust you found the beer to your liking?'

'I did, sir, very much so.'

'Good, so you should be well set up to help Mary. I think she has a few things you can do before the evening meal.'

Ned opened his mouth to utter a protest but I put my stern look on and indicated my housekeeper, who at that moment stood at the door as though ready for trouble. He obliged, albeit downheartedly, as his heavy head indicated. As he passed Mary, she looked at me, and we both exchanged wry smiles of amusement.

Jane had embarked on a first attempt at baking a pie, which now served as our late meal, having been given instruction by Mary and it succeeded beyond expectations: the beef inside was succulent and flavoursome, the gravy thick and rich. I ate in my dining room, alone, apart for the accompaniment of a bottle of Merlot. My exertions of the day had given me a good appetite and I indulged it by having a second slice of the pie, which pleased Jane no end.

Once I was replete, I adjourned to the drawing room with another bottle of wine, the fire in the hearth chasing away the chill that had arrived with the dusk, leaving Jane to clear up.

I sat reading quietly when I heard a knock coming from the front door. Ned, summoned from the deep recesses of the house, obliged by performing the duty his rank demanded by attending on the caller. I resisted the urge to find out myself whom had knocked and instead just cocked my ear to listen, but the voices were low and I could not discern the nature of the conversation. A few minutes passed and I began to think that the caller had been for Ned, Mary or Jane when the door opened and Ned's face appeared.

'Excuse me, sir, but you have a lady visitor. A Miss Thompson is outside in her coach and has asked whether you could spare her a few minutes of your time.'

'Miss Thompson? I am not sure I am acquainted with a Miss Thompson but show her in by all means.'

'Sir,' he said and then withdrew.

I placed a marker in my book and laid it down. I had dressed casually but decently enough for the formality of receiving unexpected guests. I stood up and waited, ready to welcome my visitor.

A couple of minutes elapsed, then I heard footsteps in the hall and then the front door closed. Ned appeared once again and held the door open to admit two young ladies.

'Miss Thompson and her companion, Mr Hopgood,' announced Ned.

The young ladies stepped inside, then Ned closed the door behind them. Stood in front of me were two girls, both wearing gowns of quality: one I took to be around sixteen years and a little over five feet tall, the other, around nineteen or twenty, maybe three inches taller. The younger stood a pace behind the elder, so I took her to be the maid and I noticed that her attire was not quite as fine. The elder wore a fur-lined cape about her shoulders to keep out the evening chill but beneath I could see a silk sacque style gown in a light pastel shade of blue, her waist narrow, with a neckline that enticed, being low but trimmed with lace. She wore a small bonnet upon her head, covered by the hood of the cape, though I could see strands of dark mahogany coloured curls escaping. She had an oval shaped face with dark brown eyes, a small straight nose above a wide full-lipped mouth, a girl that would turn many a head.

'Thank you for agreeing to see me, Mr Hopgood. I am Elizabeth Thompson, daughter of Jonathan Thompson.'

'Pleased to meet you, Miss Thompson,' I replied, with a little polite bow of my head. 'Please take a seat and may I get you some refreshment?'

She shook her head. 'No, thank you, Mr Hopgood. I will not take up much of your time.'

I hid my disappointment that our acquaintance was going to be so brief; however, she removed her cape, gave it to the girl and then sat down, adjusting her gown for comfort.

'Trudi,' she said. 'Could you please allow Mr Hopgood and I

to discuss in private. I am quite safe, I am sure.'

'Indeed, Miss Thompson,' I replied, sitting down in my chair. 'You are as safe in this house as your own.'

'Thank you, Mr Hopgood. Trudi, will you wait just outside the door, I will call you should I need your assistance.'

'Yes, Miss,' answered Trudi, somewhat reluctantly.

Once the maid stepped outside, Elizabeth Thompson seemed to relax a little. She eased back and regarded me, meeting my gaze and not looking away. 'I hope you do not mind me intruding like this but my father indicated where you reside and I felt I needed to speak with you.'

'Not at all, Miss Thompson,' I answered, 'please continue.'

'Thank you, Mr Hopgood. I understand from my father that you are making enquiries into the death of Thomas Sorley for the magistrate?'

'That is correct, Miss Thompson,' I replied, not expanding further as I wished to hear why she decided to visit me at this hour.

She hesitated for several moments. 'Mr Hopgood, let me be plain. I knew Thomas quite well; we were on friendly terms and this occurrence has been distressing. My father only related the bare basics of poor Thomas's murder to me, to prevent me from suffering too much shock, I suppose, but I have a strong constitution and I wish to know more about it, therefore I have come here this evening, hoping that you would speak to me of it.'

'Does your father know you have come?'

'No,' she replied, honestly. 'I have been visiting friends and decided to call on my way home.'

I tapped my lips in thought. 'Miss Thompson, I can hardly go against your father's wishes, as I'm sure he has your best interests at heart; you have already indicated that you are distressed and I do not want to add to that distress.'

'That is very kind of you, sir, but believe me, you will not be adding to my distress, only alleviating some of it. I may appear to you to be of a delicate nature but I can assure you that I am far from that. I am distressed but only because I have lost another friend, someone whom I held dear. As to me being sheltered from life, I am far from that. I have helped at the warehouse and you can imagine the things I have heard and the people I have met down on the wharf.'

Indeed, I could: the men; the swearing; the fights; the urchins begging; the whores looking for customers; the thieving; the poverty; you could find all manner of things down at the riverside. I considered what she had said but something made me repeat in my mind the words she had spoken.

'You said you had lost another friend; what did you mean by that?'

She looked down to her hands on her lap, then back up to me, taking a deep breath. 'I mean that we had two clerks working for us: Thomas and Joseph Morton. Joseph has been sent to Newgate for a crime he did not commit, both of whom I consider to be friends.'

'Really? Close friends?' Straight away, I could see the letters in the box signed with the letter "E".

She hesitated a little as if unwilling to share a confidence, then she looked away to stare at the wall and I saw her shoulders tense with her hands gripping together tightly. When she turned her head back to me the answer was all too plain and she lowered her gaze to her lap again.

'I searched the room that Thomas and Joseph lodged in, and amongst other things, I discovered some letters in the box I think belonged to Joseph: would these letters hold some interest for you?' She looked up at that and I could see plainly the distress my admission had caused. 'The letters to Joseph were signed with the letter "E"; could that letter indicate the name of Elizabeth?'

Her eyes narrowed slightly and I could see her tension increase; she held her back rigid as she sat opposite me in the chair. 'Mr Hopgood, that correspondence was private,' she said, stiffly.

'Indeed, Miss Thompson, and shall remain so. I have no wish to pry but from the little I had read, I believe that you and Joseph Morton were somewhat more than just close "friends."'

She looked away again sharply and, after a moment, she sniffed, then reached into her purse and pulled out a piece of linen, which she used to dab her eyes. She sighed and I could see some of the tension slide from her body. I stood up and went to the door, opened it, smiled at the now seated Trudi, who had Jane keeping her company and then walked over to my dining room where I picked up a glass. I returned, shut the door and poured Elizabeth a drop of wine.

'Here,' I said, handing it to her. 'I think you may need this.'

'Thank you, Mr Hopgood,' she said, her eyes avoiding me, though she took the glass and sipped the wine, then toyed with the stem nervously. After several moments, she raised her dark eyes to me and I could see a little determination creep into them. 'Joseph and I... it is nothing sordid, we are just two young people who met and fell in love.'

'Then I am sorry for how things have turned out. Is your father aware of your affection?'

She shrugged a little. 'Not exactly.'

'He would not have approved if he knew how deeply you felt?'

'I think he would have. Joseph and I are both from similar backgrounds. Joseph came to our company to learn the business.

My father made a promise to his, as they were old friends. Joseph's father died having lost all his money, so my father agreed to help Joseph.'

Ah, I thought, that explains the feeling of betrayal he spoke about. 'It still begs the question of why you never mentioned the strength of your feelings to him.'

A wry grin appeared on her face. 'Joseph said that we should wait just a little longer; then, unfortunately, this accusation of theft came. I know Joseph; he would never have done this thing.'

I nodded solemnly; I had come across many a young man who would never contemplate doing something illegal, until they did something illegal. She painted me a picture, of a sad story but I had seen the indictment, and from what I saw, they caught him with the items upon his person.

'I hope you're right and that he is cleared of the charges,' I said to placate her. 'Tell me, Miss Thompson. Were you aware of Thomas Sorley's religious inclinations? That he followed the Catholic faith?'

She fixed me with her eyes and slowly nodded her head. 'Yes, it made no difference to me. Thomas was just Thomas.'

'And that he was a Jacobite?'

'Yes, I knew that too.'

'And you?'

She shook her head. 'No, nor is Joseph. Neither of us are Catholics, but that did not stop us being friends with Thomas. We understood why he supported the Jacobites, though we do not support them ourselves.'

'And why did he? You cannot harm him by telling me now and it may just help me in my investigation.'

She took another sip of wine, giving her time now to consider her response and I watched her closely, saw the colour come back to her cheeks, the way her lips parted as she lowered the glass, her small pink tongue as she licked her lips. Why Joseph Morton had not already declared for her, I do not know.

'Thomas was born in Scotland, in February, nineteen. His father was a Jacobite who fought at the battle of Sheriffmuir in fifteen. In nineteen, he liaised for the Spanish forces when they landed at the castle of Eilean Donan in Loch Alsh.' She took a moment as if reflecting and also, maybe, judging me. 'Thomas was proud of his father,' she continued, 'for what he did and that he fought for what he believed, but the English sent ships to capture the castle, bombarding it with their guns, destroying it, with the consequence that the Spanish surrendered.' She gave a tight smile. 'All this came from his mother, as Thomas was just a baby in her arms who stayed with her husband at the castle.'

'Go on,' I encouraged. 'What happened then?'

'From what Thomas said, his father survived the attack but when the English rowed across to take control, they came with a squad of armed men. Thomas's father attempted to get his wife and son away from the castle, as he was scared for their safety. A ship's officer spotted them and gave a warning but a sailor shot his father with a musket before he could respond: a fatal wound.'

'Oh, they were captured?'

'No; apparently, the officer did what he could for Thomas and his mother, keeping them from harm, even aiding them to travel south, to Devon, to set up a new life. That is why Thomas was a Jacobite, he had learnt this story from his mother and he wished to follow in his father's footsteps.'

'That is unfortunate; how came he to London?'

She smiled ruefully. 'The same as any young man from the rural shires. He came to make his fortune in the city and because London has many who shared his beliefs. He thought he would be better able to move his cause forward.'

'He was lucky he did not get arrested.'

'Thomas meant no harm. He did not hanker for rebellion; in reality, I think he just wanted to be able to practice his faith openly and without penalty. He supported the Jacobites mainly for his father's memory.'

'But he did support them. I saw the documents he held.' I took a breath and then a sip of wine. 'Tell me, did he mention being concerned at all, frightened of something happening to him?'

She shook her head. 'No, not at all. If he did then it had occurred since I saw him last week. He only wanted to find a way to help Joseph. Mr Hopgood, you still have not told me how Thomas died.'

No, I had not. I hoped that through our conversation she would forget that element and leave without knowing how her friend had died, but looking at her determined demeanour, I should have known better. So I related truthfully the circumstances that led me to observing the body of Thomas Sorley and she listened without a flicker of emotion and my estimation in her grew.

When she left, a little later than she planned, she went with the letters, tied up with her own red silk ribbon. I had no more need of them and I did not want her to think that I might keep them just for the sake of it. I was pleased that Jane had kept her maid company; they were of an age and, from what I gathered, had a lot in common. A friend then, I hoped, for the girl from Northampton.

What now then? I thought. I decided that I would wait until morning and then when I had my night's rest I would be better able to formulate a strategy.

CHAPTER 8

Following the visit last evening of Miss Thompson, I changed my initial plan of discovering more about William Gutteridge. I realised now that my investigation must take me to Newgate prison and an interview with Joseph Morton. I did not view the visit with any great enthusiasm, so I sat eating my breakfast of slices of ham, eggs and a hunk of bread with a heavy heart.

I requested Mary to put together a few morsels of left-overs which I could take with me to the prison as I knew from my several visits to that establishment that food could be used as a commodity and would be either bartered or consumed by the inmates. I thought that Joseph Morton would be more open to answering my questions with a bag of homemade treats sitting in front of him.

Instead of me seeking to find out about William Gutteridge, I tasked Ned to do it for me, to find out a little more about his movements and acquaintances, warning him to be discreet. I did not want him acting as a bull let loose in the market; there could be something hiding beneath the surface, so for the moment, we just needed to be aware of it.

*

Newgate's grim edifice stood ahead of me. Either side of the gate were two towers acting like buttresses to the whole, while above the gate were four statues, Liberty, Peace, Plenty and

Concord; on the city side there were three more statues, Justice, Mercy and Truth. I passed under the gate to the city side and then turned to my right. I joined the queue to gain entrance, many of whom carried nosegays to ward off disease and to lessen the rank smell emanating from the prison. Others appeared to be used to the smell and I suspected that many of the women were street-girls looking to make some money by selling themselves to the prisoners. The turnkey at the door scrutinised the visitors as they came in, judging them by their dress and deportment in order to see how much he thought he could charge. Once the visitor paid the fee, they could then move along the corridors between the various wards quite freely, until, of course, another turnkey wished to charge a fee for access to a ward. I incurred further costs as I did not know where to find Joseph Morton and so had to enquire, which took both time and money. Eventually, I discovered he had been incarcerated in the Common Fellows side in the Lower Ward in the ground floor basement; at least he had not been consigned to the Stone Ward, just next to it, which is a dark depressing place with little air, no light and as foul a countenance as could be imagined, only the poorest felons ended up there, those who could pay no fees, shackled and sleeping on the bare stone floor.

I moved through the corridor to where another turnkey stood guard by the door in the dark fetid atmosphere. I passed the obligatory coin and made another enquiry about Joseph. This turnkey knew him and joined me as we continued to walk down the dark corridor, lit only by cheap tallow candles in placements and breathing the rank foul air.

'You wish for private conversation with Morton?' the turnkey asked, not too discreetly.

I hesitated briefly but then thought it might be easier than trying to converse with many an eavesdropper listening on. I nodded and saw the turnkey grin.

'I have the very place for you, sir. Just down here a bit and I will rouse out Morton from his slumber.'

I hardly thought Morton would be slumbering with all the row and racket going on around us, as the noise seemed to increase in volume through the corridors. The turnkey opened the cell door with his key and I entered. I stood at the threshold and viewed the poor incumbents, some of whom were lying prone on the floor and hardly stirred as the turnkey walked amongst them. I recoiled from the powerful stench of human waste, made more so by the restricted light that permeated the cell. The dark and dismal place seemed oppressive as if a great weight pressed down but then I thought the simile crass, as I knew that just above me, the Pressing Room still functioned, where prisoners who refused to plead could have great weights put upon their chests to encourage them.

The turnkey kicked a prisoner and I heard his shackles rattle as he pulled his legs up to his chest. 'Move Morton,' said the turnkey. 'Up you get you lazy little bastard. Gentleman wants to see you, though only the good God above knows the reason why.'

'And, presumably, the gentleman,' I heard in reply.

'Don't cheek me Morton; get yourself off that floor or I'll see what other ironmongery I can find for you.'

I saw a grey shape move in the shadows, heard the clank of the chains and then the shadow slowly grew to the shape of a man. Rats scuttled across the floor, disturbed by the movement and then the shadow shuffled towards me following the deeper outline of the turnkey. When Morton approached, I could see confusion upon his face.

'Joseph Morton?' I asked, in a brisk tone.

He nodded once and continued to regard me, the same as I

did to him. A young man of average height with greasy unkempt light-brown hair that hung limply down to his shoulders. His eyes were just dark shadows, the light being too bad to discern the colour. His features were fair and I could understand the attraction Elizabeth Thompson had for him. His clothes, such as they were, hung off him, presumably because he had lost weight during his incarceration. Around his ankles were iron shackles linked by a chain of about eighteen inches in length, limiting his walking stride.

The turnkey ushered Morton through the door and then down the corridor, he turned and looked at me and raised his eyebrows in question. Two shillings and sixpence passed between us and then he showed us into a large room with rough benches and tables. Other felons were already there, conversing with visitors: we were in the Gigger, below which, if you had the coinage, lay the tap-room, where a prisoner could purchase alcohol and judging by the noise coming up, it was already doing a brisk trade.

'This be as private as you'll get, sir,' said the turnkey. 'Unless, of course, you have the wherewithal and the Keepers grace.'

'This will do,' I replied, viewing the room.

There was no natural light, nor much in the way of ventilation and the reek of urine, sweat, ordure and the smell of alcohol and tobacco rising from below created an unwholesome atmosphere.

Joseph Morton shuffled towards a table, sat down then looked up at me, expectantly. I sat opposite and regarded him in the flickering light of the candles. I could see him better now and he appeared to be suffering from his circumstances; he looked tired and worn out, though his eyes, which I could see now were dark brown, held an intelligence with hope not quite extinguished.

'My name is Richard Hopgood, Joseph.' I began. 'Before we

begin conversation, I have some unhappy news to impart to you regarding your friend, Thomas Sorley.'

He gave me a sharp look and squeezed his hands into tight fists. 'He joining me in here, then?'

'Alas, no, Joseph. I am sorry to have to tell you that he was found in the Thames not two nights ago. He had been attacked and suffered a fatal knife wound.'

'What?' he exclaimed as the words penetrated. 'You mean he is dead?'

I nodded slowly, solemnly. 'I am afraid so.' I hated to inform people of the demise of someone close to them. Most people have some expectation if the person has gone missing in peculiar circumstances, or who had received threats of some kind, but this news for Joseph had come from nowhere and it shocked him. He sat back, stared at me, and then leant forward, his elbows on the table, his head in his hands. He trembled and then I could see a tear form in his eye. 'I am sorry, Joseph,' I ended lamely.

He took some moments to get himself together and then I saw him let out a long great sigh. 'You have not come here just to tell me that, have you?'

'No,' I conceded. 'But it is because of that that I am here. I have been given the task of investigating his murder and I hope that you may be able to shed some light on the matter.'

'Me? I'm in Newgate, if you haven't noticed.'

'And not doing so well, either, I imagine.' I pointed to his shackles. 'You haven't paid the garnish?'

I saw his face break out into a rueful smile. 'I did, but my money was stolen and my clothes are worthless, so I cannot sell them. I had more comfort upstairs in the Middle Ward but with no money I cannot pay the dues, so the irons went on and I came down here, which is only marginally better than the Stone

Ward just along; which I am sure to inhabit before too long.'

'Have you no friends to visit you and supply you with money?'

He barked a laugh. 'Only Thomas and now I will never see him again.'

'He gave you money?'

'He did but he has not visited these past two weeks and the money he did give me was stolen the very next day.' Another ironic laugh. 'Who would have thought there would be honour in this foul place?'

'Honour amongst thieves is a rare commodity,' I replied.

'Honour is a rare commodity anywhere, I think; hence my incarceration here.'

I looked at him steadily. 'Do you claim innocence of your crime?'

'Of course I do; I have committed no crime. My only "crime" as it were, is to be the recipient of someone else's malice.'

The words were bitter and heartfelt and I could not help but believe him; his face displayed no hint of guile as he spoke, just an honest appraisal of how he came to be in Newgate.

'Then who is this person and why did they do it?' I asked.

He shook his head sorrowfully. 'That is the question I keep asking myself. I have no idea; I wish I did, then I would be able to get free of this place.'

'What happened, Joseph?' I asked, wanting to hear the story from his own lips.

'What happened? As I say, I wish I knew. All I know is that Loxley drew a watch and a ring from my coat pocket but I know not how they came to be in there.'

'Then explain to me the circumstances.'

'I thought you came here to speak of Thomas?'

'I have, but indulge me for the moment.'

Joseph's eyes brightened a little and I thought I detected a little hope in them; he nodded once, as if to himself.

'It is quite simple really. We were busy in the warehouse and a ship needed to be unloaded. Mr Gutteridge wanted the cargo in as quickly as possible so we all were involved in getting it in and under cover. It was hectic and even though it was cold outside, we all worked up a sweat. I had my greatcoat on to start with but as I got hot, I took it off and placed it by the door to the wharf. Men were coming and going everywhere; we had gangers and porters and Mr Gutteridge even saw some men standing idle and engaged them with the promise of a few shillings to help. The flow to the offices was continuous as men were going up and down with papers and manifests, as were Thomas and I as well as Mr Gutteridge and Mr Cummings.

'We all worked hard that day but eventually we got everything in and under cover, stacked in the appropriate place and Mr Gutteridge thanked us all for our endeavours. Our finishing time had long gone, so he allowed Thomas and me to go home and finish off the office work in the morning. Then Mr Cummings rushed down the stairs and spoke urgently to Mr Gutteridge who then ran up to the office. A few seconds later he stood at the top of the stairs and commanded Loxley to carry out a search as some valuable items had gone missing: a watch and a ring.

'Loxley did as ordered and began to search everyone. Thomas and I stood chatting until our turn came. I then remembered my coat and stepped away to pick it up. I slipped it on and then waited as Loxley checked Thomas, and then my turn came, and Loxley pulled the watch and ring from out of my pocket.

'I could not believe my eyes; I believed Loxley had pulled a conjuring trick. I protested my innocence but Mr Gutteridge was angry and just shook his head, demanding that Loxley call a watchman or a constable. When the constable arrived, he just took me to Bow Street and now here. I am innocent, Mr Hopgood, but no one will believe me.'

'But you had taken frequent trips up to the office?'

'Yes, but so had Thomas, Mr Gutteridge, Mr Cummings, Loxley and many others. I did not commit this crime, Mr Hopgood, as God is my witness; I did not do it.'

'I believe you, Joseph,' I replied, and I did.

The story had the ring of truth and I had watched him carefully throughout his description of the finding of the watch and ring. With so many people wandering about, it would have been easy to place the stolen goods in his pocket. But why would someone want to do that? Maybe one of the workers saw an opportunity and intended to waylay Joseph outside on his way home to retrieve the items. Maybe it could even have been Thomas; the Jacobites needed funds and perhaps he had placed the items intending to get them later and then sell them. There could be any number of reasons but at that moment, and having just listened to Joseph, I believed that he did not do it. I could normally tell when someone tried to dissemble but Joseph showed no signs of that, just frustration and confusion. However, I had to temper my belief with a degree of pragmatism: he could just be a very good liar.

'Maybe,' I began, 'something will turn up during my investigation into Thomas that will shed some light on your sorry story, Joseph, but in the meantime, I would like you to tell me about Thomas and whether you know of any reason why someone would wish him dead.' Joseph leant forward and wiped his grimy head with his grimy hands. 'I know that he was a Catholic as well as his support for the Jacobite cause,' I said, as I watched him wrestle with his conscience.

He looked up at me and paused for a moment. 'Then I can speak freely of him as there is nothing to hide,' he said and then sighed. 'Thomas took his faith seriously; he is, was, a staunch Catholic. He would help the priest during their Mass, wherever they held it.'

'How would he know where they were to be held?' I asked, interrupting.

'A note would be passed to him; at a tavern or in the street; there were places where Catholics would meet up and the notes exchanged.'

'Do you know these places?'

'No, he never told me that, thought that the less I knew the better for me; but he didn't hide it from me, though I do know he'd become disillusioned with the Jacobites.'

'Really? Why?'

'I think London had done that to him. He'd been brought up believing in the Stuarts but when he got here, to London, he began to think more for himself and he now wished to withdraw from their influence. He'd attended gatherings and had handed out pamphlets and newssheets but the last few weeks he'd not done that quite so frequently. He told me he wanted to put that all behind him and move on in his life. I believe that there is a bit of irony in that now, considering what has happened. How exactly did Thomas die?'

I gave him the brutal truth, without embellishment and as I watched his face contort in emotion, I wondered whether I should have been gentler with him. I realised that as a sensitive young man his incarceration in prison would be more difficult to bear; the things he must have seen and heard would play on his mind and I wondered too whether he knew that he would likely be found guilty, with a visit to Tyburn as a reward in the not-too-distant future, for a crime he may not have committed.

Once I finished relating events, he nodded. 'Thank you, though it is no comfort to know that someone mistreated him so. Have you learnt anything that could lead you to the perpetrator of this deed?'

I shook my head. 'Not as yet, though I'm building up a picture of Thomas in my mind. You can help me further by adding some more details.'

'Like what?'

'Like the people he socialised with, the taverns he frequented. Did he have any worries or concerns? You have mentioned his faith and the Jacobites but I want to know as much about him as I can—'

An argument had broken out at a table close by and we both looked over, our attention diverted, as the row became heated and violent. The felon leant over, grabbed his visitor by the throat and squeezed, his knuckles whitening under the pressure. The bench crashed over and the table scraped across the floor. The attacker let a punch go and it smacked into the head of the other; then the visitor punched up with his arms trying to break the hold on his throat whilst kicking out beneath the table, trying to connect with anything soft and yielding. From the heated words exchanged, I gathered that the visitor had paid a serious amount of attention to the other man's wife and would likely to continue to do so for some time to come. The turnkey let the fight go on for a few moments, a grin on his face, until he deemed it prudent to interfere with the assistance of another turnkey from the corridor. Blows rained down on the felon and then they dragged him from the gigger, the felon yelling promises of vile retribution towards his visitor.

Everyone then carried on as if nothing had happened.

Joseph and I returned our attention to each other. I raised an enquiring eyebrow and he just shrugged in reply, then we continued our conversation.

'You were telling me about Thomas,' I prompted.

'Yes,' he replied. 'But there is not much more to tell. We worked and we rested. Neither of us spent much time in alehouses on our own. We went together and largely kept ourselves to ourselves. Our circle of friends is small; he, of course, had his faith which introduced him to others but I never knew who they were; there was an obvious need to keep those acquaintances secret.'

'What about the company of the fairer sex?' I asked, hoping that Thomas had led some sort of life of enjoyment.

Joseph shook his head. 'No, not really. As I said, being religious, he believed in chastity before marriage; neither of us took advantage of the vices on offer, the ones that are so readily available, you know.'

'In that case, you're in the minority.'

'Thomas just thought it sinful to lay with a woman other than your wife. I... I just did not want to become afflicted.'

'You mean the pox?'

He nodded. 'Yes.'

'The great Doctor Cundum's Machines would prevent that, Joseph, as you well know.' As I did. I always kept one about my person and kept more at home. So far, I had been blessed with health but I stay mainly to the better class of house where you could be assured of cleanliness, those that catered for the gentlemen of the city. I could never deny myself those certain pleasures, as an evening of carousing always ended up in a seraglio. I could understand Thomas's attitude far more than Joseph's, even accounting for his interest in Elizabeth Thompson, though she did not strike me as being innocent of life. 'Who murdered Thomas, Joseph?' I asked, hoping my blunt question would elicit a blunt response.

'I do not know, Mr Hopgood. I wish I did,' he replied mournfully, twisting his hands together.

'Then think on it,' I said, as I pulled some coins from my pouch. 'You can always get a message to me at The Brown Bear should you remember something that may help me. Here,' I said, offering the bag of food. 'I should think you may be in need of this too.'

He drew the bag towards him first and smiled as he saw what I had brought him. The coins he pulled over last and I made sure he had enough to get him back to the Middle Ward with the shackles off and a little bit of comfort. 'Thank you,' he said, as he gripped the treasure. 'Though I doubt that I'll be able to repay you.'

'No matter, I am sure Miss Thompson will reimburse me.'

'Miss Thompson?' His eyes widened at the mention of her name.

'Yes, she came to me last evening. I've seen her letters to you, Joseph. I had no option but to see them. I did not know your box from Thomas's.'

'How is she?' He asked, putting aside my invasion of his privacy.

'She is well, though concerned for you. You are a lucky young man to have gained her affection.'

'I think my luck has now run out, Mr Hopgood,' he said, indicating his surroundings.

CHAPTER 9

To say I was glad to leave Newgate behind me would be something of an understatement. The stench and reek of the place still clung to my clothes and I resolved to get them cleaned as soon as I could; there was no telling how many fleas and lice had attached to me and I itched just thinking of it. The interview with Joseph had fleshed a few things out for me with regards to Thomas. I now had a clearer picture of a pious young man whose main driving force appeared to be his faith; the fact that he had become disillusioned with the Jacobites and had taken a step back from their activities, interested me too. I wonder how deep into their intrigues he had become, because if they considered themselves vulnerable, they certainly would not think twice about rectifying that situation. So, my problem now is where to go from here?

I pondered the question as I walked up Snow Hill and when I came to The Saracen's Head, I decided that I had earned a little refreshment. I walked through the gatehouse to the court beyond and saw, behind the Inn, the tower of St Sepulchre's church, the bell of which tolled whenever a prisoner made their last journey out of Newgate before being turned off at Tyburn.

The Inn, a large three-storey galleried establishment sold good ale and served reasonable food, it had many rooms for travellers coming to and from London for the northern counties. I had spied Jane here when she first arrived in London. I ordered a pot and a piece of rabbit pie and settled down to my thoughts.

Unfortunately, for me, I had now found a second investigation. It could complicate things unless, of course, the two crimes were connected. Normally I could see a clear path to travel, instead, my way seemed clouded in fog and the forks in the road were devoid of signposts...or were they? I had the Jacobites and I had Thompson and Gutteridge where Joseph and Thomas both worked and where, if Joseph told me the truth, someone placed the watch and ring in his coat. So two signposts, although both a little indistinct.

My pot and pie arrived and as I eagerly began to eat, my thoughts turned to Ned and how successful he had been in finding out a little more about Gutteridge. I would find out later when I returned home, until then I had a pie to finish and then perhaps, another pot of ale.

*

The sun bathed me in its warmth as I walked and there were a few fat white clouds gambolling across the bright blue sky. The streets were busy with hawkers and traders and the people going about their business were largely in a benevolent mood, albeit the traffic was heavy, as it seemed the whole of London had come out and about in the good weather. I fought through the crush of people, wary that for a diver, pickings would be good, and no sooner had I thought it, than I felt a brush against my arm and then a tug on my coat. I snatched down quickly and caught the wrist of a boy about twelve years old who had his hand deep within my pocket. Fortunately, I had nothing in that pocket apart from the thief's hand and I gripped the thin bony extremity without regard to the pain I inflicted. The boy looked up and cast fearful eyes at me as he struggled to run away.

People walked by with knowing looks on their faces, immediately grasping the situation and some of them stopped, ready to assist in the apprehending of a young street-felon.

'No, you stay there, boy,' I said, as he tried to break my grip.

'T'was an accident, sir,' he protested, as he looked to his future and saw it somewhat curtailed. 'I tripped and fell against you.'

I felt a twitch of a smile touching the corners of my mouth. I looked at the poor wretch's ragged clothes and haggard features. 'Like I am the King of Denmark,' I replied, putting as much menace into my voice as I could. 'You are coming with me.'

'Well done, sir,' cried a man not two feet from us. 'Little bastard deserves what's coming to him,' he added, as he cuffed the boy about his head.

I let the people around me take a good look at the boy in order that they could recognise him should he venture back to continue with his thievery. I then dragged him off, still protesting, until he realised the futility of his protestations. The river Fleet was close by and I intended to make good use of it. We came upon Holborn Bridge and we then turned north towards The Swann Inn and I think the boy now realised my intention. He recognised that a little summary punishment would be more preferable to the one he would receive at the magistrate's; hanging, transportation, branding would all come under consideration, and he walked more easily towards the uncovered part of the river.

'Can you swim, boy?' I asked, as we came abreast of the Inn.

Reluctantly, he nodded.

'Good, but you will barely need to in this,' I said, observing the water. 'I suggest you keep your mouth closed.'

There were a good few spectators following us to observe the boy's punishment and they eagerly anticipated the ducking I intended for the miscreant.

I selected a spot where the boy could easily clamber out and then I cast him into the stinking rank morass of a river, full of excrement and all manner of unsavoury flotsam. A cheer went up from those witnessing as the boy disappeared beneath the surface only to reappear covered in filth. One man held a length of wood, which he proceeded to prod the boy back into the river whenever he tried to climb out. I watched for a time and then indicated that the boy had had enough and allowed him to drag himself out of the mire to stand on the bank, dripping and covered in excrement.

I grinned at him and he surprised me when he grinned back, so I found a sixpence and threw it toward his grubby hands, which he caught dexterously, snatching it out of the air.

Not wanting to become personally acquainted with the boy, the crowd began to disperse and with a final nod, I too left, leaving him in his stinking state; it would be hard for him to sneak up on anyone else until he had managed to cleanse himself from the result of his dunking.

I arrived home to find Ned absent and so too were Mary and Jane, whom I supposed had accompanied one another as they went perusing the shops at St James' market. It was late afternoon and it felt strange to have an empty house but as I relaxed in my chair with my pipe and glass of wine, I revelled in the peace, knowing that it would be short-lived.

Within half an hour, I heard Mary and Jane enter the front door, directing a barrow-boy to carry whatever they had bought through to the kitchen.

'Ah, you have returned, sir,' said Mary, stating the obvious as she saw me through the open door. 'Careful with that,' she yelled down the hall, admonishing the barrow-boy as she saw him being careless with something. 'If you have made a mark then you can carry it back to your master and I do not think he will be impressed by your explanation as to why it is returned.'

I heard a mumbled reply and shortly Jane chased the boy out with the end of a broom as he shrieked with laughter, no doubt having given a colourful response to Mary's admonition.

'A bolt of velvet,' Mary explained, when she appeared at the door. 'For curtains,' she added to my raised eyebrow. 'The little horror had not wiped his hands.'

'The folly of youth,' I replied, hiding my smile. 'I assume he has done no damage?'

'No, sir, but not for the want of his trying.'

'In that case, you have no need to worry, Mary.'

She harrumphed at my reply and then went to check again, in case she had missed any mark on her precious curtain material.

I allowed Mary free reign with most of the house's furnishings, trusting to her judgement, especially where it required a feminine touch and I must admit that she had a far keener eye than mine and the house had been complimented by many a visitor.

'Oh, sir,' called Mary, hastening back from the kitchen. 'You have not forgotten your reception this evening, have you?'

'My reception...?' Oh, God, yes, I have. With all my running about it had quite slipped my mind. An auction at the new Foundling Hospital, where they hoped to raise funds for the building of the new home. At the moment they were in temporary accommodation in Hatton Garden, opened just a couple of months ago. Lady Amerskill invited me, her being an intimate friend of Mr Hogarth, the painter, so I dare not upset her by not attending.

'Mary,' I called. 'As Ned is not here, can I ask you to sort out something suitable to wear?'

'All done, sir,' she answered. 'I have laid everything out in your bedroom.'

She had, too, even down to that infernal wig. I did think that I should arrive dressed as a pauper as then they would not expect to raise much money from me; however, I had already paid my entrance fee, so if I did not find something I wished to purchase, then at least I had made a contribution.

Ned arrived back just as I was leaving, so I had no time to hear about his day. He just indicated that he made good use of his time, so I looked forward to hearing about it later. Jane had gone to fetch me a hackney, which now waited outside and I hurried to step aboard, should he decide to charge me for the waiting time.

I thought of the irony, as I arrived in Hatton Garden, close to where I had dunked the young boy in the Fleet just a few hours ago. Here I was, now ready to give my money to save the poor unfortunate children from the ravages of destitution, helping them to get an education and teaching them morals, which would no doubt help them in their later life. The boy earlier had not that option, being too old for the hospital, but the hospital had been founded for just such a child, there to help, to stop them from doing what many a pauper had to do to survive: thievery and skulduggery. The impoverished orphan or illegitimate child at least had somewhere where they could have a chance to lead a productive life.

People were alighting from their carriages and I joined them, allowing the couple before me to enter the building as I followed behind. Footmen conducted us through the halls to the auction at the back of the house, and then guided us to the refreshments. A hubbub of noise rose as people mingled and sought out friends and acquaintances.

There were a few people that I had met briefly before but most of them were strangers to me. I spied Lady Amerskill with a glass in her hand and talking animatedly with a portly gentleman in his middle years. I caught her eye and she beckoned me over. I gave a leg and bowed my head.

'Ah, Mr Hopgood.' She greeted me with a warm smile and then turned back to her companion. 'This is Richard Hopgood, Captain Coram.'

'Pleasure to meet you, sir,' he said, with a slight bow and then held out his hand.

'Pleasure is mine, I believe, sir,' I replied, returning the bow and accepting his hand, his grip firm. 'You are celebrated throughout London for the work you've done to establish this hospital for children.'

'Thank you, sir,' he said. 'But the hard work begins now. This house is only temporary but I have high hopes that evenings like these will move us closer to building a far larger home. The Earl of Salisbury has kindly allowed us, should we come up with the money, a plot of land in Bloomsbury Fields, near Great Ormond Street. A splendid acreage surrounded by green fields. It would be good for children to grow up in the countryside.'

'It would indeed, sir,' I said, warming to the man and his enthusiasm. 'How many children do you hope to take in?'

'As many as I can, Mr Hopgood. We have only room for thirty here but I envisage many more, perhaps into the hundreds. There is a sore need for shelter.'

'London can be an unkind place, Captain.' I replied. 'I just hope that in some small way I can help you achieve your desires.'

Lady Amerskill placed her hand on my arm, looked up at me and then turned back to Thomas Coram. 'I have not seen Mr Hogarth, Thomas. Is he here?'

'Oh, William is around somewhere, my Lady Amerskill. You know what he is like, always on the move. I often say that I need to nail his shoes to the floor in order to have a conversation with him.'

An ample lady with a dominating voice came up and immediately began talking to the captain, ignoring our presence. I felt that Lady Amerskill was about to say something of a derogatory nature as she took a sideways look at the woman, so I guided her away, lest she say something inappropriate; as we moved, I cast a look over my shoulder and saw Captain Coram wince under the onslaught.

'Rude woman,' said Lady Amerskill, pointedly.

'Yes, but let it not spoil the evening,' I replied. 'You know as well as I that there is always one whom everyone wants to avoid, I suspect she is the one.'

We moved through the crowded room exchanging pleasantries to a few people and I managed to take some wine from the tray of a footman for both of us. I looked around and could see many members of the aristocracy along with government ministers, bankers and physicians, all with their wives, and I suspect, one or two mistresses. It was a gathering of the great, the good and the wealthy, though mainly the wealthy.

'Ah, there he is,' said Lady Amerskill, as she honed it on her target. 'Billy,' she called. 'I was just suspecting that you were avoiding me.'

The chubby face broke out in a wide smile. 'Lady Amerskill; delighted to see you. I would never try to avoid seeing you, my dear, as well you know. However, I cannot say that for everyone here,' he added, in a lower voice, for our ears alone.

'Like the woman talking to the captain?'

He looked over. 'Oh, yes; poor Thomas, he will not be able to get away from her.'

'No, she pushed us out of the way when we were talking to him.'

'Did she? And you never said anything?'

'No, Mr Hopgood here steered me away before I could.'

He inclined his head towards me. 'Probably well you did, Mr Hopgood. We have met, have we not?'

'I believe we have, Mr Hogarth. I was with Colonel De Veil.'

'Ah.'

'I was *with* him,' I said. 'But only as an acquaintance, not as anything else.'

He nodded at my implication. 'Wise to keep your distance from our odious little magistrate, Mr Hopgood,'

Hogarth and De Veil could not abide each other. I do not know where their antipathy came from but De Veil has detested Hogarth ever since I have known him. I believe they used to live near each other in Leicester Fields, I can only surmise that something must have occurred then to set them at each other's throats.

'I hope you'll not view me in the same light as you do De Veil, Mr Hogarth.'

'Not in all this world, I would trust Lady Amerskill's judgement above all else. If you are friends with her, then indeed, we can be friends too.'

I inclined my head in thanks for his consideration. 'I'm honoured that you can think so well of me. Tell me, Mr Hogarth; have you many works for sale here?'

'I have some engravings; most of my original work has been sold already. Should you wish to commission one, then I am sure we can come to an accommodation.'

I laughed. 'Maybe, Mr Hogarth, I'm a great admirer of your work, so perhaps in the future.'

'Billy offered to paint a portrait of me,' said Lady Amerskill, smiling sweetly. 'Do you think he should, Mr Hopgood?'

Hogarth glanced admiringly at Lady Amerskill and I came to the conclusion the he would not think it arduous work. She had long flaxen-coloured hair, fine cheekbones, azure blue eyes and flawless skin; her lips were full and smiled easily and she covered her envious figure with a soft yellow silk gown with a low neckline showing a pleasing amount of décolletage. Widowed at twenty-nine, just two years ago and childless, her husband leaving her with a title, an estate and wealth to go with it.

'I do indeed, my Lady. If anyone can do you justice then I think Mr Hogarth is that man.'

'Splendid,' cooed Mr Hogarth, clapping his hands in glee. 'Then we must arrange a sitting.' He turned to me. 'I have been attempting to get our dear Lady here to pose for some months now, so I am indebted to you, Mr Hopgood.'

'My pleasure, I am pleased to be of assistance.'

He smiled again and then someone called him away to begin the auction and he reluctantly left, I felt certain that it was not my company he was reluctant to leave.

Lady Amerskill and I walked around studying the items due to be auctioned, all of them donated for the benefit of the hospital. A series of engravings by Mr Hogarth, caught my eye, which he had entitled "A Rakes Progress," about a young man inheriting a great deal of money from his father and then squandering the wealth away in debauchery; it could well be a mirror of my own life should I have been that way disposed.

'I will bid for these,' I said, indicating the engravings on the wall. 'But I will insist on Mr Hogarth signing the reverse.'

'I am sure he would not object,' said my companion. 'Providing you pay a good price. Now, my interest is taken by that one,' she said, pointing to a painting of some ladies dancing. 'It is just full of life, is it not?'

'It is, my Lady. I'm sure you have a suitable place for such a painting.'

'I will find somewhere, Mr Hopgood. Now, look at this

portrait of Captain Coram; Billy has given it gratis to the hospital but it is not for sale. A good likeness and full of personality, I hope he does as well with me.'

'I for one will be his firmest critic if he does not.'

She laughed and gave my arm a squeeze. 'Very gallant of you,' she said, and then steered me away as our glasses were empty and we desired another.'

'So, Mr Hopgood, what intrigues are you up to at the moment?'

'In truth, something quite puzzling,' I answered. She knew that I delved into mysteries and crime. 'A young man murdered and another in Newgate who claims to be innocent of the theft he is charged with, both of whom worked and lodged together.'

We studied some jewellery laid out on a table. 'Sounds dreadful,' she said, as she fingered a necklace. 'Could not one have committed the crime on the other?'

'No, the theft happened first and the murder after.'

'But could not the thief engage the services of another?'

I shook my head. 'No, the thief did not know his friend had been murdered.'

'Oh, that is a shame; I thought I had solved your mystery. You will have to let me help in another way.'

'I wish that you could...' and then a thought occurred to me. 'Tell me, Lady Amerskill; do you count the Duke of Newcastle amongst your intimates?'

'Newcastle? What the devil do you want with him?' Her eyes widened in surprise.

'Information, as it happens. I wish to know a little about a certain group of malcontents and I very much doubt that he would entertain me should I appear at his office.'

'Well, well,' and she tapped her lips with her finger. 'I do not know Newcastle personally, but I do know someone who works under him.'

'Really?' I said, hopefully.

'Oh yes, and it is someone who owes me a favour.' She touched me lightly on my chest and smiled. 'Of course, one favour should lead to another, you know.'

'Then, in that case, you just have to mention what you require of me,' I replied, returning the smile.

CHAPTER 10

I awoke just as the dawn light broke through the window. I untangled my feet from within the sheets of the bed and turned over onto my side, propping myself up on my elbow and looking down as the sun caught the long unbound hair, giving it a golden shine. She lay on her front, her arms above her head, which angled away from me, her hair draped over her back and across the sheet beside me. I touched her neck and drew the hair away, then lowered my head to kiss her, slowly, softly. I heard a sigh of contentment and then I saw a twitch at the corner of her mouth as if in a smile. I continued to kiss, down her back, little by little, my hand stroking her soft silky skin until I met the small of her back and she moved her hips, then she sighed again before turning over. I felt her hands in my hair as my ministrations caused her breathing to quicken, then she pulled me up so that our lips could touch in a warm moist urgent kiss...

'You have taken advantage of me, Mr Hopgood,' she said, as we lay back, her head upon my chest, our waking urge now satiated.

I grinned. 'Hardly, Lady Amerskill. I think it more that you have taken advantage of me.'

She pulled at a hair on my stomach.

'Ow,' I said. 'That hurt.'

'Serves you right, Richard, for not taking responsibility for your outrageous behaviour.' She said, turning her head so that her chin now rested on my sternum. 'I am just an innocent creature at the mercy of your desires.' She licked her lips and then smiled, wickedly.

'Olivia, since when have you been innocent?' I asked, grinning.

'I was once, you know.'

'A long time ago.'

She turned her head again and deftly plucked another hair from my body.

'All right,' I said, quickly. 'You win.'

She laughed, shook her head then looked at me, biting her bottom lip coyly. 'Of course I win,' she said playfully. 'I am winning again now; do I detect a little return of life down here?' She added, exploring.

I was pleased to say she did and that she decided to give a little further encouragement.

'I am surprised your lovers do not expire through exhaustion,' I said, quietly, as I lay back, my eyes closed, a smile upon my lips.

'They do,' she replied, after several long moments. 'I have a pit in the garden when they fail to live up to expectation. However, I do believe that *you* might survive.'

Even though Olivia and I had known each other for some years, her husband and I were friends before he died, we had not ventured this far in our relationship, one that I now regretted not kindling before. She had other lovers, I knew, but being a free spirit, she had no need of another husband to keep her, being determined to enjoy life's small pleasures. I certainly could not complain about her little peccadillos.

I finally left her house late-morning, a discreet servant had provided us with a little breakfast and I now felt ready for what remained of the day. I may have been fifty guineas lighter after securing Mr Hogarth's series of engravings but Olivia had furnished me with the name of one of her admirers, one who worked for the Duke of Newcastle at his office in Westminster. She had penned a short note to him and had sent it earlier that morning asking that he indulge me in my request for information; suggesting the meeting for the morrow and I had no doubt he would be well rewarded for his trouble.

Olivia resided in Hanover Square, the distance allowing me to walk, and I must admit to having a spring in my step as I walked down towards Piccadilly and then a little further to home.

I received a disapproving look from Mary as I entered my house; she bustled about making a noise loud enough to wake the dead, banging this and crashing that, so much so, that Jane pleaded feeling unwell and disappeared to her room to recover.

Ned sat in the kitchen oblivious to Mary's bad temper, a newssheet on the table, a pot of small beer and a plate of leftovers from, I presume, last evening. He looked up as I entered and raised his eyebrows and rolled his eyes.

Mary finished putting away the pots and pans then brushed her apron down as she turned to regard me. 'Good morning, sir; or should I say, good afternoon.'

I smiled then pulled out the chair opposite Ned and sat down. 'Good afternoon, Mary,' I replied, whimsically checking my watch. 'I trust everything is in order? You seem a little fractious, if you do not mind me observing.'

'Concerned, sir, not fractious. You did not indicate that you would be absent from the house last night.'

'No, I did not, because I did not know I would be absent from the house. However, circumstances dictated otherwise but now I'm here, so you have no further need for concern.'

'No, sir, I can see that.'

'Good, so let that be an end to it.'

She held her head up high and walked stiffly out of the

kitchen, not deeming to look in my direction.

Ned sighed as she left. 'Been like that all morning, she has. No peace for me nor Jane.'

'Cannot be helped, Ned; you know she likes to keep her chicks close to the coop.'

'Yes, but you're the master of the house, you can do what you like.'

'Mary does not see it like that, she worries when any of us are not accountable; she did the same a couple of months ago, if you remember, when both of us were chasing that thief in Whitechapel. She made us feel like rapscallions.'

He nodded. 'You have the right of it; let's hope she settles down soon. I can't be having all that banging about and foul temper.'

'Never mind that; now, what news from your endeavours yesterday?'

Ned took a sip of his drink to ease his talking. 'You want me to start at the beginning?'

'That might not be a bad idea, let the narrative work its way to the dramatic finale.'

'Huh, not much of a finale.'

'Do not spoil the anticipation, Ned.'

He looked at me quizzically. 'You seem in an uncommonly good mood, sir, if you don't mind me observing.'

I wondered whether he had an idea of where I had spent the night, the reason I felt so light of mood. And then I knew that he did.

'Lady Amerskill well, sir?' he continued, pointedly.

'She is very well, Ned. Now, leave it alone or I will request the pit to be cleaned out.'

He grinned. 'That were done last month, sir, a way to go yet afore it needs seeing to again.'

'Gutteridge, Ned.'

He held up his hands. 'All right, sir; just coming to that. Now, I reckoned on starting at the warehouse, so I went there to see if he had returned, but he hadn't. So I spoke to Loxley and Cummings, said it were a matter of urgency but they hadn't had sight nor sound of him. Loxley reckoned he would likely be dealing with his other business, you know, the slaves, and that he sometimes went to the Jamaica Coffee House. Cummings reckoned he must be at his country house and when I said you'd visited but he had gone elsewhere, he just said he would probably be back by now.'

The Jamaica happened to be where a lot of the slave trade conducted their business, because of that, I had never stepped foot in the place. I urged Ned to continue.

'So, I went back to The Salutation but he weren't there and no one had seen him this past day or so, then I wondered if he had been in the other taverns down that way, so I took a look at The Dog and Duck going down to The Kings Head and all those in between, but he weren't in any of them neither, most didn't know him.'

'All of the taverns?' I asked, aghast. I knew Ned had hollow legs but even a tankard in each...

'Small beer, sir. I kept responsible but I thought you'd want me to check everywhere.'

I could not really argue with that but it occurred to me that whilst I suffered the degradation of Newgate, he was slowly getting to the state of inebriation. I closed my eyes and then waved my hand for him to carry on.

'So, I made me way to the Jamaica and had a bite to eat. You been there?'

I shook my head slowly.

'All sorts in there, which meant I didn't look out of place; you had ship owners, you had ship masters, you had traders in rum and sugar and the rest, you had speculators, you had common folk like me risking a shilling or two on a cargo, you had plantation owners, you had—'

'All right, Ned. I get the picture. Go on,' I said, as I knew he would carry on until he had gone through them all.

'Well, I sat at a table and started chatting, saying I got a few pound that I wanted to invest and that I had heard Gutteridge's name mentioned as someone worth knowing, like. They all knew him and said he were worth considering, but, they said, there were others in the place that were a better prospect because Gutteridge's ship wouldn't be going anywhere for a month or two, perhaps even longer. Two of them had ships victualling now, so I said I would think on it but I said a friend of mine had put money with Gutteridge afore and wanted to do the same again, so I used that as an excuse as to why I wanted Gutteridge. I asks if anyone knows where he is and one of them suggests the Thompson and Gutteridge warehouse, but then up steps another who said Gutteridge has a place down Deptford way.'

'Deptford?' I asked, incredulous.

'Yeah, that's what I thought. Arse end of nowhere is Deptford.'

'Did you go and look at the place?' I asked, hopefully.

He shook his head. 'No, too late for that and I reckoned you'd want to know, so I came back just as you went out. The man said he had a house at Blackheath, too.'

I thought a little on this. 'In that case, then, you and I can take a horse today and go to take a look. Ned, you can finish that off then go and secure us two mounts from Mason's Yard. In the meantime, I will change and refresh myself. We go armed, Ned, as we are to venture into uncivilised territory.'

Hoping to save ourselves a journey, we called first at the warehouse to see if Gutteridge had made an appearance but we were to be disappointed in that. Instead, we had the seven-mile trip to Deptford but first we had to cross the Thames to Southwark and that meant taking the bridge, which could take up to an hour or more to cross.

We joined the queue at St Magnus's and waited for a few minutes before the crowd began to move, slowly, inch by inch, a sense of frustration already building up. I disliked trying to cross over the bridge; normally, if I needed to get to Southwark, I would take a wherry, a far quicker way but we could hardly do that with a horse each, so the bridge it had to be. The carter's, the barrow-boys, the carriages, the pedestrians, the mounted riders like us, all had to follow at the pace dictated by the slowest. We kept to the left of the narrow roadway, the oncoming traffic doing the same; though if a horse collapsed, or a cart or carriage lost a wheel, then we were stuck until the obstacle could be cleared; no one would be able to manoeuvre as the crush going either way allowed for no overtaking. The cacophony of noise screeched into my ears, as everyone seemed to be shouting at once, together with the rumble of wheels on the roadway. Finally, after perhaps ten minutes, we managed to get onto the bridge proper and it seemed as if we were entering a gorge, such were the structures that rose up on each side of the bridge. There were houses, shops and booksellers; there were chophouses and taverns; there were sellers of silks, of fruit, of meat, every kind of commodity, all sitting cheek by jowl along the precincts of the bridge. Above the shops, there were rooms for living in, offices for accountants, solicitors, clerks, all manner of sedentary occupations, it seemed as if the whole city had gathered in one tiny place and all that balanced precariously on a long thin edifice stretching across the Thames. Finally, after many fits and starts, we stepped between the last buildings and out onto The Borough, leaving the bridge behind us, however, I could not remove the thought from the back of my mind that we would have to return the same way later.

The crossing had been reasonably quick, taking only thirty minutes this time; I did have a fleeting temptation to slake our thirst, to rid ourselves of the dust in the throat at The Boars Head as we passed and Ned looked pointedly at me for several seconds before I adjusted my sword for comfort and then kicked my horse forward, with Ned reluctantly following suit. We had to get to Deptford and I knew that one drink would lead to another and we would still be in London until late into the afternoon. We passed St Thomas's hospital and then hurried by the Marshalsea prison. We turned left by St George's church and then took the Kent Road out into the countryside beyond, where I could breathe again and the traffic became light, with just a few scattered farms to break up the expanse of green fields and country lanes.

After about a mile we came to The Bull Inn, next to the Lock Hospital for Lepers and Ned and I looked at each other, both thinking the same, that maybe we should pass by this Inn and break our journey further down the road. Ned began to assail me with reports of the ale at The White Horse, just a little further ahead, and so for the sake of my ears, I relented and we stopped briefly and partook of a couple of pots of ale, which, unfortunately, did not quite live up to Ned's recommendation. However, I used it as a good excuse not to linger and after a short while, we continued on, to the North Fields and then further to New Cross to take the road left towards Deptford itself.

We rode by the Deptford Bridge and then passed the gravel pits on our right and then came down Church Street, where the Church of St Paul's lay to our left. The busy street had many shops and stalls crammed onto the pavement, some leaching into the road itself. People were everywhere, despite it being the middle of the afternoon and it seemed to be as busy as The Strand back in the city. Work was plentiful in Deptford: ship building being the main trade. The Kings Yard built ships for the navy and there were many more wharfs and slipways where private ships were built.

Ned had learnt that Gutteridge has interests in a warehouse near to the old East India warehouse so we stabled our horses at an Inn and made our way down by foot.

We forced our way through the crowds of people and dodged the seamen as they staggered from tavern to tavern, many with a doxy on their arm. Idle men were just hanging around talking and drinking while victuallers looked for stores from the shops and traders. Painted women stood around looking for custom, their paint hiding the sores beneath. The dirty tenements and houses strangely juxtaposed the wealthier homes that lined the street. We were in Upper Deptford but moving down towards the river we came to Lower Deptford, where the workshops and timber yards, the blacksmiths and sailmakers, all clustered together in a stinking, steaming, smoking mass besides and behind the warehouses. A little further on we came to the riverbank and the dry docks where the skeletons of ships lay on slips with workers scurrying between their timbers. Out on the river I could see lighters, cutters, barges, ships of all sizes with skiffs, wherries and pinnaces rowing between them and the shore. I could see frigates and brigs downriver towards the Kings Yard, presumably waiting for repair. There were sloops and luggers and also larger ships, used as merchant vessels, but sometimes as slavers.

As Ned and I stared out at the teeming mass, the smell of the river assaulted our nostrils, the excrement from London passed this way on its journey to the open sea, and adding that to the smell of the workshops, the tanneries, the smoke and Deptford's own sewage, it all increased the stench enormously. All the industry about the small area of town created a deafening noise that I could never get used to.

'This place don't get no better, do it?' said Ned, regarding everything with distaste.

I shook my head. 'No, I think this town will always have this uncivilised undercurrent about it. Remember, it's largely a town for ships and everything that goes with it; there's a plethora of nationalities and colours, all mingling, which inevitably leads to trouble and fights. The shipwrights and sailors are hard men and take no prisoners; London is big enough for everyone to get lost in, but here...'

'Aye, you have the right of it,' agreed Ned. 'So why don't we just do what we need to and then we can get back to civilisation.'

'We still might need to go to Blackheath, so don't get your hopes up yet for an early return.'

'Oh, bugger. I forgot that.'

We wormed our way westwards around the back of the warehouses and workshops by way of the narrow alleyways and lanes, coming back to the river by the Middle Water Gate, where, from what Ned had learnt, we would find the old East India warehouse, now leased to private merchants. We found it easily enough, the letters of The East India Company still legible on its walls. Next to the warehouse, a ship, upon blocks above a slipway, seemed near to completion.

Thinking it better, and quicker, to be forthright as opposed to discreet, we approached a group of men as they gathered, seemingly discussing the ship as they were gesticulating towards it.

'Good afternoon, sirs,' I began with a smile. 'I am seeking William Gutteridge, whom I believe, has business interests hereabouts.'

They all turned their gazes towards us and then one of them nodded and stepped forward. 'He has indeed, sir. You are looking at his new Barque.'

'Then I have come to the right place; can you tell me where I might find him?'

'Alas no, sir. He came here yesterday after seeing to his concerns at Blackwall but I know not his whereabouts now.'

'Blackwall?'

'Yes, sir. The old East India dock there. When this is ready, we will tow it down there to be fitted out.'

'Oh, that is unfortunate. I've some business to discuss with him.'

'Business, sir? You are an investor?'

I smiled noncommittally.

'Then maybe you would like to see how your investment is progressing, sir? Mr Gutteridge is most keen to accommodate those whom he deals with.'

'Thank you, that would be most kind, Mr...er?'

'Darnley, sir, Master Shipwright, at your service. Mr...?'

'Hopgood, Richard Hopgood.'

He spoke a little more to his company and then they broke up their gathering and Mr Darnley came over to us.

'Follow me, sirs. Let me show you the ship.'

We followed him on board where a few timbers lay scattered about the deck; men were busy working, using various tools on the wood but I could not tell you for what purpose. Mr Darnley had an infectious enthusiasm as he showed us about the ship and we learned a great deal about the business the Barque would undertake. It would ply its trade between England and the shores of Africa and then over to the west before returning back to England. It would have a full hold on each of its passages and Mr Darnley took great pleasure in showing us how he had designed the hold to carry the maximum cargo in a humane way. The trade in slaves had good profit margins and he wanted to maximise those profits by ensuring all would make the passage. He showed us how the hold would be compartmentalised, how the bunks could be easily dismantled and then put back together, depending on the cargo being carried. He showed us the fittings of the shackles where the cargo could be kept in place and indicated the room, far better than most, at around two feet and nine inches between bunks. Safety and comfort were important to get a high return on investment.

'We aim to carry four hundred of them,' he said with a degree of pride. 'They will be quite comfortable down here, all snug so they can chat with their friends.'

He painted rather a pleasant picture of the enterprise and I wondered how much of it he actually believed. Listening to him speak I began to feel a little hypocritical of myself because I knew where my father's fortune had come from, and in turn, the fortune that sustained me. I abhor the idea of slavery — now. In seventeen eleven, a group of men formed a company and the government granted it a monopoly to trade in the South Seas and South America, they called it The South Sea Company and my father invested heavily in their enterprise because it aimed to help reduce the national debt. He saw his investment return good profits, so he poured more money into it, even to the extent of mortgaging his own property so that he could add that money too. The dividends kept returning and he kept putting more and more money into it. He did this for several years until he began to get a little nervous. He studied everything to do with the company and calculated how much he could make by selling every share he had. The money would be vast, so in seventeen twenty he sold — everything. As luck would have it, he had the foresight to sell at that most opportune moment, the share price went a little higher for a time but it did not last. Shortly after he sold, a scant few weeks later, the South Sea Company collapsed and all investors lost all of their money; except for a few lucky exceptions, including my father. He became one of the richest men in the country.

The South Sea Company traded, to a large part, in slaves: the money in my pocket and the fortune that I would one day inherit, had come from the very trade that I now stood against, but I could reconcile it by knowing that my father had no idea about it at the time and only invested for the betterment of his family. I still feel awkward about it, and will probably continue to do so but it sustains me in my lifestyle and despite its provenance, I am not of a mind to give it all away. What is done is done, but I will join the campaign to curtail the trade.

We finished the tour of the ship and Mr Darnley gave us directions to Gutteridge's Blackheath house, in the hope that he had stayed the night there. We bid him good day and then returned to the Inn to collect our horses, paid the ostler and put the town of Deptford behind us; neither of us were too disappointed to leave and even Ned did not request a pot at the Inn. Darnley had been free with his information and we knew that Gutteridge was building his own ships at Deptford and Blackwall and that he had interests in the warehouses at both Deptford and Blackwall. Add that together with his business with Jonathon Thompson, then his fortune must be immense; or could he be borrowing the money in the hope of paying it back when the voyages were completed and the profits made, using his standing with Thompson to get the loans? That was a question that might be worth investigating in the future.

CHAPTER 11

We found Gutteridge's Blackheath property situated close to Dartmouth House, a relatively small house compared to his Chiswick residence, lying to the west of Greenwich Park in which stood Wren's Celestial Observatory. I could see the hospital building just visible in the distance, on the site of the old Palace of Palencia that fronted onto the river.

Ned and I rode up to the house and before we even had the time to dismount a servant appeared from around the side and approached us, wiping his hands on a rag, a hoe balanced against his shoulder. A gardener, I surmised from his attire and implement.

'May I help you, sirs?' he enquired, looking at both of us.

'Mr Gutteridge,' I replied. 'Is he at home?'

He shook his head. 'No, sir. He left this morning, back to London,' he answered simply, placing the rag into his pocket. 'Our William don't like the dust to settle on him; just a night, then away he goes.'

'Our William?' I asked, now not quite sure of my initial thought.

'My cousin William, I should say. You are not the urgent business he had to attend to, are you?'

'Possibly,' I said, guardedly. 'I have been trying to meet with him.'

'Then you had better hasten to London, sir. He'll not be happy should you be here and he be there.'

I inclined my head in thanks and bid him a good day. Ned and I then left without even getting off our horses. All in all, it had largely been a wasted journey. William Gutteridge had eluded us again; a man difficult to pin down and I again wondered whether he just did not want to answer my questions.

We returned to London along the same route as we came, but this time we broke our journey at The Castle, which served far better ale, and we indulged in a pot and a bowl of oysters each to slake our thirst and to fill the hole in our bellies.

London Bridge was thankfully light in traffic and we crossed easily. I thought to go back to the warehouse again but I felt tired from the day's ride and I still had to catch up with the sleep that Olivia had deprived me of last night. I had one more visit to make before I could go home, so Ned and I headed to Bow Street so I could bring De Veil up to date. Unfortunately, he had gone out but had left instructions with Digby, asking that should I visit, he would be obliged if I waited for him to return.

I decided to wait across the road at The Brown Bear, so sent Ned back with the horses. At least I would be able to catch up with news from those in a like trade and get something more substantial to eat, as I had the feeling I might be waiting for some time. I had the beef with onions, turnip and gravy which I soaked up with hunks of bread, all washed down with a pot of ale.

I learnt that a knight of the road had been taken up Black Mary's Hole, above Clerkenwell, caught when he tried to hide out behind The Fox at Bay Inn; he had plagued the roads around there for weeks, had shot one man with his pistol and had intimately assaulted a young woman. The quick-witted coachman had used his whip and lacerated the robbers face, and a passenger, John Donahey, who happened to be riding in the coach for the very purpose of catching him, wrestled a pistol from his grip. The felon had managed to gallop off but had, for some reason, thought to hide in the locality; Donahey had spied the horse as they drove by the Inn and he managed to apprehend the villain. I willingly partook of the celebratory jugs of ale and quite forgot my reason for being there until Digby intruded as I reminisced about the burglar who tried to hide in the privy of a house that he had just gone through.

'Ah, sir. The colonel has returned,' said Digby, appearing at my elbow as we all laughed.

I looked at him and felt my lips pursing as I thought to ignore the summons but then remembered that De Veil could be a vindictive bastard should the mood take him and wished to keep on the right side of him. 'I will come directly,' I replied, tapping my pot with my finger. 'Just as soon as I finish this.'

Digby waited, standing close to my elbow, which had the effect of making me feel a little uncomfortable, so I upended my pot and bid farewell to my colleagues. Coming out of The Brown Bear I realised a lot of time had passed. Dusk had crept up, leaving just a faint glimmer as the sun took its final bow of the day. I followed Digby as we crossed the road to the court and then up the stairs to the private apartments of the colonel. De Veil had seated himself in an armchair close to the hearth, which emitted a warm glow. He held a glass of wine and sat back relaxed in a mien of contentment.

'Hopgood, there you are, sir,' he said, through his thin lips, which cracked as if in a smile.

'Colonel,' I replied, stiffly.

I could see his mind working as he pondered the circumstances. Ordinarily he would keep a thief-taker standing whilst he issued his thoughts and asked the questions but my class stood above him in social standing, which dictated how he should behave. He offered me a chair opposite him and

133

instructed Digby to pour me a glass of wine.

'Tell me,' he said, once I had settled and had the wine in my hand. 'How goes the investigation?'

'Slowly,' I admitted, with a sigh of frustration.

I outlined what I had discovered since I had last seen him and complained about the situation in regards to Gutteridge, how he had eluded me these last days. He waved a hand at me dismissing my concerns.

'William Gutteridge came to see me today, which is why I wanted a word with you.'

'Gutteridge? Here today? Damn the man,' I replied, leaning forward. I had chased after him through Chiswick and Kent and always a step behind.

De Veil nodded. 'Yes, he was and having spoken to him regarding the death of his clerk, you can now leave him out of your investigation. He knows nothing about it.'

'Really? And how did *you* come to that assumption?'

'It is not assumption. It is fact. I held the inquest today and William Gutteridge made an appearance. I took the opportunity to question him and am satisfied as to my conclusion.'

'The inquest? And you didn't consider me pertinent to it?'

'No, I was present at the discovery of the body; you came after at my invitation. You did not need to make an appearance. That man Cummings identified the body and I concluded that Thomas Sorley died as a result of murder by a person or persons unknown.'

My face must have registered the anger I felt, as De Veil seemed to sink back into his chair as I returned his look. 'You notified Gutteridge of the inquest but you didn't inform me when you knew I wished to speak to him?'

'An oversight. I am a busy man.'

I briefly thought to curtail my investigation and wipe my

hands of it, pushing it back to De Veil and walking away. But then I thought of Joseph Morton and my suspicion of his innocence and of Elizabeth Thompson and the love they had for each other. Morton and Sorley's death had a connection and I could not just leave Joseph to the hangman. I stood up quickly, banged the glass down on the table and made to leave. As I got to the door, I turned. 'What one man misses, another discovers. I am not yet finished with William Gutteridge.'

'You are, Hopgood,' returned De veil. 'I am instructing you to leave him alone.'

I slammed the door and then stomped down the stairs but a servant got to the front door just before me and opened it, saving me the trouble of wrenching it off its hinges. People going about their business must have wondered what had befallen me as I left the court but I did not care what they thought. I just focused my mind at what I wished to do to De Veil at that precise moment and imagined the satisfaction of wrapping my fingers around his throat and squeezing it tightly. The man was just a pox-peddling magistrate. I stomped down Bow Street as if the wind blew me and I suddenly remembered Hogarth warning me last night about De Veil. By the time I reached Russell Street my temper began to cool. I turned right and walked more slowly up to Covent Garden and the square where they held the market. Most of the stallholders and pedlars had long gone but there were a few left, still trading, hoping to catch those who had been drinking and so would be freer with their spending. Revellers had already begun to congregate around the taverns and chophouses and the cheap penny-whores in their rags and their sores were trying to entice custom from those already too inebriated to realise what they were doing. I ignored the calls, the clutches, the endearments and the promises of having the best time of my life and walked past the crowds, along Henrietta Street and through the courts and alley's aiming towards Leicester Fields and then beyond towards home, thinking that by the time I got there my mind would be clear of animosity.

I had just passed the stables in Cock Yard, off The Haymarket, when I heard footsteps quickly approaching from behind. I turned and could discern a shadow against the light from the night sky and I saw an arm raised and more movement behind that. There were two of them and I raised my arm to protect my head from the blow. I felt an impact, hard and powerful on my forearm from a cosh or a baton. My attacker grunted from the effort and quickly attempted a second blow.

'Do 'im, Nate,' I heard from the other man.

I clenched my fist and sent a round-arm blow to the side of my assailant's head, I heard a grunt and he staggered back a step, at the same time I saw a glint in the light of a piece of metal and it dawned on me that the second man carried a knife. I scrabbled at my waist to draw my sword when the first man rushed me, pushing me down the alley so that I thumped against the wall. He had his face close to mine, so I threw my head forward onto the bridge of his nose. I heard a crack and felt warm fluid spray onto my face. I brought my knee up into his groin and he gasped as the force pushed the air out of his lungs. He groaned and then collapsed, holding himself between his legs, moaning and writhing as he fought to catch his breath. This time I managed to slide my sword from its scabbard and the second man must have heard the rasp as he hesitated in coming forward, my blade being several times longer than his. He stood snarling just out of my reach but I could see his blade waving as he sought a point of attack.

'Do not be a fool,' I said, breathing hard and holding my sword in readiness. I edged away from the wall to give myself a little room.

'You're the fool,' he answered. 'Sticking yer nose in where it ain't wanted.'

I gave the fellow on the ground a wide berth as I stepped around him. 'And where might that be?' I asked, trying for a definitive answer.

'You know,' he growled.

Unfortunately, I did not for certain. It could relate to any number of arrests I had made; some people bore grudges and had long memories. 'Be clearer,' I replied. 'If I do not know what you are referring to then I cannot desist, now can I?'

'Your problem, not mine,' he said, with a snarl.

The man on the ground rolled over onto his knees and attempted to rise. I kicked him, hard, in the ribs and he gasped again before rolling back onto his side. 'Who sent you?' I asked, trying again.

'No one sent us, we volunteered.'

Ah, I thought, an organisation. 'I think you may have made a mistake.'

He shook his head. 'No mistake,' he said as he jumped at me.

I twisted aside as I saw the knife descend and I flicked his arm, deflecting the blow. I brought my sword up and smacked his head with the pommel, sending him sprawling into the deeper shadows on the ground. As I faced him, I found my breathing had quickened and my pulse pounded in my ears as I waited. I heard a scrabbling noise coming from behind and it dawned on me that I had one behind and one in front; not a good position from which to defend oneself. I turned my head and saw the man on the ground getting to his feet, one arm protecting his ribs, the other clutching his nutmegs; his breath coming in gasps as he stood half-crouched and I could see a pinprick of light reflecting off his eyes as he stared at me. I transferred the sword to my left hand and spun around, my fist clenched, and I landed a vicious punch to his jaw; I heard a crack as my knuckles connected and he dropped like a sack of coal, his head smacking onto the slimy stones of the cobbles. I turned my head and just had time to see a blur of movement erupt from the shadows and the second man rushed towards me. I put up my left arm, not having time to present my blade and smacked my forearm into his throat but the hand holding the knife came beneath my arm, the point angled towards my guts. I pushed away, sucked in my stomach, and twisted, stepping back a pace at the same time and fortunately, the knife found only air. Then his free hand came over and I felt a fist strike my head, I just began to bring my right hand up to take my sword when I felt a sharp pain in my forearm, just below my left elbow and I knew I had suffered a wound. I let out a yell of defiance and anger and spun away from the man, slicing down with my sword at the same time. He screamed out in pain and I heard the clatter as the knife fell from his grip. I should have finished him then but I hesitated which allowed him enough time to turn and rush away, his hand clinging to his wounded wrist, leaving his accomplice lying unconscious in the alley. I transferred my sword back to my right hand and I felt the pain in my arm where the knife had caught me. I did not know how bad it was but suspected it was deep. I sheathed the sword and tried to catch my breath. The wounded man had escaped, leaving me with the unconscious one.

Even though I felt a little shaken by the attack, I decided to wait for the man to regain his senses, so in the meantime, I crouched down and began to search him for any form of identity when I heard a group of men coming down the alley towards me. Damn, I thought, it would look as if I were the attacker and was stealing from him. I looked up and could see several men, silhouetted against the thin slither of light and I began to creep away, keeping low, trying to stay in the darkest part until I came near to the exit of the alley. Then I ran, out into St James' market.

I heard a shout behind me as I ran and I turned my head to see two men come running out of the alley and looking around. Fortunately, the lanes in the market crisscrossed, so no sooner did I run down one lane, I could then turn down another. The men following soon gave up, leaving me to return home at a more sedate pace with time for me to calm down.

'Sir,' exclaimed Mary, as she walked through from the back of the house and saw me holding my arm, the specks of blood on my face. 'You are hurt.'

'Calm down, Mary,' I said. 'It is only—'

'Ned,' she yelled, interrupting me, shouting back towards the kitchen.

She hurried forward and prised my hand away from my wound; blood had soaked into my coat-sleeve, though not as much as I had feared. Ned came rushing through as Mary probed the tear in the material.

'What happened?' asked Ned, urgently.

'I was attacked in Cock Yard. I injured one, who ran off and the other lies unconscious as I left.'

Ned grabbed the door handle and flung it open. 'I'll go find the bastard.'

'Wait, Ned. A group of men came along forcing me to flee. They might still be there.'

'No matter, I'll just be passing as far as they are concerned.'

As soon as Ned had gone, Mary took me through to the kitchen and sat me down. She called to Jane to come down and help and before I knew it, the two women were fussing around me, easing off my coat and waistcoat. My blood had ruined my shirt so Mary cut it away from my arm while Jane brought a bowl of hot water and together they cleaned my injury.

'Was this a knife?' asked Mary as she dabbed away.

'Yes'

'Then let us hope that it was clean; this will hurt a bit,' she added, as she reached for a bottle of gin.

My arm stung like it had been set on fire as she poured the potent spirit directly into the cut and I exclaimed briefly before clamping my jaw shut again. Not content to doing it once, Mary poured and dabbed some more until she had upended most of the bottle over me, and I suspected she enjoyed the opportunity to cause me a little distress.

'It is not a large wound,' said Mary, peering close, 'but it will need drawing together. I will send Jane for a doctor.'

'No,' I said, holding up my hand to stay Jane. 'There is no need for that. Can you do it, Mary?'

'Me?' She exclaimed, wide-eyed.

'Why not? You do sewing, do you not?'

'Yes, sir, but it is not quite the same.'

'I can do it,' said Jane, shyly. 'I used to sew my father up after his fights.'

'Did you?' I replied, eagerly.

'Yes, sir. He were a right brawler, always getting into trouble but he always picked on the bigger man and lost more times than he won.'

'Then this little cut is not a problem to you?'

'No, sir. All I need is a needle and a waxed thread. Silk would be good.'

Mary stared at Jane in astonishment until, prompted by me, she went off on her errand to find the things that Jane required. She returned a few minutes later and we both watched her as she cut the thread of silk and then pass it through the beeswax candle.

'That'll do,' announced Jane, as Mary handed her the needle and thread. 'This'll sting, sir,' she warned.

I smiled at her. 'Just do it, Jane. Do not worry even if I yell the house down.'

I will admit that it hurt more than I thought it would do, even taking into account the beer I had drunk earlier but Jane worked most diligently on her stitching and it did not take very long before she sat back and nodded to herself. My arm ached but I could see that she had made a fine job, with four neat stitches holding it together. I just had to hope that it would stay clean and not putrefy as I was quite fond of my arm and would not like it to be taken off.

Mary found me a clean shirt whilst Jane passed a piece of clean linen around my arm and then I had to sit and listen to a lecture from Mary regarding my choice of business. Not for the first time had I suffered this and I knew it would not be the last. Thankfully, Ned returned mid-harangue, which quite put her off her stride as she was just warming up. Jane had watched and listened with an amused expression on her face, which pleased me to see, as it indicated that she had become content enough to be relaxed around me, but I resolved not to utilise her newly discovered skill too much in the future.

'Gone,' announced Ned. 'No one there when I arrived. I had a look all around, even the stables, then went up the road but still nothing, so I went back to the market and had a look around there too. Still nothing. Whoever it was had got up and gone, or someone had carried him away.'

'That does not surprise me but the attack indicates that we have stirred up a nest and from what those men said, they belong to an organisation.'

'There's only one organisation that we've been asking about,' said Ned, thoughtfully.

'Precisely. The Jacobites.'

CHAPTER 12

I lay awake mulling over in my mind how and what had instigated the attack upon my person. Beside me, a lone candle flickered and beside that, a restorative glass of brandy, a large restorative glass of brandy, as I felt that I deserved it. It felt strange to be lying in bed with a glass of spirit at hand but I must admit, I found it quite pleasurable. My arm still ached and throbbed but Jane had done a fine job and I had no restriction in my movement.

The Jacobites, I mused as I took a sip. To whom had I spoken regarding them? Not many, I thought, just a few people and those questions just generalities. I could not think what other group could have organised the attack; the man let slip that they had volunteered, so they belonged to a large group, indicating that my probing had triggered a reaction. Had I stumbled upon something of a greater scale than murder? Maybe I jumped to conclusions and that the Jacobites were not involved at all; maybe they were Wharf Rats who plied their illegal trade along the riverfront. Thomas could have been immersed in their operations, stealing from ships and warehouses but that seemed unlikely as my dealings with them in the past showed that they were honest thieves and would have no doubt told me why they were roughing me up. No, I could think of no other group but one: it had to be the rebels.

Now, I thought, I should make a list of names of the people I had spoken to; so not having pen, ink and paper to hand, I got up, threw on my robe and headed downstairs to my study. I lit my pipe, swallowed a mouthful of brandy then got to work.

I wrote down all those I had spoken with, including a couple of associates at The Brown Bear, Hal Bryant and Josh Hampton and then studied them: now, which names could I discount?

In truth, none of them, but some were highly unlikely and I poised my quill above, ready to strike a line through them; First, I put a line through Olivia Amerskill's name, I had known her for a long time and I could certainly discount her as a rebel and a Catholic.

De Veil and Digby received a strike through too and I also put a line through Joseph as he was in prison; he would have to be a major influence to arrange something from there and I just could not see that he could be.

I put a line through Elizabeth Thompson's name next, because... and here I thought a little more and decided that I could not discount her yet, so I rewrote her name at the bottom.

The watchmen, Griggs, Howard and Brice were unlikely too as they spent most of their time at sea, sometimes for several years at a time but could I discount them? I decided no, I could not.

Hal and Josh got a strike through, as they had no time to organise an attack.

That left me with Loxley, the three watchmen, Cummings, the two Thompson's, Grace, Ella and even though I had yet to speak with him, Gutteridge.

It must be one of them, and they certainly had a hand in the death of Thomas Sorley, but which one?

*

I slept into the morning, I did not rise until nine o'clock, perhaps because of my late-night deliberations or perhaps because of the brandy, though my head felt clear and without the fug of inebriation. I rose, washed my face in the bowl and dressed. I had an appointment later in the morning but in the meantime, I could make Ned a happy man and send him out to investigate the two women, Grace and Ella.

Mary waited for me in the kitchen, a cloth covering some ham with a hunk of bread and cheese. She had the pot boiling on the fire and Jane made me a bowl of tea.

'We will have a look at your wound, sir,' said Mary, with a stern expression that brooked no arguing as Jane put the bowl in front of me.

I sighed, then removed all my upper garments under the gaze of the two women, both of whom watched without embarrassment. Jane untied the linen bandage and inspected the wound, Mary too inspected it and then applied a fresh bandage and both of them agreed that it looked clean, as it should be.

'Does it hurt?' asked Mary.

I shook my head. 'A little ache but that is all.'

'Then I say that you are a lucky man, sir, because you could be sitting here dead from your wounds and that would not serve you well at all, now would it?'

I thought to point out the incongruity of her reply as I replaced my clothes but realised that she only meant concern for my welfare, so I would do well not to take it lightly. 'You are correct, Mary, so I will endeavour to take more care in the future.'

She nodded acceptance and then bustled about, picking things up and putting things down and I could tell that she had a nervous air about her. Jane caught my eye and I cocked my head in Mary's direction and gave a quick wink, making her smile.

Ned then came in carrying a basket of clothes for washing

and dumped it on the floor by the back door. 'How's yer arm today, sir?' he enquired, turning around.

'Good, thank you, Ned,' I replied, moving my arm in all directions to show the women how well it worked,

'Then I take it we will be trying to find those that did that to you?'

'Not exactly, Ned. I have to see a man at Westminster today which will leave you at Mary's mercy, unless you would prefer to look into the background of those two ladies from the lodgings of Joseph and Thomas?'

His eyes lit up and a grin spread across his face.

'My attackers have disappeared into the city but we'll find them by eliminating our suspects. You can start with those women; find out all about them, whatever you can, specifically whether they have any connections to the Jacobites.'

'Right you are, sir. I'll find out what I can.'

'Good, but take care and no unnecessary risks as we don't want to cause Mary anymore angst.'

Mary's head whipped around and I saw her lips purse in indignation. 'You can mock me, sir but I am only saying what I seem fit: someone has to.'

I held up a hand and smiled. 'You are right, Mary, and I promise that both of us will bear what you say in mind. Is that not right, Ned?'

'Indeed it is, sir. I don't intend to become food for the maggots, at least not for a few years yet.'

'See, Mary.' I said, holding out both my hands. 'We have taken your point.'

Jane turned her head away but not before I saw the amused expression on her face.

Ned left for Botolph Street shortly after, a few coins in his pocket for sustenance, and if needs be, a little bribery. I lingered a while longer having decamped to my study, hoping that by looking at the names I had written down during the night I would miraculously discover a connection. Try as I might, I could not see one, so eventually decided to take a slow trip down to Westminster, to take the air, as the day appeared to be a fine one with plenty of sunshine and moderately warm.

I left home then headed south, traversing St James's Square and taking a moment of leisure at the lake in the centre, then down to Pall Mall, worming my way across St James' Park. I again took a few moments to relax on a bench in the park, watching as the people conversed and paraded amongst the trees and the lush green grass. Further away the cows grazed and I could see the booth where you could buy fresh milk straight from the cows. Some children were playing tag, running after each other as their guardians watched over them. After a few minutes of losing myself in the tranquillity, I rose from my bench and continued around the head of the canal and over to the parade ground of the Guards where, at the edge, a wide alley led down to White Hall. No guards were parading at that time but there were a few strollers wandering and studying the armaments. I came out onto White Hall opposite the Banqueting House, where the first Charles met his end, and turned right, heading down, past the Privy Gardens and taking the left fork into Parliament Street, a little further down they were building the new bridge, only the second to cross the river which would hopefully alleviate some of the congestion on London Bridge, and then I came to The New Palace Yard.

I stood for a moment and pulled out the piece of paper that Olivia had written upon, giving me directions to the office of the gentleman she had sent me to see, a Sir Chauntley Ambrose, whom it pained me to think, must have had intimate knowledge of her, or wished to have intimate knowledge of her and thus would be prepared to offer her a favour. I knew that she had several lovers and did not feel particularly aggrieved by that, but now I was probably going to speak to one of them and I did not know for certain how I felt.

New Palace Yard lay in front of Westminster Hall with the Exchequer building to its left; I had to look for the alley that ran between them. In the Yard itself many people milled about amongst a cacophony of noise: taverns, chophouses, coffee houses were built hard up against the hall, roughly put up, they looked like temporary constructions which would collapse in anything more than a breeze, but they had been there for years and would certainly be there for a few more years yet, selling their wares to all who worked in the government buildings. Within the yard, there were hawkers and traders selling their goods from barrows and stalls as well as the ever-present whores looking for business, hoping to snare a rich benefactor.

The Palace of Westminster was like a city within a city; a collection of various buildings connected by a series of alleyways, lanes and winding covered corridors. Behind the Hall and the Exchequer lay the Chapel of St Stephen where the Commons sat to debate the great issues of the day.

I looked up at the gable end of the Hall and the main entrance, above which, a massive arched window looked down onto the Yard, to either side were two towers, rising nearly to the roof. A steady stream of people walked in and out, some to visit the shops inside which sold all manner of legal paraphernalia: wigs, ink, quills, vellum, paper and others who sold cloaks, gloves, hats and capes, serving those who had business in the court.

Pushing through the crowd, I aimed to the left of the Hall and came to the alleyway described to me and thankfully the crush of people had thinned out and I could move more freely. I had to look for an arched door some few yards down on the left, behind which a set of stairs led up to the floor above. I hurried up the stairs to the corridor and then followed it down, passing several doors until I came to the sixth and then I knocked, hoping that Olivia had written down the instructions correctly.

'Come,' barked a voice in reply to my knock.

I turned the handle and then entered into a cramped untidy office. A large desk sat beneath the window with the walls hidden by cupboards and shelves, stacked full of parchment rolls, books and ledgers. Behind the desk sat Sir Chauntley Ambrose, who rose from his chair as I came in and we both nodded a polite bow. He stood a little under my own height with a sturdy proportionate build. He wore his own hair, wavy and thick about his head, coloured a dark brown. I would think women would consider him fair looking having dark lively eyes with plump lips that broke easily into a smile. He looked around forty years of age, which I thought a little old for Olivia.

'You are Hopgood?' he enquired, as he indicated a chair in front of the desk.

'I am, Sir Chauntley. You have received the note from Lady Amerskill?'

He nodded as he sat back down and flashed a grin. 'A scant note but I understand that you wish to ask me some questions?'

'That is correct, Sir Chauntley,' I replied, as I sat down. 'I am hoping that you may be able to assist me regarding an investigation I'm currently undertaking on behalf of Magistrate De Veil; and no, I am not a constable or an official of the court, before you ask.'

He raised his eyebrows. 'Then in what capacity are you investigating?'

'As a private individual, sir, though under the direction of De Veil.'

'Oh, I see. A thief-taker then?'

'I have been called that but I prefer a Gentleman Investigator.'

He smiled and leant back. 'What is in a name, Mr Hopgood? The result is the same, as long as you do not take after Jonathan Wilde or have his aspirations.'

I sighed in frustration: Jonathan Wilde was a thief-taker in the early part of the century, famous for taking thieves but also as the leader of the biggest criminal gang operating in London at the time. He used one side of his operation to benefit the other. He used blackmail, extortion, murder, theft, the disposal of stolen goods, anything illegal to further his riches and to control the other criminals and their gangs as well as their victims. Eventually, he was caught and they hanged him in twenty-five. In some ways, he should be admired for his audacity in managing to keep on both sides of the law. 'I think the less said about Wilde, the better we will be, Sir Chauntley.'

'Quite right, Mr Hopgood, though I have no doubt that some of your number look to Wilde for inspiration.'

'There are always a few bruised and rotten apples in the barrel, sir, but that is true for all society, regardless of profession or standing.'

'Well said, sir,' he said, waving an arm languidly. 'Now, let us get down to business. What questions do you wish to ask?'

I took a deep breath, knowing that the ground I would be stepping on could be a little bumpy. 'Jacobites, Sir Chauntley. The London Jacobites. I wish to know about them.'

'As do we all, Mr Hopgood,' he replied, after a brief pause. He steepled his fingers in front of his nose and looked steadily back at me.

'I will be clearer then, sir,' I began. 'A young man has been murdered, stabbed in the back and dumped in the river. I've discovered that he was both a Catholic and a Jacobite, although I believe he recently stepped back from his Jacobite activities. I'm working on the assumption that his association with that group has some bearing on his demise.'

'A reasonable assumption, by the sound of it.'

'I believe so; which begs the question: what does the government know of Jacobite activities at the moment?'

His face broke into another grin and then he laughed. 'Not a little question then, Mr Hopgood. However, as much as I would like to help, I am afraid that you are speaking to the wrong man.'

'Then who could?'

'Ah, that would be the Duke, sir. I am one of the bees, buzzing around gathering honey for the Queen; the Queen being the Duke, if you excuse the analogy.'

'Would I be able to see him?'

'He is a busy man, Mr Hopgood; there is a great demand on his time.'

'Perhaps if you ask he may find he has a few minutes to spare me?'

He went quiet for a few moments, thinking, I presumed.

'Who was the young man murdered?' he asked, in the end.

'Sorley, a Thomas Sorley. A man who worked at Thompson and Gutteridge of Thames Street.'

He smiled, nodded and then seemed to come to a decision. 'Would you mind waiting here for a short time, Mr Hopgood?'

'Of course not, sir. I would be grateful for any consideration.'

He stood and walked around the desk, heading for the door, then he stopped and turned. 'On second thoughts, perhaps I can find you somewhere a little more comfortable to wait. Follow me, please.'

I hid my disappointment as I had thought to take a look at all the bits of paper scattered across his desk, I reasoned that it could not all be boring. He must have realised that I would not just sit quietly, ignoring the temptation.

We walked through the building, along dusty corridors and up and down rickety steps and stairs; men hurried past us, scurrying around like rooks in their dark clothes. I had now lost all sense of direction as he led the way through the labyrinthine passageways. Eventually he showed me into a room in which two clerks busied themselves, scratching away with their heads bent low over their work. A bench sat against the side wall.

'There you are, Mr Hopgood. I will just make an enquiry,' he said, indicating the bench.

The two clerks looked up briefly but then continued with their work, ignoring me completely. I sat there quietly, staring into space, occasionally catching the eyes of the clerks as they returned my scrutiny and I wondered whether they were used to having strangers deposited upon the bench in their office without so much as an explanation.

I sat there for nearly an hour waiting for Ambrose to return and I found that it did not overly concern me that he was *friendly*, as it were, with Olivia. I perceived him as little threat to any future encounters Olivia and I would have and I just began to mull over what those encounters might be when the noise of the door opening startled me. A gentleman I had never seen before summoned me to accompany him.

'Mr Hopgood?' he asked, brusquely.

I nodded, indicating that he had made the correct assumption.

'Follow me, sir,' he replied, turning on his heels.

Along further corridors, tunnels and more stairs, I followed in the wake of the sullen uncommunicative fellow ahead of me. Occasionally, he turned his head to make sure I still kept pace with him but apart from that, he just trudged on relentlessly, eventually climbing a set of stairs to enter into a bright corridor with a window overlooking the Old Palace Yard, beyond which I could see the Abbey. We were in the Court of Requests, or to be more precise, above the Court of Requests. He steered me down the corridor and then we entered another office, a sumptuously furnished office with an ornate oak desk, leather covered chairs, a hearth and shelving containing a number of books. Behind the desk, I could see another door, to the sides of which a few portraits hung on the wood panelling of the walls. Behind the desk sat an austere looking man, bewigged and wearing his formal gown. Thomas Pelham-Holles, Duke of Newcastle, the first Secretary of State, second only to Walpole in importance, looked up and waved his hand absently towards the chair in front of the desk whilst studying me keenly with sharp intelligent eyes. I got the impression that this man did not suffer fools of any capacity, under any circumstances, whatsoever.

'Sit,' he barked. He then turned to Ambrose standing a little away from him. 'This your man Hopgood?'

'It is, Your Grace,' replied Ambrose. His demeanour now one of servitude.

'Then leave us, Sir Chauntley and I thank you for bringing him to my attention.'

'Your Grace,' answered Ambrose, inclining his head in a short bow. He then cast me a quick look, perhaps one of sympathy, before heading for the door, closing it quietly behind him.

The Duke of Newcastle regarded me for some moments in silence and I fought the temptation to look away, instead I returned his gaze steadily, each of us weighing up the other as if we were combatants ready to fight.

'So,' he said, breaking the impasse. 'You are asking about Jacobites. What do you know of them?'

'Your Grace, I know that they are disaffected citizens looking to replace our King with the Catholic James Stuart. That there have been several battles over the years in support of putting the Stuarts back on the throne, that it is mainly to the north of the country and Scotland where it has the biggest support, as it has in the south west of England and of course in Ireland.'

'That is true, but it is also supported by the French and the Spanish, they would wish to see regime change for their own ends. Put a Catholic back on the English throne and they, especially the French, would have a great say in the politics of this country. So, it is not simply a matter of exchanging one King for another. It is an invasion by proxy that we are preventing. Unfortunately, there are those within this building who support it, I am of course talking of Tories.'

'Yes, I am aware it is not only a Catholic desire, it is a Protestant one too, those who want their high church back; but there is also the line of succession, they believe that the Stuarts should be on the throne by dint of primogeniture.'

He nodded. 'So, what is your interest in them?'

'I am investigating a murder, which has revealed a Jacobite connection, so I am forced to look a little closer at their activities.'

He nodded again, accepting the relevance of my interest. 'You are a private citizen, are you not?'

'I am but Magistrate De Veil requested that I take this investigation on.'

'That might well be the case, sir, but has it not occurred to you that you may well be stepping on unstable ground?'

'Yes, Your Grace, which is why I look to your office in order to clarify where I may step.'

He barked a short laugh. 'Ha, very shrewd of you, sir. You ask so that you can appear to appease us whilst at the same time look at where we wish you to stay clear, is that it?'

'Not at all. All I wish is to solve a murder and bring those responsible to justice. To do so I may have to put a stick into a hornets' nest.'

'I would rather you did not.'

'And leave a murder unsolved?'

'If the rebels have murdered one of their own then I am not too concerned. Ambrose told me the name. Sorley, is it not?'

'Yes. A Thomas Sorley.'

He sat back in his chair and then drummed a finger upon his desk. 'Sorley was unimportant,' he said after a while. 'We knew of him, a mere foot soldier. He carried messages and handed out pamphlets. We keep track of their activities, of course, allowing them a little rope with which to hang themselves. As you well know, occasionally they do that and we put them in a place where they can do no harm.'

'I understand that. I have learnt that Thomas Sorley intended to step away from his involvement in them, so I'm wondering whether he was privy to some information or activity which could have had a bearing on his murder, that someone or some people decided that they could not risk him revealing anything that could jeopardise something that they had planned to do.'

Newcastle frowned in thought. 'That is a valid point, Hopgood, one that we may have to look at more closely. We were not aware that Sorley had become disillusioned. It is a shame, as had we known, we may have been able to exploit it.'

'You mean you would have made a spy of him?'

'Of course, that is the nature of things. To keep this realm safe, we have to use every resource we can.'

I nodded, easy with the concept and easy with the reality. Information regarding a cadre or a gang from within was part of the stock in trade that I knew so well. 'So, Your Grace. Will you allow me to delve a little deeper, now you understand why I believe Thomas Sorley was killed?'

The finger began to drum on the desk again and I surmised that he used the action to think through a problem or an idea. Eventually, he seemed to come to a decision as he stood up abruptly and went over to the door behind him. He opened it and called through to someone on the other side. 'Is Jarmin still in the building?' he asked the unseen person. He waited a few seconds and then nodded. 'Good, get him back here immediately.' He closed the door then returned to his desk, sat down and recommenced the finger drumming.

'Your Grace...?' I asked, wondering what he had decided.

He raised a finger for me to hold my tongue. 'Patience, Hopgood. You came here looking for information. You must forget Ambrose now; what you will learn, he is not privy to, though I suspect he gave indication that he is involved in some capacity. He is not. Jarmin is though, so you must listen and act on his advice, for not to do so could put not only yourself in danger, but more importantly, others. Do you understand that, Hopgood?'

I felt my eyes widen at the last two sentences and I nodded my compliance but now I wondered whether I had done the right thing in coming here, for not only had I involved a government agency, that government agency had now given me a resource: I may not now be the driver in this, it seemed to me that I had handed the reins over and had inadvertently become the passenger.

CHAPTER 13

Jarmin arrived at the office within a few short minutes, about my height, no wig, light-brown hair cut short, hazel eyed with a pleasing face though lined with stubble, as if not shaved for a day or so, perhaps forty years old and wearing plain clothes of good quality. I would not want to argue with him. To enable me to pass muster with Sir Chauntley Ambrose, I wore my best clothes and wig but now I felt just a little overdressed. My attire had even outshone the duke's in style and tailoring, giving the impression of a gentleman of means and refinement; though accurate, my ensemble impressed Mr Jarmin not one whit. He cast his eyes upon me disdainfully.

Newcastle quickly dispatched me to the corridor outside, to wait upon his pleasure — or so I thought. Instead, after several minutes kicking my heels in the corridor, the door opened and Jarmin came out, looked me up and down again, then indicated that I should follow him. We hurried down the corridor, then descended some stairs, all the way to the basement and then along another corridor to a suit of small dark rooms, lit only by safety lanterns. Two burly men sat in the first room we entered, sitting at a table and playing cards by the weak light. They looked up as we came in but quickly returned to their game, speaking to neither of us. Jarmin led me past them and into the further room, furnished with a simple desk and two chairs. Arranged along the walls were shelves, upon which were stacks of brown folders containing sheets of paper. He walked to a shelf and pulled a file out, looked at it, then closed it again, turned and sat at the desk and indicated that I should sit too.

'This, Mr Hopgood, is our office. What you see around you is the result of years of endeavour. All the information that we have gathered on France, Spain, the America's, Ireland and others, including the Jacobites, is here in these rooms down here. We have names, places, events. As you can see, it is rather full and soon we will need to find bigger premises, but at the moment, we make do. Not many people know about our little home here, so you are privileged to see it. Of course, you will not disclose its location to anyone, ever. Do you understand?'

I nodded dumbly as the enormity of what I was being shown dawned on me.

'Good,' continued Jarmin. 'Welcome to our company, Mr Hopgood.'

'Er...?' I replied, not quite understanding, but aware that something had shifted and it had gone from my control. I had the uneasy feeling that I had somehow been recruited as an intelligencer, albeit not a willing one.

'You sound a little hesitant, Mr Hopgood,' said Jarmin, as he made himself comfortable.

'Not so much hesitant, as a little confused, Mr Jarmin.'

He gave a knowing half-smile in response.

'I have not come here to participate in your discreet activities, as it were, but for information that would help me in my investigation into a murder.'

'So I understand, Mr Hopgood,' replied Jarmin. 'The information you desire is here, upon these shelves,' he continued, waving a lazy hand in the air about him. 'It only leaves you to decide what you are willing to give us for access to them.'

'You mean there is a price?'

He had the half-smile fixed upon his face. 'As in all things, Mr Hopgood.'

'And what is the price I have to pay?' I asked, not with any enthusiasm.

'Your loyalty to your country, Mr Hopgood,' he replied. 'In return for looking through these files, His Grace, just asks that should the need arise, we could call upon your assistance. Does that sound too much of a burden? He may never call; you may never hear from us again; who knows what the future holds for any of us?'

I turned my gaze away from his and looked towards the shelves, stacked with national secrets. I should have run away, very quickly, but my curiosity anchored my legs as I mulled over the dilemma. Newcastle and Jarmin were trying to draw me into their world and I had no doubt that should I agree, then I would be at their beck and call forever more, something I had no wish to be or do. Enticing though the prospect was of looking into those files, I thought the cost prohibitive.

I returned my gaze to Jarmin and shook my head. 'Thank you for your offer, Mr Jarmin but I will decline. I have no wish to enter your world of espionage any more than I wish to gouge out my own eyes.'

Jarmin regarded me and I could tell my response surprised him. 'Do you not wish to think again on that, Mr Hopgood?' he said, as he pushed back the chair and stood up. He walked a couple of steps over to the files, pulled out the file he looked at when we first came in and one other, then returned to the desk. He looked up and patted one of the folders. 'This contains information on thief-takers in London,' he said, a serious expression on his face. 'Including you, I might add. This one,' and he tapped the other folder. 'Contains information about the group of Jacobites Thomas Sorley was involved with. The Duke anticipated your reticence so has allowed me to show them to you. If you agree to help us then you can spend as much time as you like reading them, and all these too.' He waved his hand around again. 'If you wish to, that is, though you may need a few months to go through them all.'

I shook my head slowly. 'My answer is still no, Mr Jarmin, though I thank you again for the offer. The price is too high.'

'Very well. In that case you must cease your investigation.'

'I beg your pardon?' I looked at him, stunned.

'I'm afraid so. Jacobites are my problem, not yours.'

'But murder is my problem, not yours.'

'I am sure, Mr Hopgood, that by now, you realise that what you want is not necessarily what you get. The security of the realm could be at stake here, you can work with us or work against us. I think you know who might win.'

'You're trying to push me into a corner, Mr Jarmin.'

'No, you have put yourself in the corner; I am trying to help you out of it. You came to us, after all. All we want from you, all the Duke wants from you, is for you to agree to help us from time to time.'

'I have no wish to enter your line of work. I get enough problems with my own.'

Jarmin laughed. 'Believe it or not, Mr Hopgood, you are already in our line of work. If you looked at this file,' and he tapped the one to do with thief-takers, 'you would find out how.' He looked at me for a few seconds and then gave a small nod to himself. 'I will make a bargain with you, Mr Hopgood; I will give you one name, just one.'

'And what would you require of me for that name?'

'A promise.'

'For what?'

'That all information you discover you will pass on to us, the

Duke and I.'

'You will not ask me to join your merry band of men?'

'If you are not prepared to help your country, then what use are you? No, but the Duke did say that he would give you a little assistance; hence the single name.'

'And the catch is?'

He smiled and then shook his head. 'There is not one, Mr Hopgood. I will give you the name and then you can leave; just tell us what you find out.'

He was lying; I knew that my very presence here indicated that I would be drawn into the Duke's web, eventually. I reasoned that by taking the stand I did now, then at least I might have some control over events in the future. They want to know what I find out, which is fair enough, I will tell them. I could walk away and not take the name, which would salve my conscience, but it would not help Joseph Morton or the memory of Thomas Sorley; and Elizabeth Thompson would remember me for what I could have done but chose not to. Then there were these rooms, these files, these men. I now knew of them, what they were for, what the men did that worked here. I had been admitted into something, if not into the inner circle, then at least on the periphery. They had caught me, whether I liked it or not.

'Show me the name, Mr Jarmin,' I said in the end, reconciled to my fate.

He grinned and then picked up a sheet of paper, opened the file in such a manner as I could not see within, and then dipped a quill into ink and wrote a name and address. 'Courier,' he said. 'Thomas Sorley worked alongside him. A Catholic, like Sorley. He will show you what you need to know; if you are discreet and clever enough.'

Jarmin escorted me out of the building and into The Old

Palace Yard where I quickly moved away, not wanting to linger, feeling a little sullied by my clandestine experience. Of course, I knew that people like Jarmin existed but I had hoped I would manage to avoid them. Some hope, I thought, as I began to walk away from Westminster. I had now become embroiled in the machinations of the state: where did my common sense go when I needed it?

Walking back up White Hall, a thirst began to tickle my throat but I wished to be away from Westminster, so I continued up towards Charing Cross, in the hope that a little distance would put my morning's activities into some sort of perspective. The Golden Cross Inn, opposite Northumberland House, appeared very busy with travellers departing to various destinations and offered me a degree of anonymity where I could sit amongst the many in relative obscurity and contemplate the name Jarmin had given me.

I found an unoccupied booth at the rear of the Inn in a dark corner with just the glow of the candle on the sconce behind me. I ordered a pot of ale from the girl and settled down to ponder upon the steps I would need to take next. Ahead of me, I could see the patrons of the Inn in discourse on every subject under the sun, their voices raised and forceful, indicating that they had been there some time, drinking and conversing.

Jarmin had written upon the sheet of paper in a peculiar manner. At the bottom were two names, Thomas Sorley and Henry Musgrave of Lombard Court in Seven Dials, both with the annotation of "Courier." Small letters and numbers accompanied their names. Above the names were lines, leading up to boxes with small numbers and letters beneath them too. It seemed as if he had abstractly drawn a little tree; there were several boxes, all of them blank. He asked me to fill in those boxes.

Jarmin had explained that there were small groups of activists about London and he had shown me one such group. He had not been content to just give me the name of Musgrave; he had to do it in this way, a way that would garner my interest and without doubt, he had been successful in that. The small numbers and letters must relate to other files, to other people, presumably to names he already knew; but what if he did not know the names, or at least, not all of them. He insisted that I go to him when I discovered something, so would I be confirming for him or giving him a new name to add? I could go round in circles with this, I thought. The danger for me would be that I could lose sight of my task, to discover a murderer. I put the sheet of paper down on the table and took a long drink of ale. I could not be distracted, I decided. If I found something of interest then all well and good but I would not get lost along the path. Just concentrate on finding Thomas Sorley's killer, I thought; everything else was just politics, a game I had no wish to play.

My finger tapped upon the name of Henry Musgrave, residing in Lombard Court in Seven Dials, a slum area attached to St Giles, where gin-shops, brewhouses and taverns were in abundance. I had no indication of his professional occupation, so I decided he likely had none, residing where he did, so probably lived by felony and his wits. I would soon find out, as I would make a distant acquaintanceship with him.

Having finished my ale, I relieved myself out in the yard and then left; my intention now to go to Seven Dials and see what I could find out, but I would not last five minutes in that area dressed in my good clothes, so I would have to visit Barty again and dress in a way that I could blend in with the surroundings.

*

Barty shook his head ruefully as I finished donning my St Giles finery and packed up the clothes in which I arrived. He had noticed the bandage on my arm but I dismissed his question with a wave of my hand. 'A little accident,' I said, making light of it.

'Sometimes, I rather think you enjoy going about in a poor man's garb, Richard; your countenance always seems to change,' observed Barty.

'It can be refreshing, I have to admit,' I replied, practicing my slovenly walk. 'Unlike most, I can adopt a new personality, albeit for a short time and see things from a different perspective. It can be edifying; you should try it one day.'

He shook his head again but in a different manner. 'No, thank you. I'm content just to stay as I am, just a poor man of the law.'

'Hardly poor, Barty. Hardly poor,' I responded, as I took my leave with a grin.

I walked brazenly out of Lincoln's Inn, past the lodge and out into Chancery Lane as if I had a perfectly legitimate reason for being there; no one would give a messenger or a workman a second look as long as he did not skulk along suspiciously, and so I proceeded and adapted to my new persona as I went along.

Barty was correct that I did enjoy walking in a poor man's shoes for a short period of time but I knew that should I have to walk in those shoes permanently, I would not be quite so sanguine about it. The poor had a hard, fierce life which could end all too soon for many of them, for disease, violence and hunger was rife within their society. A Gentleman lived in wealth and privilege, which went some way to dispel the ravages of destitution. Although I enjoyed stepping into this poor man's life, I could count myself fortunate that I had been born to another.

Henry Musgrave lodged in a tenement in Lombard Court, just off Little Earl Street, where the alley diverged to branch off east. The alley could be described as squalor personified; a narrow rank thoroughfare full of waste and degradation, a pall of smoke hung above the rooftops, belched from the chimneys all around. Families lived cheek by jowl with other families in single rooms and there appeared to be no peace from the struggles of life here. The intense smell assaulted my nostrils; the scent of foulness concentrated within the constraints of the alley, of tobacco, of alcohol and of human waste, which invested the area and left a harsh tang at the back of the throat.

People milled about as I entered the Court, some slumped in doorways, lying in their gin-fuelled stupors as opportunists rifled pockets for pennies, all in broad daylight without thought of who would be watching. No one seemed to care for the fortune of those inebriated, even though they could be robbing a neighbour or a friend.

Not being able to recognise Henry Musgrave put me at a disadvantage, however, I knew which room he rented, so I would have to contrive a way of entering it, hopefully with him being in residence at the time.

I elbowed my way through the crush back to Little Earl Street where I could at least breathe once more and give myself time to think.

The simple solutions were usually the best, so I purchased a jug of possibly the worst gin in London and began to cast my eye about, looking for the most pox-ridden hag I could find. It did not take me long — I had too many to choose from. I soon made friends with Adah, a buxom broad-hipped woman of about forty years with dyed dark hair. Her breath stank, her eyes barely focused but I could not argue with her willingness to lay on her back for a shilling and a swig of my jug. She would do.

Adah appeared keen, though I could not decide whether she yearned for my jug or me, though she did drop her hand to give me a measure. She then announced satisfaction with what I had and that we could continue, if only I allow her to take control of the jug. I relented and then steered her into the Court and down towards Musgrave's lodging room, where I would be given "the time of my life," as well as a dose.

I pushed the front door open and we lurched drunkenly inside; the stairs led directly up and we stumbled against each other as we climbed the rotten staircase to the first floor. She swayed as she stood on the landing and I grabbed her before she tumbled back down the stairs.

'Oh, yer a keen one, ain't ya,' she giggled, as she lurched back and pressed against me. 'Too eager by half, but you'll be in 'eaven soon, my lovely, just you wait an' see.'

I recoiled from her breath and turned my head away just before she planted that odious mouth against mine; though I did wrap my arms about her hoping that both her weight and mine would suffice for the job I had in mind.

Musgrave's door was ahead of us, closed, but I did not know whether locked or not, neither did I care, just that the frame seemed distressed enough to give, should I apply enough pressure.

I held Adah tightly and then carried her towards the door in a running stumble. We crashed against the door, which gave with a splintering crack and burst open.

'Oh,' exclaimed Adah, as we recovered from the stumble. 'Friend of yours?' she asked, as she noticed another man lying on a mattress in the room.

'His birthday,' I said, thinking quickly. 'You're to give 'im yer man-trap.' I will say this for her; she still kept hold of the jug.

On the mattress lay a man of around thirty years of age, red haired and sporting a face full of freckles. He appeared unconscious and judging by the bottle beside him, alcohol was the cause. He wore a dirty grey shirt without breeches, his thin white legs stretching out. The shirt had ridden up exposing a small limp worm of a member below a red bush.

'Two shillings,' I said, as I pushed her towards him. 'And you can keep the jug.'

She turned her head to me. 'Two shillings? I want that in advance,' she said, putting the jug down on a stool.

I paid her the money and then stood briefly at the door and watched as she hitched up her skirts and sat over Henry Musgrave's groin, giving his member a bit of a tug then squirming to allow an access.

I winced as Musgrave came back to his senses; but at least I now knew what he looked like.

Across from the lodging, I found a single roomed brewhouse with a rudimentary bar, which consisted of planks of wood resting on some barrels up against the back wall. A door behind it led presumably to the back room where they did the brewing. Several tables and benches were scattered about with perhaps fifteen customers. No one paid any attention to me, so I found a seat by the window in order to keep an eye on the door across the way. The brew itself tasted like sewer water with a thin skin of scum sitting on the surface. It cost a halfpenny, which was a farthing too much, however, the view made up for it.

After a few minutes, Adah made an appearance, standing in the doorway and smoothing down her skirts before setting off back up to Little Earl Street, where she would presumably be looking for some more custom. Musgrave appeared at the door just as she left and he followed her with his eyes. He scratched his head and then looked up and down the alley with a confused look on his face, no doubt seeking his anonymous benefactor, who unbeknownst to him, sat just a few feet away. He rubbed his groin quite fiercely, as if the contagion had already hit, then turned and walked back in.

I did not wait as long as I feared, as after no more than twenty minutes, Musgrave re-emerged from the doorway, still wearing a baffled look, this time he did not return to his room, instead setting off down the alley. Leaving a good half-pint of ale in my pot, I stood up and left the brew-house, hurrying after, thankful to leave that foul brew well and truly behind me.

Musgrave's distinctive red hair acted like a beacon amongst the crowds in the alley, making him easy to keep in sight, allowing me to keep a safe distance behind, as I did not want to rouse any suspicion in him. I watched as a couple of children harassed him and to their delight, he responded in an aggressive manner which only made their attention worse; finally, he backhanded one of them quite violently, casting the boy to the ground and the pair gave up their baiting, one sporting a bloody nose.

We emerged from the alley into the centre where the sundial stood prominently at the junction of all seven streets, a tavern on each corner. I waited a moment to see which way he would go and then followed him briskly as he headed up towards Broad Street, St Giles, where he turned right and then threaded his way through the crowds and crossed the road, dodging the carts and scattering a couple of sheep, which were undoubtedly on their way to slaughter; the owner of the sheep causing some uproarious laughter as he desperately tried to bring them back under control. Musgrave only gave the scene a passing glance as he disappeared into Plumptre Street.

The crowds thinned here a little as we were now on the outskirts of the slum and so it had an element of affluence as compared to the rank poverty of just a street or so away. There were a few hovels and lodging houses at the lower end of the street, as well as a gin-shop and a tavern, but there were also some shops selling second hand clothes, a few stalls selling trinkets, foodstuffs and the like, some craftsmen working leather and other traders. Musgrave did not stop to look at any of the wares on offer, instead, he just walked up towards the end of the street, where the condition of the houses improved slightly, not hesitating to enter a small establishment selling books and pamphlets.

I stood thoughtfully for a few moments and then decided to wait for him to emerge, finding a spot a few doors away where I could observe unobtrusively. I staggered against a wall and then slid down to the ground, sitting slumped as if I had imbibed a skinful of drink, blending reasonably well into the surroundings. Folk stepped over and around me, none of whom passed even the remotest interest in my pretended predicament, for which I was eternally grateful as the minutes passed with me sitting slack-jawed and dribbling and peeking out from beneath the brim of my hat.

A good thirty minutes must have gone by until the door of the bookseller opened and Musgrave stepped out, carrying a small package tucked beneath his arm. I would not have put him down as a man interested in the written word, but as I have learned over the years, it is not well to judge too quickly, given that folk are prone to surprise you when you least expect it.

Musgrave hesitated outside the shop for a few moments and then the door opened again and another man emerged, he stood with his back to me and appeared to utter some words to Musgrave before they exchanged a brief nod. Musgrave then turned and walked away. I became a little animated now and rolled over and climbed unsteadily to my feet, bracing myself against the wall, preparing again to follow my red-haired friend when the other man turned towards me and I felt my eyes widen. I quickly hid my face as the man walked close by, practically brushing shoulders with me. It was Nicholas Cummings, Thomas Sorley's superior at Thompson and Gutteridge.

CHAPTER 14

The appearance of Cummings surprised me, to say the least, but that emotion did not last long as I stared at his back as he walked away. I had a decision to make: continue to follow Musgrave, or abandon him and follow Cummings instead. Cummings won. I already knew where Musgrave lived so would be able to pick him up again but the appearance of Cummings and his obvious acquaintanceship with Musgrave whetted my interest: he could well be a fellow Jacobite. I had to find out what he was up to.

Cummings appeared to be in a hurry. I saw him check his watch and then he increased his pace as he walked along Castle Street, then he crossed the road and shortly we were passing St George's church heading towards Bloomsbury Square. He did not look around, he just hurried and I struggled to be discreet as I kept pace with him. We quickly passed the Square and took Orange Street where he checked his watch again and began to slow his pace at last. Cummings halted at the corner and looked towards the north side of Red Lyon Square, where, a few houses down, a carriage had drawn up, its attendant waiting patiently. Cummings checked his watch again and continued to wait; he appeared to be nervous as he could not stop fidgeting and smoothing down his coat. I sought shelter in the lengthening shadows as the light of the day had begun to dim and watched, slightly perplexed. I saw the door, opposite the carriage, open and immediately Cummings began to walk again, purposefully towards it. I saw someone emerge from the house, a young lady whom I recognised as Elizabeth Thompson, together with her maid, Trudi.

Dressed in silk, the colour of a fine claret wine, the hues shimmering in the late evening's light, Elizabeth walked with her back straight and her hands clasped upon her purse in front. She looked demur and beautiful, her countenance, confident. Cummings approached her and I could hear him bid her a good evening and that it was such a pleasant surprise that they should come upon one another. Their voices then lowered so that I could not hear their intercourse but I could see that Elizabeth did not quite feel entirely at ease with the circumstances. Cummings moved close towards her and quite without invitation and with extraordinary presumption, placed his hand upon her shoulder, an intimacy that appeared far from welcome. He let his hand stay there for some moments before eventually withdrawing it and I could see a little relief pass across her face. Cummings appeared not to notice as he continued to talk, although he no longer had his hand upon her person, his very close proximity appeared to make her feel uncomfortable. Eventually, Elizabeth took a step towards her carriage and the attendant opened the door for her. Cummings took a step to follow her movement but then halted and offered a small bow of his head as Elizabeth, followed by Trudi, stepped aboard.

I waited by the wall, still blending in with the shadows and watched as the carriage drove off. Cummings watched too, though he seemed mesmerised, keenly looking until he could no longer see Elizabeth. I could see that he held her in affection and he obviously desired a return of that affection, but from what I had just witnessed, that hope had no chance of being realised. He had timed his appearance to perfection; no doubt he had said that it was a fortuitous happenstance to be passing at the exact moment that she had come out of her door. I did wonder that if Cummings could contrive a situation like that, what more could he do?

I resolved to follow him a little more but he hastened from Red Lyon Square via Princes Street and then hailed a chair, which carried him off quickly. I decided not to continue, so instead, retraced my steps in order to study the bookseller; but here too I ran out of luck as the establishment had closed for the day.

As it would be foolish to try and find Musgrave again, and with nothing more to occupy my time, I headed back to Lincoln's Inn and Barty's office, where I could change back into my normal clothes.

I entered Barty's office to find him still hard at work, his desk illuminated by two candles, which must have been expensive beeswax owing to the lack of odour. He lay down his quill, sat up, and stretched.

'Hungry?' I asked, as I felt my stomach churn through lack of sustenance.

'Yes,' he replied, instantly. 'I have not had a morsel since this morning and am fair fainting away.'

'The Cock?' I asked, knowing he favoured that Fleet Street tavern, though whether for the ale or the fact that next door you could find Mrs Salmon's Waxworks, I could not be sure. I did know that he frequently visited the establishment, always on the lookout for a macabre addition to the collection.

'I trust I will not be bringing my purse?' he said, grinning.

'No, even if you wish to avail yourself of one of the other houses along there.'

'I have not the energy for an evening of pleasure, Richard. I would fall asleep before I got going. Though another night I might be more willing and able.'

'Then it'll be just food and ale and all the cheaper for me.'

In fact, I felt relieved, as my day had been a busy one and I did not feel up to an evening carousing. I just wished to have something to eat and drink with a friend for an hour or so and The Cock served good ale and good food and it would give me an opportunity to churn over what I had learned with a legal mind, albeit Barty's.

Having donned my clothes, I watched impatiently as Barty finished off his work and then snubbed the candles, at long last, ready to proceed. The hour of nine approached, so it made a change for him to finish early; though well and good to be diligent in your work, and Barty strived to get a partnership, but if he continued to do most of the work, they would be hardly likely to elevate him in case their workloads should increase. I had spoken to him many a time on this but still he would not listen, believing that diligence would bring him the reward.

We left the chambers and walked down, emerging shortly after into Fleet Street where we turned right and threaded our way through the girls plying their evening trade. The Cock was just a short walk away and we made it with hardly a verbal rebuke from those we turned down.

Although full of people, we managed to spy a booth at the far end where three men were just leaving. Barty hurried and just managed to secure the seat before two other lawyers got there. I followed and squeezed in beside him. I was just adjusting my seat when I heard a hail.

'Mr Hopgood, good to see you, sir.'

I turned my head and saw Mr Hogarth a few tables down; I had passed him by unseen, hidden amongst a group of men full of merriment.

'Good evening to you too, sir,' I replied, with a nod of my head.

'Sent those engravings around this morning; did they arrive safe and secure?'

'Alas, I have been away from the house all day, sir, but I am sure they have come to no harm.'

'Splendid, please tell me if anything is awry. Lady Amerskill would take it personally and I have no wish to upset that particular lady.'

'Indeed not, sir: I neither.'

'I understand you escorted her home?'

'I did, Mr Hogarth; an arduous task but someone had to keep the lady safe.'

'Then we are grateful for your diligence, sir, in ensuring no harm came to her.' He grinned as he said that and I wondered if he suspected how diligent I had been. 'Your health, sir,' he added, raising his pot.

'Yours too, sir,' though I had no pot to raise as Barty had only just given the girl our order.

I relaxed back and waited until the girl arrived with our ale and we managed to quench our thirst. I had already told Barty some details regarding the investigation, so I briefly summarised before bringing him up to date. His eyes widened noticeably as I described my interview with the Duke of Newcastle and he gave a low groan of dismay.

'As I understand it, Newcastle is no fool. He is a political animal and has his sights set high. He expects results from those he engages and it sounds very much like he has engaged you.'

'The trouble is that I need the information he has, if I'm to get to the bottom of this murder, because I am certain there is a political aspect to it. He gave me one name, which is enough to take me forward and I believe he knew the right name to give. I believe they want me to confirm what they already know.'

'So, he has made you an Intelligencer of the Crown.'

I shook my head. 'No, I declined that invitation.'

'From what I hear, you do not decline Newcastle, even if you believe you have. Be warned, Richard, you're getting deep into something you may later regret.'

'Thank you for cheering me up, Barty.'

The meal arrived; two plates with slices of beef, red and bloody with an assortment of vegetables along with gravy and bread. We both set to as if we had not eaten for a week and soon there were just a few smears left on our plates.

'From what I have told you, Barty, who do you think murdered Thomas Sorley?'

He sighed and sat back then called for two more pots of ale. 'From what you say there is only one answer, which you already know. It must have been the Jacobites.'

This last he said very quietly even though the noise in the tavern would drown out most conversations.

'I agree,' I said, nodding. 'Though I do need to know more about that bookseller, what his connection is to Musgrave and what Cummings was doing there.'

'They are probably all part of the same thing.'

'Jacobites? Yes, I had already deduced that.'

He nodded. 'Booksellers are sometimes book printers too, do not forget, and if they can print books, then they can print pamphlets as well.'

I was being muddleheaded, as I should have thought that straight away; I think I may be too tired to think properly at the moment. The package under Musgrave's arm must have been pamphlets meant for distribution and Cummings surely knew that when he spoke to him. Now I must figure out what to do next. I thought back to when I informed Cummings of Sorley's death and how distressed he had seemed. I thought then that he had to be innocent but now I might have to revise that opinion.

It seems as if he is hiding a secret; Sorley was a Jacobite and it looks as if Cummings is too.

'What about this William Gutteridge, have you spoken to him yet?' asked Barty.

I shook my head. 'No, De Veil has warned me off. He told me Gutteridge came to see him and De Veil is satisfied as to his innocence in this.'

'You believe him?'

'No, which is why I intend to ignore De Veil. I'm certain that Gutteridge is avoiding me, he knows I am trying to speak with him, which is why he spoke to De Veil.'

'Could Gutteridge be a Jacobite as well?'

'It is possible; which would mean that Gutteridge, Cummings and Sorley were working together.'

'At a shipping company,' observed Barty, with a knowing look. 'Where goods come in as well as people.'

'Yes, at a shipping company...' I felt like someone had slapped my face, such a jolt it gave me as I realised the implication. Sorley became disillusioned with the Jacobites cause and wanted to leave but, as I thought previously, if he knew things that should not be known then the Jacobites might want to silence him, especially if things were being brought in to further the cause, whether it be people or goods. Gutteridge's successful business and investments made him a very rich man, he could not afford to have a scandal, it would bankrupt him at the least, with even the rope being a possibility.

'I see you have made a connection, Richard.'

'I have, Barty, thanks to you. A tentative one but a connection all the same, one that definitely needs exploring.'

'Well, you certainly will not be exploring tonight,' he said, tapping the pot in front of him. 'So, we may as well have a couple of refills.'

We had some more refills after that and then we spent an hour at the waxworks but much to Barty's disappointment the mad old woman had not put her skill to crafting any new exhibits: we could only look at what we had seen before, like the death of the first Charles as he knelt at the scaffold; a depiction of Boudicca and her daughters; various scenes of cruelty and misuse; the woman who gave birth to three hundred and sixty five children, all at the same time and many other exhibits to look at in wonder; all, I admit, expertly crafted with the figures dressed sumptuously in expensive cloth. I could not garner the same enthusiasm as Barty but I did admire the lifelike details. As we left, I managed to dodge the clockwork figure of Mother Shipton, the old prophetess from the last century, who gave a kick to all departing visitors but Barty always enjoyed that part most and laughed as she kicked him out of the door.

Midnight had gone when I finally arrived home; my house was in darkness with the front door locked and I had no key. I could wake everyone up but I decided to try and gain entrance through a window.

I knew how the catch worked and also about the weak spot where I could slip a knife through to raise it up enough to open the window.

When I recovered my senses, I saw Mary, Jane and Ned standing over me. Mary wore a fierce expression, Jane, one of concern, and Ned with amusement. I had made so much noise that it woke the household anyway and Jane, thinking we had an intruder, hit me with a saucepan she had quickly grabbed from the kitchen, just as I placed my feet down upon the floor. Fortunately, for me, she just caught me a glancing blow, which stunned me for a few moments rather than rendering me unconscious, which happened to be her intention.

Mary berated me in her usual fashion, treating me as an errant child and if my ears were ringing from the blow, they were now chiming a cascade. Ned saved me from further admonishment by suggesting a restorative, which I instantly agreed and very soon, he liberally distributed my expensive brandy to all.

I rued my foolhardiness when morning dawned. My head ached, though I believe that had more to do with the alcohol rather than the blow that Jane had given me and it took a while before I could face the day ahead. Conversation was muted and Mary once again gave her opinion on my activities of last night, lecturing me on the perfidious nature associated with excess consumption of the demon drink as she changed the dressing on my arm; rather roughly too, I might add.

Ned came in, took one look at me, and then proceeded to make as much noise as conceivably possible in the process, taking an inordinate amount of pleasure in returning the compliments that I had frequently paid him in the past.

Ignoring Ned and his largely successful attempt at discommoding me, I adjourned to my study to quietly recover my equilibrium. Jane, bless her, entered with a concoction of lemon balm, sage and thyme infused in hot water and bid me to drink it all up and that I would feel much better shortly.

An hour later my head began to clear and my jumbled thoughts became more orderly. I could function as a member of the human race once more. Stacked up against the wall were the engravings from Hogarth, The Rakes Progress, and again I pondered the aptness of such pictures of a young man of good quality whose descent into vice, debauchery and alcohol led him into debt, imprisonment and finally madness. I would die happy should the last three not happen to me. I decided the dining room would be a perfect home for them as they could act as a conversation piece should the talk stutter to a halt when I entertained. I called to Mary and gave instruction on how she should hang them and then called for Ned, as I felt now in a suitable condition to find out what he had learned yesterday.

Ned arrived and sat down, still with a grin on his face.

I held my hand up. 'You can now desist from your gloating as my constitution has recovered, though I may add that my temporary incapacity is as nothing compared to your all too frequent lapses.'

'But I am just a poor down-trodden servant, sir, drowning my misery in the only way possible for someone of my situation. We poor folk have to have something to look forward to.'

'I can always make you poorer, Ned,' I replied, taking aim at his tender spot. 'Servants are two a penny.'

'Maybe you are correct, sir, but reliable, loyal servants are expensive.'

I again wondered why I give my staff so much leeway, because they all seem to play upon my good nature. I dread to think how they would survive should they have a less tolerant master, one that did not appreciate the occasional playful round of ribaldry. I disarmed Ned with a smile and held up my hand to signal that the time for serious business had arrived.

'What occurred at Botolph Street?' I asked, as I settled in my chair.

Ned shook his head and settled too. 'Nothing, I'm afraid, sir. I discovered the owner of the property is a gentleman by the name of Blaston, so pretended to be his agent inspecting his property as I spoke to the neighbours regarding the tenants. They were all surprised that Joseph Morton ended up in Newgate and were shocked at the demise of Thomas Sorley. The two ladies, Grace and Ella, are both widows, husbands lost at sea only a few months ago. All in all, it was a waste of time.'

I shook my head. 'Not a waste of time, it means we can cross them off our list which narrows things down even more.

However, after yesterday, from what I discovered, the people I met and followed, we now have a target.'

Ned raised his eyebrows in question and so I related my experiences of the day before, of my meeting with Newcastle and Jarmin and the information provided. I told him about Musgrave and the somewhat distasteful way I crashed into his room and what followed; of my following him to the bookseller's and how I saw Cummings emerge and the strange meeting he contrived with Elizabeth Thompson. He listened with wide-eyed shock and I think a little jealousy as I related the events, somewhat different to his.

'Could he not just be buying a book?' queried Ned.

'Cummings? Possibly but he conversed with Musgrave as he came out.'

'He could have just been passing the compliments of the day. I would not have put Cummings down as a man of deceit.'

'Neither would I, but my eyes told me differently. They knew each other and then the way Cummings accosted Miss Thompson disconcerted me. If nothing else we need to see what Cummings is up to, even if he is totally innocent.'

'You want me to follow him and find out more?'

'No, I will do that. I want you to concentrate on Musgrave, see what he will show us. In the meantime, as Cummings will be at the warehouse, I will take a closer look at the bookseller.'

Jane's concoction had evidently done the trick and my head had eased enough for another day's work, now I would at least be able to think straight once more. I gave Ned Musgrave's details and description and then we prepared to leave.

CHAPTER 15

I left Ned where Little Earl Street met Monmouth Street, bidding that he would do his best but not to put himself at risk, though sometimes he could not see the risk until he had already sunk knee deep into the mire. I hoped that the mire would at least be shallow should he find it. I continued up, heading towards St Giles and I again felt the stirring in my breast, the stirring of pity or at least the semblance of a little shame at my fortune, where here, the imbalance of society was laid bare. The shops, such as they were, were crowded with people, all searching the baskets for clothes, twice worn before, sometimes thrice and more. The ragged garments passed from hand to hand from one pauper to another, by the payment of coin or sometimes by barter. Monmouth Street had many of these types of establishments, all selling previously used items; from clothes to wigs to shoes to pots and pans. Even though the clothes I wore this day were old and well used, most people here would not be able to afford them, should I offer them for sale.

Worming my way through the crowds, I eventually emerged into the relative peace of Broad Street. I turned right and headed down. As I passed Dyot Street, a thought occurred to me. Kitty Marham, whom I helped not a few days ago, resided there and I wondered whether she might know something about the bookseller. Her trade would put her in contact with all manner of people and gossip would be rife. I hesitated only briefly before turning and making my way up towards her lodgings, sidestepping the urchins playing and avoiding the barrow traders and rickety stalls. I soon entered Kitty's building and climbed the stairs. I would elicit no comment as to my reason for being there; I was just another cull visiting his trull.

I knocked upon her door and waited, not wanting to venture in without invitation, in case she entertained.

'Who is it?' she called, a muffled sound, breathless, a little distant and I admit I felt a pang of disappointment that she continued in her trade.

'Richard,' I replied. 'But I will return when you are alone.'

I heard a scrabbling sound and then a thump and then a few seconds later the door opened hastily.

'Richard, come in, come in,' she said, enthusiastically. 'I had no idea you would come to visit.'

She opened the door and smiled warmly, her eyes, now recovered, shone brightly. As soon as the door closed, she stepped towards me, threw her arms around my neck and pressed me close. 'Have you come for your three shillings worth?'

I smiled back and shook my head. 'Alas no, dear Kitty.' I had my hands around her tiny waist and felt her as she pressed up against me and it took all my willpower to resist the temptation. 'What I need from you is a little information.'

She sighed and I could discern the catch of disappointment. 'Information?'

'Yes, just information.' I gave a smile and stepped back, taking in the room at the same time. If I had considered indulging, it would not have been comfortable as the bed lacked a covering with just a straw filled mattress showing. All her items were taken down; the pots, the cups, the plates, all the little ornaments and I could see none of her clothes. 'What is happening?' I asked, studying it all.

'I'm leaving, Richard. I have a new room and am taking it up today. You've caught me just as I was packing.'

I could see the small chest on the floor with a large bag beside it, all ready and waiting to go. 'But where are you to lodge?' I asked, feeling saddened that she could have just disappeared without me knowing where.

She smiled and looked at me a little coyly. 'Drury Lane, next to The White Hart. I will have two rooms and it is all thanks to you.'

'Me? How?'

'The money you gave me. I've paid for six months.'

I grinned. 'Do not forget that you have more to come, I promised you half and there is another thirty due to you. Fifty to each of us so it's just as well I called as I wouldn't know where you had gone.'

She still had her arms around my neck and I felt her increase the pressure against me. 'I would send you a note to let *you* know, Richard. You know I would not just disappear.'

'I know, Kitty, I would be disappointed if you had. Drury Lane will be convenient for the theatre trade.'

'It would but I hope to leave that life behind me now. I intend to do a little trading but not my body,' she said, finally disengaging from me.

'Then what?'

'Candles. I spoke to a Chandler and he agreed to sell me some to see how I do. A good price I got too.'

'Then I wish you luck and may I be your first customer. I will take a dozen of the best beeswax as soon as you are trading.'

'Thank you, Richard, you are so very kind.'

'Not at all but in the meantime, you can tell me all you know about the bookseller in Plumptre Street. You know the one I mean?'

She nodded and sat down on the end of the bed. 'He's been there a year or so now but along with normal books, most of what he sells is allied to my former trade; you know, books and sheets that describe various forms of intimacies. Very graphic from what I understand. He has a large customer base and some of them are very wealthy.'

'You do not surprise me there. Anything else? Does he print them himself?'

'He does, he has a printing press in the cellar.'

'Then he might not just print this licentious stuff?'

'No, he would print anything if he could make money from it'

'That is interesting. Would you know if he were a papist at all?

She nodded. 'Yes, by all accounts, he is, but people do not hold that against him, not here in St Giles anyway. Live and let live and we have any number of Irish here.'

'That is true; it's a shame that the authorities are not quite so tolerant.'

'Why do you want to know about him?'

'I followed a man there, another papist, but that is not the crime. I'm looking into a murder.'

'A murder? Oh, Richard, I hope you're not taking risks. Who was murdered?'

'A young man, a Catholic, but there is a little more to it. I'm taking less risk than you did with regard to Abe Gordon, so do not worry on my account, Kitty.'

'Do you intend to visit the bookseller?'

I nodded. 'I will take a look inside; maybe buy a book or two.'

'Then, wait...' she turned to her belongings and rummaged inside the chest for a few seconds. 'You may find this useful,' she said, passing me an item in her hand. 'Someone left it here and I have no doubt they will not return to collect it. I had forgotten I had it until I packed.'

I looked down and smiled. 'Thank you, Kitty. Indeed, it may be useful.'

I left Kitty with some reluctance as I enjoyed her company but she waited for the boy to arrive with a barrow to cart her belongings to her new rooms, eager to put the damp and squalid place behind her and she became a little distracted listening out for his arrival. I found myself grinning as I walked, pleased that she had a new venture to look forward to and that she would no longer have to do what many a young girl had to do to pay her way.

From where I stood in Plumptre Street, I could see the bookseller's quite clearly. I crouched down against the wall for a few seconds and then stood up again, realising that I had not dressed as a beggar would be. Folk passing by ignored me but I could not stay static for long in a busy street. Ideally, I would gain access to one of the rooms overlooking the area where I could sit for hours, if need be, just observing, but that option did not exist. Towards the lower end, I could see the gin-shop and tavern but neither of which would allow me clear observation, so, in the end, I decided that I had to enter the establishment and hope that I would learn something to my advantage,

I removed myself from the wall and strode towards the shop, stepping up and perusing the window, studying the items on offer; a few poor engravings and some battered looking tomes amongst the display of some newer books. Many of the authors I did not recognise but some I did, like Milton, Bunyan and Moliere, some cartographers' drawings of distant shores and some newssheets. I tore myself away from the window and reached for the door, entering and taking a couple of steps down to the floor. Noise from the street immediately extinguished as the door closed behind me and like any shop that sold old books

I could sense an atmosphere, slightly heavy and subdued, though a noise did intrude into the peace, a rhythmic thumping and clattering noise coming from below the floorboards. From my limited knowledge, it certainly sounded like a printing press. To emphasise that, a smell of ink permeated the shop as well as a corrosive tang, a further indication of what lay below in the cellar. A man dressed formally as though a scholar but of an age of about fifty, wearing an old-fashioned wig gave me a nod of welcome and I returned the greeting. I then began to peruse the shelves. Unsurprisingly, there were works by Swift, Defoe and Richardson, all slightly damaged but of a good enough condition. I could see works by Pope, Dryden and even Aphra Benn, journals and encyclopaedia, as well as simple prayer books and collections. I leant down towards the bottom shelf to look at a pile of Gazettes, at the same time loosening my neckcloth; as I hoped, it released the object Kitty had supplied me and as I stood up I could see the proprietor looking keenly at me. He twitched his head then cleared his throat and then emphasised a look towards my neck. I looked down, allowed my eyes to widen and then hastily put the crucifix back within my shirt. I flashed him a rueful grin of thanks. I was the only customer.

Looking back at the shelves once more, I saw a work by William Rufus Chetwood, an adventure featuring Captain Richard Falconer which I did not have at home; I pulled it down and began to leaf through the novel.

'Excellent choice, sir,' said the man observing me. 'I can tell you are a gentleman who would appreciate a tale such as that. I found it most edifying, a joy to read.'

'Did you indeed? Then I will bow to your superior knowledge and take it off your hands.'

'And most welcome you are to do so. It is priced at five shillings, sir.'

187

'Five shillings,' I replied. 'Surely you mean four?'

'Alas, no, sir. I paid four shillings for it not a week ago and you do not appear to be a man who would cast a fellow into penury.'

'The binding is a little distressed,' I said, observing the tome in my hand. 'And I can see a little damp on some of the pages.'

'Maybe, sir, but it has had a life. I will be reasonable with you then, sir. Four and sixpence, my last offer.'

I thought about it a little and then smiled and nodded my agreement. 'Four and six it is, Mr...?'

'Armitage, sir. Andrew Armitage.'

I made a polite bow. 'Jordan,' I said, holding out my hand. 'Mathew Jordan.'

'Good to make your acquaintance, Mr Jordan.'

'Mathew, please,' I replied. 'I do prefer informality where I can.'

Armitage smiled at me. 'I believe you have the right of it. There are so many sirs this and madams that, not to mention their Lordships. Call me Andrew, as my friends do.'

I counted out the money and handed it over and we passed a pleasant few minutes chatting about nothing in particular and all of the time I could hear the intermittent noise coming from below.

'Er...?' I began, hesitantly. 'I take it you do your own printing beneath our feet?'

'Some,' replied Armitage. 'Notices, newssheets and the like, though occasionally a book or two. Tell me, Mathew, I could not help but notice that ornament about your neck a little earlier; would you be of the old religion at all?'

I hesitated briefly and eyed him warily as if I weighed up my answer and then he smiled and brought out a rosary from his pocket, quickly showing it to me before clamping his hand around and putting it back where it came from. I too then smiled and nodded.

'It is that I know most people of note in our city, but I cannot recall meeting you, Mathew.'

'Alas, no, Andrew. I have been travelling these last few years, latterly spending a little time in Rome.'

'Rome, eh? Wonderful place, I understand.'

'It is indeed. Have you not been there?'

'No, but I hope to one day. You must have found many things of interest there; it is much to my disappointment that I have yet to manage a visit; as for all our faith it is where our true heart lies.'

'I can certainly recommend it, especially a visit to the Palazzo del Re.' I smiled at him as I said this, wondering what his reaction might be. James Stuart has his alternative Court in exile in The Palazzo de Re and many a traveller had visited, both Catholic and Protestant, to look upon it in awe, bewilderment or just plain interest. I had done just that several years ago, as of interest, and came away feeling it a poor relation to the real thing here at home; somewhat pretentious and something of a caricature, but then, I am not a Jacobite. I felt my heart beating faster, a great drum pounding in my chest as I waited for a response, wondering if I had taken a step too far.

After a few moments of looking at each other, Armitage spoke. 'May I enquire what brought you to my little shop of books today, Mathew?'

I smiled again and decided that nothing ventured, nothing gained. 'Let us say that you came with a recommendation, from Rome. To be precise, the Palazzo de Re.'

I saw his eyebrows rise and a little colour came to his cheeks. 'Really? May I ask from whom?'

'Let us say that I met a young man and his followers there, a young man who might well hold high office in this country should his father not do so first.' I referred to Charles Stuart, the son of James, hoping that he would see my inference clearly, as I doubt I could be plainer than that.

Armitage nodded slowly as if a great understanding had come upon him. He then turned away and held his chin momentarily as if processing a thought and pondering its ramifications. My stomach churned, anticipating a response, and I wondered if I had gone too far, gone too quickly and ruined any hope I had of learning more. I acted spontaneously as he talked, not thinking as such but just going along with the mood. I wished to appear unconcerned so I gazed at the shelves again, though this time I did not notice any of the books. I felt my heart beating fast again and had to concentrate to keep my breathing steady. Eventually, Armitage turned back to me and I could see a glint in his eye.

'Would I be correct if I assumed that you might be interested in *helping* that young man's father?'

'I do not think we would be having this conversation otherwise, Andrew,' I replied, as evenly as I could.

'Then come back tomorrow at the same time. I will speak to another gentleman of interest.'

I gave a slow nod of acknowledgment and gave a thin smile and then I heard the door to the street open. I turned and who should walk in but Henry Musgrave.

'Day to you, sorr,' he said, in a lilting Irish brogue.

'Good day to you too, sir,' I replied and then I bid Armitage a fond farewell and left the premises.

Outside, I wanted to stand still and take deep breaths to slow my heart but I knew I could not; I had to move away at a steady pace in case someone observed my progress. Ned must be here somewhere and I hoped he would see me walking away and make his presence known.

Sure enough, I soon felt that I did not walk alone and I turned my head slightly and saw Ned out of the corner of my eye, just a few steps behind and keeping pace. I tripped a little and slowed to a stop, cursing and staring at nothing in particular.

'Am I being watched,' I asked Ned, as he drew alongside.

'Not that I could see. I saw you come out and waited a moment but no one emerged.'

'Good, then follow me. I think we can forget Musgrave for a moment.'

CHAPTER 16

We sat in a brewhouse in Broad Street just by Drury Lane and nurtured two pots of indifferent ale, though better by far from the one I had whilst watching Musgrave.

'That were a rot-gut brew,' said Ned, as he upended his pot. 'I feel sorry for the locals. I'm just grateful you warned me about that swill. Won't be going back there again. Thankfully, I were only in there ten minutes or so before he came out. Left the ale in the pot, couldn't abide drinking any more of it.'

'Where did he go?' I asked, grinning, as I knew exactly how he felt.

'Covent Garden,' he said. 'Easy to follow is your man, that hair stood out like a whore in a nunnery.'

'What then?'

Ned took another pull on his pot and I think he was still getting the taste of the last from out of his mouth. 'He started looking amongst the stalls and hawkers, eventually coming across two ill-looking coves and began talking to them. They were holding pamphlets and handing them out to anyone who would take one. Then the three of them argued before finally Musgrave swore loudly at the two men, yelling that he had just walked all the way here but now he would have to walk all the way back. Those clowes were laughing as Musgrave stomped off. So I decided to pass close to the two men and grabbed a pamphlet as I went by and then followed him to the bookseller's.'

Ned produced the pamphlet from out of his pocket and handed it over to me.

'Have you read this?' I asked, as I sighed and leant back.

'Yes, briefly,' he replied. 'It don't seem something that could change opinion.'

'No, not in itself, but like raindrops falling, each drop adds to the last and before you know it you have a puddle, then the puddle gets bigger, and then before you know it, you have a flood.'

'That's true enough; then you think this,' and he tapped the pamphlet in my hand, 'should be stopped.'

'Yes, Ned, I do, but not because I do not agree with it, they have valid points, but this could be said to be an incitement to violence, of retribution against the government. It is calling for civil disobedience.'

'Suppose so.'

'There is no suppose about it, Ned.' I lay the pamphlet back on the table and took a mouthful. 'Which would explain the presence of those villains handing them out and I suspect there were a few more in the background, just in case things turned ugly.'

Ned took a pull of his pot. 'But you want to leave Musgrave now, even though you just found him?'

'I did not find him, Jarmin showed him to me. For a purpose. I think Armitage was that purpose. Yes, we forget Musgrave; we need to concentrate on Armitage. I only wish we could watch the shop unseen as I believe we would be rewarded by identifying some of the people frequenting it, also, I would like to know when Armitage leaves his shop because I wish to follow him.'

We both lapsed into silence for a few minutes, thinking upon a solution and it is at times like these that I wished I had my pipe with me, as the very act of drawing in the smoke and the stimulus it supplies relaxes my mind to give order and clarity of thought. I could have hired one from the landlord but I had an aversion to putting my lips around a stem that had been between another's. And then the answer came to me.

'Ned, I wish you to speak to the owners of the houses opposite the bookseller's. I wish to rent a room overlooking the street. Offer them what you think fit.'

'It will have to be ready money, sir, not a promise.'

I nodded and delved into my pockets, retrieved my small purse and handed it over. 'I would go, but I do not wish to be seen there at the moment. Try to drive a hard bargain as we'll not need the room for long.'

Ned grinned as he weighed my purse in his hand. 'I'll do my best, sir. Stay here and I'll return as soon as I can.'

As he left, I relaxed back on my stool and leant against the wall behind me. I looked around and watched as most of the patrons drew on their cheap clay pipes and I wrestled with the desire to join them. Shortly the girl came to clear Ned's empty pot and I ordered another but as she moved away I stayed her by catching her arm. 'I've a yearning for some fogus,' I said, giving a grin. 'And I've inadvertently left mine at home.' I fished out a few pennies. 'For you, if you can tip me a gage: new, virgin, unused?'

She was a pretty little creature with an abundance of dark wavy hair, an easy smile came upon her lips and her eyes brightened at the prospect of the easy money on offer. 'Certainly, sir, we 'ave a few and I will fetch one immediately. Would there be anything else I can offer you while you are at your leisure? I can keep you company fer a while, upstairs,' she said, indicating with her eyes, making her offer obvious.

'Maybe another time,' I replied, putting as much regret into the words as I could. 'The gage will have to suffice for now. The delight of your company I'll keep in mind for my next visit here,' I said, dropping my hand from her arm and placing it upon her waist, smiling as I did so.

True to her word, she returned shortly with a fresh pot and the gage, newly filled with the stem bereft of the marks teeth made when clamped to it. She handed me a spill and I proceeded to light it from a flame nearby and set it to the pipe, luxuriating in drawing the smoke into my lungs.

An hour passed, perhaps a little more before Ned returned to the little brewhouse. He wore a smile of success as he settled opposite me. He quickly caught the eye of the girl and a pot for him and another for me appeared in front of us.

'Good service here,' observed Ned, as he wet his lips.

'Better than you may think, Ned. I have spent the last hour in pure chastity despite intense provocation.'

His eyes widened slightly as he turned to cast his eye properly over the girl. 'Her?'

I nodded and let my breath out slowly.

'Hmm,' he mused. 'In that case, I may drop by here again, when you give me a little time away from your employment.'

'Be my guest, Ned, just don't complain if you end up pissing pins and needles.'

'No fear of that, I takes me precautions,' he said, tapping his pocket.

'Never mind all that; were you successful in finding a room?'

He grinned. 'Of course, it will be ready in about half an hour. Cost you three pounds, though you can keep it for three days.'

'Steep,' I observed. 'Why is it not empty now?'

'He's turfing the incumbent out and going to give it a sweep and a clean mattress.'

'The tenant is evicted?'

'Only for a time, he was willing for a consideration.'

'Why the clean mattress?'

'Er... because I told him my master wants a place to entertain a lady. You know, privately.'

'Oh, I see, and when just you and I turn up, what will they think then?'

'Ah, that may be a problem. You can always hire her over there,' he added, pointing a finger at the pot-girl. 'I don't rate being thought a Madge.'

'Me neither, so we will have to get a girl but not that one. I saw Kitty Marham earlier, perhaps she might oblige.'

'Kitty Marham? Then no wonder you are not particular 'bout her over there.'

'I just wanted to know if she knew anything about the bookseller, and she did. Nothing else occurred, so you can wipe that smile from your face. Besides, she said she has ceased that trade now, moving her lodgings to just around the corner in Drury Lane, next to The White Hart, which is where I hope to find her,' I said, putting his speculation to rest but somehow thinking I had made it worse.

We found Kitty easily enough, the comings and goings of tenants provided plenty of gossip and a pretty girl taking up residence on her own was fuel to the fire. My appearance with Ned, just as she moved in would provide another log for the fire and I only hoped she would forgive me for adding a burden.

I need not have worried as she just laughed off my concern as to her reputation. 'People will think what they want to,' she replied, as I apologised for the intrusion. 'And in truth, they wouldn't be too far off the mark, considering how I made my money up 'til now and there are plenty of jades living in this street anyway. But enough of that,' she cast her eye to Ned. 'You are after more information?'

I shook my head. 'No, but perhaps a little help if you are feeling charitable.'

She listened as I explained that the bookseller was probably a Jacobite and that with the use of the crucifix she had given me, I had managed to engage him in conversation. When our conversation had ended, he stated that he wished to speak to someone, which prompted us to seek a room so that we could keep watch. She readily agreed to assist us and found it hilarious that we required her just so that folk would not think Ned and I indulged in backdoor games. She had yet to unpack her scant possessions, so the chest and the bag lay on the floor but she took pride in showing us the rooms and how they compared to her last residence, how much cleaner and drier they were.

We crossed the road and she linked her arm through mine companionably as we walked towards Vine Street, intending to cut through the back alleyways by The Bell, which would bring us out close to the bookseller's and the room that Ned had procured. We chatted as we strolled, or rather, Kitty chatted and Ned and I listened. I took delight in the easy form of her voice, its soft tones, the gentle rise and fall, the husky sensuality which I had previously failed to notice. Ned turned left as we reached the tavern and we entered the narrow byways, stepping around and over that which we had no wish to step upon. Walkways above us connected one side to the other and washed clothes hung out to dry on ropes strung between the buildings. Some of the alleys allowed only single file, the light dimmed by the encroaching tenements. After a few minutes, we emerged from the alley, a few doors down and across from the bookseller. We stepped into the street and almost immediately took a turn into a passageway that led to a door. Ned used a key and the door swung open, revealing a staircase that bent around to the left.

'Up here,' said Ned, as we began to climb.

At the top of the stairs, a corridor headed to the front of the building with four doors leading off, two either side. A door opened and a man's face appeared. Ned smiled and cocked his head towards Kitty and me.

The man nodded and sent a lecherous grin Kitty's way. 'All ready for you, sir,' he said, speaking to me but looking at Kitty. 'I 'ope you finds it satisfactory.'

'I am sure I will,' I replied, following Ned to the last door on the right, then putting on the arrogant air of the gentry, I said. 'Providing I am not disturbed.'

The man chuckled as he continued to follow Kitty with his eyes and only caught my gaze as I spoke.

Ned had done well. The room, in fact two rooms, overlooked the street with a window in each and gave a clear view of the bookseller's. To my enquiry as to two rooms, Ned explained that he told the man that he would need to accompany me but that he should have somewhere where he could keep out of the way of our activities, as it were.

The first room had a table with four bare wooden chairs, the hearth had a hook with a pot hanging upon it in order to cook; other pots and pans sat on the floor next to the hearth. A cheap cupboard and a dresser lined the wall. Ornaments, there were none. The back room had just a bed with a small table beside it, upon which a candleholder stood. A chest sat against the dividing wall. A pot for pissing in completed the furniture.

'Comfortable,' announced Kitty, casting her eye about the place. 'Though I believe this mattress has seen a lot of use,' she added, as she pulled back the blanket and inspected the bed.

'He promised to change that, though I expect that may not be the case,' I said, as I looked out through a cracked pane of glass to the street outside. 'However, it will not be needed for the purpose the landlord thinks it will.'

'You two had better stay in here,' said Ned, as he stood at the door. 'He,' and he cast his head in the direction of the entrance, 'will have his ear pressed to the door, listening; probably with a hand down his breeches.'

'Then he will be sorely disappointed with the performance,' I replied, finding amusement with that thought. 'Though I expect the door will have a crack within its timbers, so will you hang that blanket in front of it, Ned. It'll muffle any noise and prevent him from attempting to see.'

'Are we to just sit here?' asked Kitty, as Ned hung the blanket and pulled two of the chairs through to the bedroom.

I nodded as I placed the chairs in front of the window. 'Yes, Kitty,' I said, giving her a smile. 'I want to see who comes and goes and I want to know when Armitage leaves, as I wish to follow him and see where he goes and whom he visits.'

'Then we could be here for quite a while, until the shop closes, at least.'

'Probably, which is why I wanted a room to wait.'

'We'll get hungry,' she reasoned, as she sat upon the bed.

'Ned will go out for provisions soon. We'll not want for sustenance.'

I settled in front of the window and stared out, already preparing myself for a long wait. I could see the front of the shop clearly, as well as the approaches from either side. I reasoned that customers would be infrequent due to the nature of what he sold but hazarded that genuine customers would be amongst those there for nefarious reasons. I would not know one from another, so hoped that one of us might be able to recognise some of them.

Kitty came and sat opposite me and she too stared out of the window. I could hear Ned next door grunting and sniffing as he took up his position for the vigil.

In that first hour, only one gentleman entered the shop, a well-dressed man of about fifty years, unknown to the three of us. He emerged clutching something and then hurried away.

'I wonder what he's bought,' I asked, aloud but as a thought to myself.

'Under the counter material; salacious,' said Kitty, confidently. I looked at her and she grinned. 'I can tell the type.'

We lapsed back into silence and then I sent Ned out to get some food and drink and also to empty the pot, which had received a decent amount of the brewhouse's ale. Kitty and I just continued to watch the people in the street as they went about their business; the children playing and getting up to mischief; we watched a diver relieve a man of his purse; a couple of whores fishing for custom. Ned returned with some pies and a flagon of ale and we watched some more until the day began to turn to evening. Three more men visited the shop and then Musgrave returned but he went in alone and came out alone, just a minute or so later. Shortly after that, Armitage appeared at the door and took a look up and down the street before stepping back in and shutting the door. I surmised that trading had finished for the day, which was confirmed when the light dimmed in the shop.

Ned came into the bedroom. 'What do you think will happen now?' he asked, as he checked to see if we had left any food.

'The printers are still there, so I imagine he'll wait for them to leave and then I hope he will take a walk to see this "Gentleman" of his, regarding me.'

'We still going to follow him?'

'Wherever he goes, we will go.'

'Does that include me?' asked Kitty, a touch of hope in her voice.

'No,' I said, a definitive reply. 'It might be dangerous.'

'Dangerous?' she queried, interest in her tone.

I then realised I had said the wrong thing. I had been telling her that it was not going to be dangerous and she had accepted that, now I had reversed it all and said that it might be dangerous. 'Only that we do not know where we will go,' I said, lamely.

'Then you should take me,' she replied, a confidence now in her voice. 'If nothing else, I could call an alarum should you find yourself in peril. I'm not some innocent tib, remember. I know these streets as well as you.'

I could not argue with that but, I thought, she would know the streets far better than I did.

We argued about it a little but in the end, I relented, and agreed that she could accompany us. Her assertion that she had spent a boring time looking at a shop when she had only moved lodgings a few hours before because we needed her to "save our reputation," as she put it, won the day for her but I hoped she would not regret it later.

'Movement down there,' announced Ned, still looking, despite taking enjoyment from the discussion between Kitty and I.

Three men emerged from the shop and quickly melted away into the darkening light, followed shortly after by Armitage, who took his time locking the door and looking furtively down the street before heading up.

'Come on,' I said, standing up. 'We cannot lose him.'

CHAPTER 17

We ran out of the rooms, rushed down the stairs then out. I then remembered I had left my book in the room but reasoned that we had rented it for three days, so I could retrieve it later. We stood for a few moments until I caught sight of Armitage in the gloom, hurrying away from his shop, his gait somewhat pronounced as if he continuously stepped over something. There were few people about at this end of the street, so we hung back a little, as I knew the street ended with no means of progression. Armitage turned into the narrow unlit path of a court that led to Dyot Street. We waited a moment and then followed. The path seemed to belong to the slum as it was ankle deep in rubbish and dirt, the construction of which became obvious as the foot stepped down, breaking the surface and releasing the pungent odour. We slipped and slithered along, following Armitage, whom I suspected wore protection for his footwear. My coat kept scraping along the walls, leaving a residue of mould and muck sticking to it, which I was actually thankful for, considering the direction Armitage seemed to be aiming towards. A stranger who dressed well could easily become a victim in this area. Kitty and Ned kept pace with me as we negotiated the twists and turns, eventually breaking free of the alley, all of us appearing in a more dishevelled manner than when we entered just a few minutes ago.

I could see the outline of Armitage across the street, his peculiar stepping motion making him easy to spot. A few curious residents took a view of us but some seemed to nod at Kitty and then relaxed, taking no more notice of Ned and me.

Armitage entered Buckridge Street, another narrow road, but fortunately, I would term it a proper street with dilapidated three-storey houses lining both sides, a plethora of alehouses and gin-shops, many of them all next to each other, cheek by jowl. We were in the heart of the slum area and I became a little wary until I remembered my attire had been somewhat distressed from the alley, besides, people knew Kitty, so I would just seem like another of her culls.

Rough men in groups of three and four, their doxies following dutifully, roamed the streets in their drunken stupors, caterwauling and screeching at each other as if vying for supremacy by want of the loudness of their voices. Several gangs, or crews, held sway within the slum, all at odds with each other, until a common foe, generally the authorities, united them in a collective until such time as the threat receded. Ragged urchins in their scraps of clothing ran and played or offered themselves as playthings to those of a certain disposition, children old before their time, destined for a short harsh life through their need to survive long enough to find their next meal.

I have said before that there is something about the people that live here that I admire greatly: through all the poverty and degradation, the depravity, the drunkenness and the desperation, there burns a flickering flame of hope, although that flame continues to gutter, it is never allowed to be snubbed out. Death and violence are commonplace but beneath it all, it is a society like no other; there is a camaraderie that transcends circumstance. The people will join hands when the need arises.

Armitage walked unmolested, which led me to believe that he was a frequent visitor, well known and accepted by the inhabitants as his dress alone was cause enough to turn him into a victim. Behind me, Ned walked easily, even receiving a few nods of recognition, while Kitty, hanging off my arm, walked with confidence and grace, bestowing a smile or a wink to those we passed. I too could claim an acquaintance with some of the people, though they failed to recognise me as they knew me as a shabbaroon, not as a man with a few shillings in his pocket. We carried on, keeping Armitage in sight in spite of the descending night, the lengthening shadows only partially relieved by the glow emanating from the gin-shops and taverns. Pigs and poultry roamed free, their owners keeping their careful eyes on them as they scavenged amongst the filth and the squalor, competing with the beggars and the vagrants for any morsel that would sustain life for a few hours more. I could hear the canting language, which, fortunately, I was familiar with, as we nudged past, though I could hear Irish and French too as well as the negro patois from the escaped slaves or free blacks, released from servitude as they grew from children of curiosity, who adorned rich houses early in their lives, but now cast adrift as their novelty lost its lustre.

We watched as Armitage turned right into Maynard Street, a street just as wholesome as the one we had just left; more thieves, cut-purses, whores and beggars filled the road, but like before, we were allowed to progress freely, without hindrance. The raucous inhabitants shielded our movements and I saw Armitage look briefly over his shoulder before quickly diving into an alley between a tenement and a tavern.

'Do you know where that leads to?' I asked Kitty, as we hesitated by the alley.

She nodded slowly and I felt her fingers dig into my arm. 'Yes, this is where I grew up,' she said, staring at the entrance.

I turned to look at her and she returned my gaze and I saw a challenge there as if daring me to judge her upbringing, her admission of the lowly status that saw her into life and then the situation that forced her into the life she had so recently led.

I did not judge her. I admired her, but I did not voice my admiration, I just hoped she could see it in my eyes. 'Are you all right to go in?' I asked, putting my hand onto hers.

She nodded, then took a deep breath and stepped forward.

We found a court behind the tavern, crowded with people, most of whom seemed in a state of drunkenness; voices were loud and some, argumentative, as they drank from jugs and pots and bowls. I could see the open barn door and smell the tang of strong alcohol wafting across the court resulting from the preparation of gin. Men groped and fondled the girls and women who responded in either encouragement or outrage; raucous laughter rang out, games of chance played, drink spilled and wild-haired children cavorted, as drunk as the adults and aping their manners. I could see across the court and spied Armitage as he entered another passage and we quickly traversed the court in pursuit.

The next dark and intimidating rank passage dog-legged with liquid running through it, though what liquid I did not want to think on. People lived in rooms in this alley, their doors opening directly into the sewerage. The next court appeared just a dark sullen place, the tenements looming menacingly, some of the buildings falling down through neglect. I could see Armitage disappear into yet another passageway on the far side and we hurried across.

'He's going to the alehouse,' said Kitty, sure in that. 'Though it's more a mumpers hall.'

'That bad? Then wait here and let me look first,' I said to both of them.

Kitty and Ned opened their mouths to protest but I held up

my hand to stop them. 'No time to argue; wait here, both of you.'

I did not linger and hurried into the passage where I could hear voices coming towards me. I rushed on, eager to be out of the confining space. I lurched out of the passage into the court where a few people collected in groups. I could see the alehouse to my left, timber framed with a low roof, shutters on the windows instead of glass; an orange glow filtering through the gaps in the timbers, two young men watched me with interest and behind them, I could see Armitage making his way through the door. Kitty was right; it was a low establishment.

One of the young men stepped towards me and I saw a flash of light reflect from an object in his hand.

'What 'ave we 'ere, Pat? he said, throwing the words at his companion.

'A tidy rum-duke and no mistake, by the look of 'im,' replied Pat.

'A bit lost are you my bene-cove?' asked the first man, with a sneer.

I shook my head, keeping an eye on the knife. 'Seen a drab come by?' I asked, dismissing their question.

'Drab, eh? Plenty of them 'round 'ere. You after one in particular?'

'The one that took my watch.'

'Ah, that one,' said Pat. 'You want to show 'im where she went, Davy?'

'Reckon I might, fer a price.'

'And what price is that then, my friend,' I replied, moving back a little, away from the arm with the blade.

'Whatever you got will do us. Might 'ave yer boots and breeches too, won't want some other cove 'ave them.' He laughed and raised the knife towards my face.

'You sure, boy?' I asked, giving him a grin. 'Like as not you'll wish you'd turned and minded your own.'

'I am minding my own,' spat the one called Davy.

For some reason he wished to spike my face, which showed he had yet to learn his trade; he should have gone for my belly to rip my guts out, the bigger target and the most disabling. However, he made it easy for me. I could see he was nervous and hesitant as he tentatively poked the blade towards me, perhaps because of my refusal to be cowered he suddenly realised I might not be such an easy victim. I did not disappoint him in this. I swayed out of the path of the knife and stepped forward quickly, inside the arc of the blade, bringing my arm up and smacking my forearm into his, deflecting the knife away, then I slid my hand down his arm and took a grip of his wrist, twisting it hard. I smacked my fist into his face, twice, quickly, then gripped him by the throat and turned him so that his back slammed against the wall. I brought my knee up fast into the soft spot between his legs and he doubled over in an instant. I heard the clatter of the knife as it fell and I lifted him and squeezed his throat harder, cutting off his breath. I then rammed the back of his head against the wall. He groaned as my hold of his throat relaxed and I kicked the knife away before turning quickly, putting an elbow into his stomach as his friend, Pat, looked on, wide-eyed in shock and surprise. I looked up and grinned at Pat as his friend Davy slumped puking to the ground.

'Your turn,' I hissed, as I took a step forward.

For some reason Pat decided against attempting to fight me and a small part of me felt disappointed as he turned and ran across the court and into the alley on the far side, leaving his friend to my mercy. A trio of men outside the alehouse had viewed the disturbance with their pots in their hands, unconcerned but with a studied interest and laughed as Pat ran to save his own skin. I turned to retrace my steps, leaving Davy lying in his own vomit.

'Armitage went into the alehouse,' I said, as I re-joined Ned and Kitty.

'I heard a yell,' said Kitty. 'That wasn't you?'

I shook my head. 'No, nothing to concern us, just someone picking a fight that he should have avoided.'

Ned gave me that look of his, the one that disbelieved everything I said. 'If you say so, sir,' he ventured in the end.

'What do you know about that alehouse, Kitty?' I asked, turning away from Ned.

She shook her head. 'You won't get in, if that's what you're planning.'

'Why?'

'The O'Rourke brothers. They control things around here. If you tried, you would just disappear.'

'Hmm,' I thought, it was what I expected.

'But there is another way if you wish to risk it,' she added, as she saw my disappointment.

'Then tell me,' I said, eagerly.

'Not tell you but *show* you.' She turned away and began to walk, down past the crumbling hovels and rank buildings to the bottom corner of the court where another passage led away. The light of dusk had now gone and we had only the night sky to light our way, that and the occasional gleam of a single candle through shuttered windows from the court.

Within that passage I could see a doorway; however, the door itself had gone long before. The room beyond stank of urine and excrement, the miasma stinging the eyes and forcing bile to the throat but I could see timbers littering the floor, fallen from above, though most things of value or use had already been plundered. Parts of the roof had given way and I could see the stars through the gaps. Kitty led us into the building and across the room to another doorway, beyond which revealed the remnants of a stairway.

'We need to get up there,' said Kitty, looking up. 'It wasn't as bad as this a few years ago but I suppose time has done it no favours.'

As my eyes adjusted to the lack of light, I could see it would not be a difficult climb as there were enough handholds to grip. With Ned's help, I managed to scramble up to stand on the rotting floorboards. Kitty looked up and then gathered her skirts between her legs and said something to Ned who showed his teeth in a smile. He aided her in the same way as he did me, one hand beneath a bent knee, the other he placed firmly beneath her buttocks. I leant down, held her arm and pulled at the same time as Ned heaved. She weighed less than a feather and the next thing I knew, she stood next to me.

'Wait there, Ned,' I instructed, as I did not think the floor would sustain much more weight; already it complained at our intrusion, creaking and groaning. 'If you came, I think the whole place would fall down.'

I heard a grunt from Ned as a reply.

'This way,' said Kitty, as she moved into the building. 'Watch where you tread, it is in a much poorer state than when I last used it.'

'Which was when?' I asked, placing my feet carefully.

'Eight or nine years ago. As children, we used to climb up here so we could work our way through to the alehouse to see what the adults were up to. There is space above it in the rafters where you can both see and hear what is going on below. I received a lot of my education by observing what went on there.'

'But surely the O'Rourkes know this?'

'The O'Rourkes weren't around then; they have only been

'here these past two years, so they may be unaware.'

'But the children, like you, who came here, who now drink here, they would know.'

'Yes, but there is an advantage to knowing something a gang leader does not. It is an unwritten rule not to divulge something that may be advantageous to you. The O'Rourkes' of this place come and go, someone will challenge the O'Rourkes one of these days and someone else will take over. Gilkes ran the area in my childhood but then he ended up in a noose and a new regime came in. Most of the children who came up here are no longer around or do not care. Anyway, we'll soon find out.'

Nimble footed, she led me through the building. I kept to the main roof-beams, hoping that they would bear my weight, dodging the fallen tiles and avoiding the holes, though we did not have to go far as she soon brought me to a wall with a gap above, a hum of noise and the waft of alcohol and smoke beyond.

'This is the alehouse,' she said quietly, pointing to the gap. 'It's still here, so we need to slip over the wall and we will then be above them.'

'You mean me; *you* will not go any further, Kitty. If something goes wrong then you can get back to Ned.'

She opened her mouth to complain but then saw the sense in what I said. She nodded, albeit reluctantly. 'Just don't kick anything that will fall through,' she warned.

I had no intention of alerting those below to my presence above them but as I clambered over, I could see that I had to be careful. Amidst the fug of smoke from the hearth fire and from pipes of tobacco which hung beneath the roof, stinging my eyes, I could just about distinguish boxes and crates and sacks and bags all over the boards, undoubtedly containing illegal goods waiting to find an alternative home. Light from below filtered up through the gaps in the boards and I eased down onto my knees and bent my head forward, fighting the urge to cough and wiping the smoke-tears from my eyes.

I could only see through the gaps between the boards, somewhat restricted, but good enough to see those below. There were many drinkers but I could not see Armitage, so I began to crawl forwards, every few moments looking down, hoping to catch sight of him. As luck would have it, the next time I looked down I paused; I did not see Armitage but I did see the man I rendered unconscious just the other night. I grinned, at least now I knew who had attacked me. I moved forward again, raised my head and then looked below; something did not seem right, so I raised my head and I could see a disparity between the boards up here and the size of the bar below. I craned my head to look at an angle and then I could see why, there appeared to be a further room to the bar. I crawled over and came alongside a large crate and my curiosity made me try to raise the lid, but it had been nailed down tight and I could not move it. I wanted to look into the bags and sacks but they were over on the far side and I did not think I should waste time with them. I left everything alone, moved forward and then I could see a partition, accommodating two private booths where I found Armitage, sitting upon a bench and leaning on a table, a leather pot by his elbow. He was in discussion with two other men, both of whom he appeared well acquainted.

A pox-faced man of large build with close-cropped fair hair shook his head. 'No, I say we hush the cull,' he said in a raw Irish brogue, slapping the table with his fist.

I could not see the face of the third man, only his back, but when he spoke, the voice was familiar. 'Not so hasty, Liam. If, as he claims, he has come from The Palazzo del Re, then he may have a message for us. He knew about your book shop after all,' he said to Armitage, 'No, I believe we must find out a little more, he could just as easily be testing us. Tomorrow, when he returns, I will be perusing your shelves.'

I tried to bring the sound of the voice to mind, I had heard it only recently, I was certain of that, so I began to crawl again in order to bring the man into view but then he turned his head and I could see him in profile and then I grinned to myself.

'What do you intend?' asked Armitage, nervously twisting his fingers.

'I intend nothing. I merely wish to view the man, although I may engage him in conversation,' said Cummings, his previous servile manner replaced with one of authority. 'If he proves false, then you can take care of him, Liam.'

The big man nodded. 'As long as you don't interfere like last time.'

'I told you I wished to land the lethal blow.'

'You did but you nearly messed up, he could've got away. I take pride in making a cull easy, even one of our own.'

'He died in the end, Liam.'

'I still do not understand why Sorley had to die,' said Armitage. 'I rather liked him.'

'You did not know everything, Andrew,' explained Cummings, sighing heavily. 'He would have gone against us, turned King's evidence. We would all be for the Tyburn tree if we allowed him to live.'

'So you say,' said Armitage.

'I do say,' replied Cummings. 'You forget yourself, Andrew. I am privy to more information than you and I have to act accordingly to safeguard us all.'

'Speaking of which,' said Liam. 'When are you going to move that lot up there?' he asked, pointing directly at me.

'Soon, Liam,' said Cummings. 'I have it all in hand.'

I looked up and glanced around me and all the items began to take on a new meaning. They were not, as I thought, stolen goods, but were something to do with the Jacobites. What did that actually mean?

Armitage finished his drink and then got up to leave, I had no need to follow him back to his shop, so I waited to see if I would learn something else.

Liam watched the bookseller go and then turned to Cummings. 'He's weak, you know. If it weren't for that press, I would've got rid of him long ago.'

'Maybe,' replied Cummings. 'But he has his uses.'

The two then got up and moved into the main bar, so I knew I would not learn anything more.

CHAPTER 18

I scrambled back over the wall to re-join Kitty, my mind churning everything over. I now knew the name of Thomas Sorley's murderer but in finding out, had I discovered something more?

The fact that Cummings had brazenly, and with much false distress, identified the body of Sorley, indicated a character of obvious duplicity. He had lulled me into feeling sympathy for him; and now to learn that he had been part of the same group as Sorley, agitating for a change of King and had also delivered the killing blow to the young man he had mentored, as well as how he contrived a meeting with Elizabeth Thompson, just confirmed his deceitful nature.

'Did you see or hear anything?' asked Kitty, as she guided my foot to the floor.

'Yes,' I replied quietly, as I helped her stand up. 'I will tell you all, once we are outside.'

Kitty nodded and then turned and guided me back through the dilapidated buildings. There must have been cloud cover as it had become noticeably darker now but she moved as if in sunshine, sure of her step. When we came to the former staircase where Ned waited, I caught her arm and put a finger to my lips then knelt down on a beam and looked keenly, seeking a man-like shadow in amongst the detritus of the floor below.

'Ned,' I hissed, into the darkness.

'Here, sir,' replied Ned, directly below us.

I let out a sigh, relieved that no harm had come to him in our absence, then lowered Kitty and he caught her in his arms. I then swung down myself, landing just by her as he put her feet to the ground.

'All quiet?' I asked.

'Apart from the rats, there must be hundreds of the buggers running around.'

'Yes, and I know where at least three of them are,' I replied, wryly. 'Come on; let us get out of here.'

We hastened across the court and through the passageway and then past the revellers of the gin-shop and back out into the relative peace of Maynard Street. I had no wish to give voice to my discoveries in this still hostile area, so we hurried away, turned right and within a few moments, we emerged onto the High Street, thankfully leaving the slum behind us. It never failed to amaze me that you could move from the cesspit of the slum to the relative wealth of the road abutting it, in just a few short steps; a stranger would never know unless he took a wrong turn by mistake and by then it would be too late, for he would be set upon instantly.

As we walked down towards the church, I related what I had seen and heard to my two companions; Ned, like myself felt his ire rise at the conduct and deceit of Cummings, while Kitty focused on my description of the third man there, this Liam, whom she identified as Liam O'Rourke, a man very familiar with violence.

Carriages clattered by, their lanterns giving a feeble light to the road ahead while people walked about, looking for entertainment in the various establishments along the way. It was becoming a busy time of the evening and the three of us became just another part of the tableau of a London street.

We passed the church, heading away from the slum, and I

began to feel a little easier; I did not realise how tense I had become but I now felt myself relax.

Kitty walked between Ned and I, with her arms linked through both of ours but she seemed a little melancholy as we walked along, lapsing into silence where before she was talkative and animated. I took a little look at her but she released Ned's arm for a moment and I saw her raise her hand to wipe a tear from her eye. I wondered if her thoughts had dwelt on the return to her childhood but she put the hand back through his arm and then looked at me, giving a rueful smile. After that, she became alive once more and by the time we reached Drury Lane she insisted on a short visit to The White Hart, where we could at least buy her a little sustenance to fortify her for the first night in her new rooms.

We took a table and ordered three pots and three fish pies. Kitty sat on the bench next to me while Ned sat opposite, our heads leaning towards each other as we continued the discussion on what I had heard.

'Surely you're not going to Armitage's tomorrow, are you?' asked Kitty, wearing a concerned look.

I grinned. 'Well, at least I will not go on my own,' I said, thinking the matter through. 'I believe I would need a little assistance to venture in there, I think.'

'Who from?' asked Ned. 'I can be there but two of us won't be enough.'

'No, not if Cummings is there too and there is always the possibility of O'Rourke turning up as well.'

'De Veil?' suggested Ned.

I shook my head. 'No, I will go to Jarmin.'

'Why him?' asked Kitty.

'Because he gave us Musgrave and I have my suspicions about what is hidden above the alehouse; I also promised him I would tell him what I had found out.'

'This Jarmin can't be that bright if he couldn't find out what we have just found out, I mean, we followed Musgrave easy enough, so why couldn't he do it too?' asked Ned.

'I believe I told you my thoughts, Ned, when I came back from Westminster. I can assure you that Jarmin is very bright indeed. I do not think he knew Cummings killed Thomas Sorley but he may have suspected it. I will find out when I speak to him but I will not be at all surprised if he already knows what we know.'

'Then you have been played, Richard,' observed Kitty, shaking her head sadly.

'I don't think so,' I said in answer. 'De Veil tasked me to find out who killed Sorley and I do not believe I would have done that had Jarmin not pointed me to Musgrave. We might have found Musgrave after a long time searching,' I said to Ned. 'But it certainly made things quicker. My hope is that I can extricate myself from Newcastle's clutches, as I've no wish to become an intelligencer for the state. However, just in case we have found out something they do not know, I feel I have to speak to him.'

I finished my pie and felt better, more optimistic, for having something substantial in my stomach. I had a feeling of satisfaction that I had discovered the murderer of Thomas Sorley and that soon, Cummings would pay for his crime. Kitty still sat next to me and I could feel her thigh pressed against mine, her shoulder against mine, her hair brushing my face as she turned her head to speak. I considered leaving things until the morning; I thought it unlikely that Jarmin would be at Westminster, so I could send Ned back home and keep Kitty company, help her unpack and then spend the night in a most convivial manner.

I dismissed the later thought as ungallant, considering the

circumstances, there was more at stake here than just satisfying my more basic urges. I resolved to attend upon Westminster at the earliest, which meant going now.

I stood up. 'Ned, see Kitty has everything she needs, then go back home, I am to Westminster, where I hope to find someone in authority.'

Kitty looked up and smiled; she then took my hand and gave it a gentle squeeze. 'Be careful, Richard.'

'I always am,' I replied, squeezing her hand back.

I left The White Hart and headed out into the Lane, fortunately, due to the theatre, there were any number of hackney's to be had and soon I was being jolted down towards Charing Cross and then along to the seat of government. The driver sensed urgency in my manner and reacted accordingly, hoping that a higher gratuity would apply should I arrive at my destination with alacrity. With all the shuddering and the bumping, I did think that I might regret the fish pie, the lack of light compounding the issue but thankfully, we arrived at New Palace Yard unscathed and the pie still in my stomach. I alighted to find the Yard crowded with people and I stood there for a moment as the hackney turned and slowly eased away, my shillings in the driver's pocket and a grin on his face.

I threaded my way through the crush as even at this time there were stalls selling goods, places to drink and eat and bodies for sale. Fortunately, the crowd diminished as I gained the Old Palace Yard and I headed over to the nondescript building from which I emerged only two days before.

I banged hard with my fist on the door for several seconds and then waited, hoping that someone somewhere in the building had heard me.

It seemed an age that I stood there and after two further attempts of banging on the door, I considered giving up and going instead to Bow Street and De Veil. Without warning, the door suddenly opened and a short stringy looking man with a mop of grey hair and sporting bushy eyebrows stood before me, holding a lantern. He raised his eyebrows in question.

'I wish to speak to Mr Jarmin,' I responded to the unasked question.

He nodded slowly as if to himself. 'And you are, sir?'

'Hopgood, Richard Hopgood.'

'Wait here, Mr Hopgood. I will see if someone is available to talk to you,' he said, as he shut the door in my face, giving me no chance to place my foot between the door and the frame.

I waited impatiently, scuffing the sole of my boot on the gravel as if I were a bored child. I studied the knots in the oak wood of the door. I turned and saw two drunken revellers, their arms wrapped about each other, giving support as they staggered into a path between buildings, bawling a bawdy song.

Eventually, the door sprang open, interrupting my musings on the drunks; the short stringy man had returned and now beckoned me inside.

He shut the door behind me and locked it with a key amongst a set of similar keys, hooked into a bunch, which went back into his pocket. He pushed past me and led the way along the corridor and down into the basement where I had been before. Two different men slouched upon chairs at the table, plates of bread and meat in front of them. They looked up as I entered, as if in passing interest and then returned to their repast.

'Ah, Mr Hopgood,' said Jarmin from his chair as I entered his office. 'You have returned and so soon too.' His mouth showed a smile that did not quite reach his eyes as he indicated the chair on the other side of the desk.

I sat down and heard the door shut behind me as the short man left. 'I believe I may have some information that might please you,' I began, settling myself in the chair. 'Or not, considering you may well know what I am about to disclose.'

'Then furnish me, Mr Hopgood. I am always grateful for information, even if it is only confirmation.'

'Very well,' I said, nodding to myself. 'I found Thomas Sorley's murderer. His name is Cummings and he works at Thompson and Gutteridge.'

Jarmin snapped his eyes wide and I got the impression that this was news to him. 'Quick work, Mr Hopgood,' he acknowledged.

'Yes, but you gave me Musgrave who led me to a bookseller by the name of Andrew Armitage.'

He nodded. 'Yes, we know about him,' confessed Jarmin. 'So, tell me, how did Armitage lead you to Cummings?'

I will give Jarmin his due, he listened without interruption as I related the events and I tried to gauge from his reactions what he knew and what he did not but apart from the brief indication when I first revealed Cummings as the murderer, he gave away nothing. When I had finished describing what I had seen and heard, when I crouched in the rafters at O'Rourkes', just a couple of hours ago, he took a deep breath and then called out.

'Fulton,' he yelled. 'In here.' He picked up his quill, dipped it in ink, and quickly began to write on a piece of paper.

Fulton entered and stood in the doorway.

'This is Mr Hopgood,' said Jarmin, pointing to me with the end of his quill. 'He has just come from O'Rourkes' alehouse where he managed to get in, and as you can see, get out again.'

Fulton looked at me and I thought I could detect a little respect in his eyes as he inclined his head in a most seemly manner.

'We have lost two men over the last few months,' explained Jarmin. 'Both tried to infiltrate the O'Rourkes' but both were unsuccessful. We pulled their bodies out of the Fleet; Fulton's brother being one of them.'

'Then accept my condolences on your loss,' I said to Fulton, feeling I should say something.

Fulton acknowledged me without a word; just a slight pinching above his nose indicated his feelings.

'Take this to the Duke,' said Jarmin, finishing his writing and drying the ink. He folded it and applied a seal in wax. 'Wherever he is and then wait for a reply. You may well have your wish, Fulton.'

'Thank you, Mr Jarmin, I shall look forward to having it granted,' he replied, and I could see a little satisfaction pass over his features.

'What now?' I asked, as Fulton left to deliver the message.

'We wait,' replied Jarmin. 'Even though I am itching to see what is stored above O'Rourkes' alehouse, we wait. I do not have the authority needed, as many men will required to destroy that particular nest of vipers.'

'All this on my say so?' I asked, now becoming a little worried.

'Yes. The Duke said he trusted you, thought you might find out things that we hadn't; from what you have just told me, he made the right assessment. I can always stop things if you are not confident in what you say.'

'No, no. I know what I heard and what I saw. What do you think is in those crates, Mr Jarmin?'

'I do not wish to speculate, in truth,' he said, surprising me. 'But the fact that there are items there that O'Rourke wants to see the back of and quickly, indicates that they could be of great interest to us.'

'And Cummings?' I wished to see him arrested but I had a feeling that I would not be the one to do it.

'Cummings is another whom we have been keeping an eye on, Mr Hopgood.'

'But you did not know he was involved in the death of Sorley?'

He shook his head. 'I confess, no, we did not.'

I hesitated to suggest that he had not been keeping a very close eye on him in that case, allowing him to commit a capital crime, instead, I nodded gravely. 'You know I wish to arrest Cummings, do you not?'

'I do, Mr Hopgood.'

'And once I identify him to De veil, then he too would wish him to be taken, but I sense a problem; am I mistaken?'

'There is not a problem. De veil's assistance will be required, if what I envisage comes to pass.'

'Which is?'

Jarmin sighed. 'The first thing we need to do is to examine those items at the alehouse: I take it you will be able to show us how to gain entrance?'

I nodded as our eyes locked together.

'Good. Once I have established what they are and that they are of interest to us, our men can move in and take the O'Rourkes and all those with them. If, on the other hand, those items turn out to be nothing more than stolen pieces, we will leave them be but we would have the advantage of being able to have men keep watch. I would also leave Armitage and Cummings free for a while longer.'

'What? You mean to leave Cummings alone and not allow me to arrest him?'

'Only if nothing is found,' he replied, patiently. 'There are larger issues here.'

'You mean larger issues than murder?'

He nodded. 'In truth, yes, though you may not think that; we believe otherwise. Content yourself with knowing who your murderer is, for he will stand trial, the only thing is that it may not be just now.'

'Unless you find incriminating material?'

'Exactly, Mr Hopgood. Then you can do whatever you like to him.'

CHAPTER 19

Within the hour, Fulton returned with the reply to Jarmin's letter and then the wheel began to turn. Newcastle had approved of whatever had been written and I felt a momentary concern again that all this had gained momentum because of what I had seen and heard. I felt responsible for it all and it did not sit easily upon my shoulders. The doubts were there, they loomed large over me; the machinery of a government department brought to readiness for deployment was down to me, and me alone. I felt the responsibility keenly as I watched Jarmin issue his orders.

Newcastle had sent to De Veil to provide assistance, while Jarmin assembled ten men, all armed with pistols, cudgels and bladed weapons. Where he found them at short notice and at the hour of midnight, I do not know but they arrived and were issued instructions and then dispatched, with Fulton leading them to assemble at the yard of The Blue Boar in Oxford Street.

Jarmin and I, along with two more late arrivals, proceeded to Bow Street, there to collect the constables and watchmen supplied by De Veil, whose assistance as Magistrate would be required following the apprehending of the felons.

As we pulled up at Bow Street, two watchmen hastened through the door, Jarmin and I followed soon after. Inside, seven men, both constables and watchmen awaited us with De Veil, who appeared alert and full of anticipation, which diminished slightly as he caught sight of me.

'Hopgood,' he greeted, without enthusiasm. 'I did not realise that *you* would be involved with this.'

'It is through his good work that we have this opportunity,' returned Jarmin, casting an expert eye on the men assembled.

De Veil made a noise in his throat, the inference of which only he knew, as he cast a sly eye in my direction.

Jarmin explained what they were required to do and then checked to make sure every man had arms adequate to the task, then he handed out armbands for identification purposes, only to be put on when the signal sounded, which would be two pistol shots in quick succession. They could allow no one to exit from the alleyways and passages leading from the court of the alehouse following the signal. Each constable and watchman would be paired with a government man once we arrived at The Blue Boar and were to act under that man's direction. All inside the alehouse and the O'Rourke residence next door were to be arrested. Pistols were only to be used as a last resort.

De Veil decided that he would accompany his men, which met with some annoyance from Jarmin, but De Veil agreed to follow instructions.

The carriages arrived to convey De Veil and his men but the colonel decided to accompany both Jarmin and I in our carriage instead of travelling with his men. As we rattled along, he admonished me for my tardiness in not keeping him informed of my progress. Jarmin looked on with a slight smile on his face as De Veil tried to wrest a little dignity from the situation.

'I have found the murderer,' I said, when De Veil had finished berating me.

Even in the half-light, I could see his eyes narrowing and his lips purse. 'What?' he barked.

'The man named Cummings, who works at Thompson and Gutteridge,' I replied, as I returned his look. 'The man who identified the body at your inquest, the man also at the heart of this,' I added, wafting my hand in the air.

De Veil stared at me for a few seconds then turned his head to Jarmin. 'I understood that this action pertained to the security of the country, not just to apprehend a murderer, albeit a deceitful one at that.'

'It is,' said Jarmin. 'However, if things do not go well then neither your murderer nor my insurrection will have a satisfactory outcome. Both Cummings and the O'Rourkes will be allowed to continue for a while longer.'

'I cannot allow a murderer to walk the streets,' countered De Veil.

'You can and you will,' replied Jarmin, authoritatively. 'You would answer to your masters otherwise and I can assure you that they would not look sympathetically towards you. It would be a shame, as you are held in high regard by them, to do something that would jeopardise some future recognition of your service.'

I had difficulty in keeping the grin off my face as I watched De Veil wrestle with his ambition, which, I imagine, won easily. To him, titles mattered; a "Sir" would certainly not go amiss.

'Very well, Jarmin,' said De Veil in the end. 'I will bow to your judgement as I agreed.'

'Wise,' returned Jarmin. 'However, let us hope that everything works as we would all wish.'

We pulled into the yard of The Blue Boar and came to a halt, a boy standing with a link lighting our way. The other carriages were there, the men standing around the nervous boy. Jarmin alighted and passed the boy some coins, which seemed to settle him somewhat.

Even though the hour was late there were many people still abroad, so we left the yard in small groups of twos and threes, a few additional people here and there would not elicit concern so much as a large group entering the slum. I left with Jarmin and another member of his group of intelligencers and we walked slowly across the High Street and entered the realm of the slum. I looked for those who left previously but they had all melted away into the surroundings

Maynard Street still bustled, still full of life, hardly differing from the noisy and raucous place of a few hours ago with many drunk men and women, some of whom had difficulty in standing, let alone walking. Grunts emanated from alleyways as girls plied their trade and I wondered how many of their customers would be in a solid enough state to get their relief.

We came to the tavern and turned into the alley. Jarmin allowing me to lead across the court where the gin-shop still had a good trade going, judging by the many people littering the front of the door, most too inebriated to notice our passing. As we entered the darkness of the second court, Jarmin snapped his fingers and from out of the gloom stepped two of his men who joined us as we traversed the court to the far side where Kitty had guided me.

One of the men produced a small lantern and after several attempts with a flint produced a flame. With a few cuts and bruises and muttered oaths four of us climbed up and proceeded carefully along the beams as I had done, leaving one man in the same place where I had left Ned. The building complained at the weight of four robust men upon its weak timbers, much more so than when just Kitty and I were there. One man waited at about the halfway point with the lantern, leaving just three of us to thread our way through the rest of the building.

We arrived at the wall with light still coming up from the alehouse, filtering through the fug, which had grown thicker and more pungent, slow to disperse, though there were plenty of holes in the roof. Jarmin nodded to his man, George Blake, and then they slipped over the wall leaving me to stay as Kitty had done.

Peering over the wall, I could see Jarmin and Blake creep slowly, testing their purchase on the boards before placing their whole weight. They moved slowly, carefully towards the boxes and crates and sacks and I felt relief that they were still there, despite my trepidation at what they might hold. Occasionally Jarmin and Blake would stop and peer down, watching the people below consuming their alcohol, at the same time wiping their eyes clear of the stinging smoke.

Blake arrived at a sack and I watched eagerly with my heart racing as he opened it and looked inside. He reached in and withdrew an object and then looked over to Jarmin and waved. Jarmin looked over to him as Blake nodded and pointed to below. Jarmin stabbed his hand at the other bags and sacks and mimed opening them. Blake nodded and carried on forwards. Jarmin had now arrived at the big crate that I had tested; the size and shape of a squat coffin and from out of the recesses of his coat he produced what appeared to be a jenny, which he then used to prise the top off. It took him a while, as he did not wish to make any noise, methodically going around it, levering a little up at a time until the point came where he had loosened it enough. He put the bar back in his coat and then raised the lid and looked inside. He stared for several seconds before letting the lid back down. He stood up, waved to Blake and then pointed at me.

Blake quickly shuffled over and I could see he wore a big grin. 'Give the signal,' he said, a hint of triumph in his voice. 'We have them.'

I did not ask what they had found, I just turned and hurried back to the man waiting at the mid-point, passed on the message and retraced my steps back to the wall.

'It is done,' I informed Blake, who grinned again.

'Then come over, you will not want to miss this.'

As I climbed over the wall, I heard the crack of a pistol followed quickly by another and Blake grabbed me by my collar and dragged me over, before hurrying across the space, now no longer worrying about stealth, towards Jarmin. I followed quickly and as I joined them, it seemed as if pandemonium had broken out below.

The door to the court had burst in and I heard Jarmin's men together with the constables and watchmen yelling at the tops of their voices. I could only see a flickering scene of confusion through the gaps in the boards but I could hear the violence meted out as batons connected with flesh and heads.

Jarmin stood by the trapdoor that opened into the taproom, a short length of rope acting as a handle. He reached down and pulled it, dragging it away, revealing the melee below. Blake sat down on the edge and then holding onto the frame, swung down. Jarmin followed suit and then it was my turn.

As I landed, I allowed my knees to bend to take the weight of my fall, using my arms for support on the floor. I regained my standing posture, only for a thug of a man to back into me, pushing me away and nearly throwing me off balance; he had his arms raised as he attempted to ward off blows by a constable. I peeled away and then kicked him hard at the back of his knee and he folded, the constable lashing out with renewed vigour. I could hear De Veil screeching away by the door, ordering men to be quick about the work, directing them as they forced those inside towards the back of the alehouse. I bumped into a badly painted whore who screamed in my ear that she was just an innocent going about her lawful business, when I spied Fulton lashing away with his baton by the corner of a booth. I pushed the whore away then gave an elbow into the ribs of a drunkard, causing him to double over. I then felt a blow between my shoulder blades, which knocked some breath out of me, but I gasped and reacted by spinning around and throwing a fist straight onto the jaw of an old toothless man who immediately crumpled over a table, sending pots and bottles and all their contents flying. Jarmin, grinning, pushed past me and then hesitated and grabbed my arm.

'With me, Hopgood,' he yelled, into my ear.

A ruffian stood in our way, brandishing a crude blade but Jarmin did not even have to think, he just raised his baton and brought it straight down with an expert flick of his wrist onto the outstretched arm and even through the din, I heard the bones crack and the lifeless fingers released their hold of the blade and it clattered to the floor. The man screamed in agony when Jarmin caught hold of the damaged arm and wrenched it forward, twisting it at the same time and then he brought the baton down again, right where the shoulder joined the neck.

We left the man thrashing on the floor.

'Enough!' cried Jarmin, as he reached the booth.

Fulton looked at Jarmin, a grim rictus of pure hatred upon his face. He panted, breathing hard and sweat glistened on his forehead.

'Enough,' repeated Jarmin, holding up his hand.

Trapped in the corner of the booth were two men, one of whom I just about recognised as Liam O'Rourke, the other I had not seen before. Both men were bloodied and only barely conscious, their heads, now the beating had stopped, seemed to erupt in various vicious swellings, livid red and spongy.

'I think you have their full attention now, Fulton,' said Jarmin, a little ironically.

O'Rourke groaned and then slumped forward, his head and arms spread out on the table, his companion lay back, his head against the wall, saliva dribbling from the corner of his mouth.

'Not nearly enough,' replied Fulton, taking a deep breath. 'They did for my brother, said he squealed as they did for him. Not our Alan, he wouldn't have given them the pleasure.'

A pistol shot rang out, sharp, harsh and close and my ears rang from the sound, my head disappearing into my shoulders in a protective reflex.

Jarmin spun around; his eyes wide open in a fierce expression. 'Who did that?' he shouted, as the noise of the battle subsided.

One of De Veil's constables waved a weapon in the air. 'I did, we wasn't getting their attention, but we have now,' and he grinned to all his friends and De Veil.

'You idiot, you jingle-brained lobcock, you totty-headed sapskull.' He walked quickly over and slapped the heel of his hand against the chest of the constable, forcing him to take a step backwards. 'I have a mind to take that barking iron, shove it right up your fundament and pull the bloody trigger! Do you know what's up there?' he asked, pointing to the rafters. 'No? Well, I do and *you* could have sent us all to the great God almighty. Did you not hear me say not to shoot unless it was absolutely necessary?' He added, thumping the man again and forcing him back even further.

De Veil did not say a word and it briefly crossed my mind that maybe the constable acted under orders.

Fortunately, the candles that had been upturned and dislodged during the fight had been stamped out, either purposely or inadvertently, so we were spared the possibility of a conflagration, especially now that Jarmin had given an indication of what he had found up there.

Blake looked on as Jarmin turned away and the whole incident had obviously appealed to his sense of humour, because he failed to suppress a grin of amusement.

Soon, all those in the alehouse were herded into a corner. I counted twenty-seven in all, five of them being female with the addition of O'Rourke and the man with him, who were still in the booth.

Jarmin prodded O'Rourke with his baton as I joined him, still keeping him at a distance until he could be certain he would be compliant.

'Who is that?' I asked, pointing to the man slumped against the wall.

'I don't know; a murderer undoubtedly. We will find out soon enough, I might even let Fulton have a further go at him.'

'I think he would enjoy that.'

'No doubt,' snapped Jarmin, jabbing the man hard.

'And up there,' I asked, pointing to the rafters.

Jarmin looked where I indicated. 'I saw muskets and Blake saw lead shot cartridges, which is why I got angry with that constable.'

I nodded, imagining the consequences of a hot lead ball finding a tightly packed bag containing gunpowder and shot, albeit a chance one. The alehouse door banged open and the men who had been searching next door pushed in two men and a woman.

'Ah,' said Jarmin, turning to look. 'And here is Eoin O'Rourke. If Liam is the brawn then Eoin is the brains.'

'Which one?'

'The one on the right,' replied Jarmin, giving Liam another poke. 'You hear that Liam? Your brother has joined us.'

I could see a short thin man of around thirty years of age with high cheekbones, sunken eyes and a mop of dark hair covering his head; he looked bemused as a watchman unceremoniously shoved him into the corner with the others.

'What about the rest of them?' I asked, thinking mainly of Cummings.

Jarmin took a breath. 'I believe we have a few hours before word of this gets out. You have those rooms opposite Armitage's for another two days, you say?'

I nodded.

'Very good. We will utilise them in that case. In the meantime, we need to get all these safely locked away in Newgate for interrogation and De Veil can arrange it all; he, after all, is a Magistrate.'

CHAPTER 20

I managed to catch an hour or so of sleep following the raid at the alehouse. I lay back on the bed in the rooms overlooking the bookseller and awoke to find George Blake staring out of the window in exactly the same position as when I closed my eyes. I could discern a lightening of the sky and hear the occasional song of a bird, indicating that dawn would soon be upon us.

Blake and I, along with three other fellows had made our way just after the raid had finished, leaving Jarmin and De Veil to find the means to convey all the prisoners to gaol and to recover the boxes and crates and bags and sacks and everything else up in the rafters above the alehouse. I did not envy them their problem but De Veil must be able to count on various resources through his office to deal with it all.

The brief period of slumber had the desired effect of revitalising me and as I swung my feet to the floor and stood up, I felt as if I had had a full night's sleep. Blake and I were to deal with Cummings, leaving the three other men to deal with Armitage. Jarmin had promised that there would be more assistance coming at first light, so their arrival should now be imminent.

I wished to send a note to Ned to say that things had taken a definitive turn during the night and that consequently, I would be tied up for the rest of the day. I told him to inform Kitty and to make sure of her safety. I scribbled a note using a piece of charcoal I found in the hearth and would find a boy to take it as soon as we left.

Cummings resided in St Clement's Lane and I hoped that he would still be there before he had a chance to make an escape. Jarmin believed he would be too arrogant a character to think that anyone would be clever enough to unmask him and having dealt with him over the last few days, I could well believe that assumption. I did not wish to take the risk of Cummings absconding, so was eager to get him safe under lock and key.

Blake held up his hand and then twitched his fingers, beckoning one of the other men. 'They have arrived; go down and bring them up,' he ordered.

I went and stood next to him and saw a lone figure ambling slowly by.

They have come through the back alleys,' he informed me. 'Safe, should Armitage look out of his window. One vagrant will not alert his suspicions, especially in this street.'

A few minutes later, four more men swelled our numbers and Blake repeated his instructions for the sake of the new arrivals. They were to wait until those men working the printing press arrived for work, then they were to enter the bookseller's and take all into custody. They then needed to secure the shop to await further investigation. He told them that only one door led into and out of the premises and that they could see it clearly and that Jarmin would not look kindly upon them should things go awry.

I had the impression that Blake's words were superfluous, as I had no doubt they all knew their business but conventions still had to be applied. Part of me wished to remain to witness the taking of Armitage, so that I could probe a little to find out his motivation in rebellion; he did not strike me as a man of violence but I have known men in the past whose surface persona far from matched that which was found within.

Blake and I left the rooms and negotiated the silent alleys, reversing the same route that Ned, Kitty and I took on our first walk to the rooms. Now we walked in that strange unworldly atmosphere that always appears in those moments when night begins to give way to day; there is a peace where most folk are still abed, their toils of the day yet to begin. Yet there is still an energy beginning to exert its ethereal influence, the dawn of a new day promising optimism, discovery, fruitfulness and bounty but in reality, in these parts, more likely to portend disaster, want, strife and heartache.

We walked down Vine Street side-by-side, conversing in low tones with the subject being mainly of the successful raid on O'Rourkes' alehouse. Blake hoped that Fulton's severe beating of Liam O'Rourke and the other man would not prove fatal, as hanging a man already dead had no sense of fulfilment, no gratification, no pleasure, no anticipation of watching the man, with a noose around his neck, his feet twisting and jerking, doing the time-honoured dance of retribution. Blake gave the impression that he enjoyed seeing a man having his neck stretched, of a criminal getting his just desserts. I hesitated to point out that many an innocent man or woman had gone to the gallows and no doubt, there would be more.

I found a boy, abroad early to catch a few pennies where he could, and bid him take my note to Jermyn Street and gave him some money with the promise that he would receive the same upon safe conveyance of the missive, which, I thought, somewhat ironic, considering we were just about to pass Drury Lane. Blake hailed a passing hackney and we climbed aboard, with me thinking that as Blake had hailed the hackney, he could pay for it. I settled in my seat and looked out, just as we passed Drury Lane and I could see The White Hart and the tenement next to it and a momentary picture flashed into my mind of

Kitty lying in her bed, alone. A picture that I dwelt upon quite happily for a moment but circumstances dictated that I cast my mind to more serious considerations, and I obscured her picture with the face of Cummings, which dealt with that all too fleeting vision of carnality.

With The White Hart behind us, the carriage carried on down Holborn, turning a right at the Church of St Andrews, travelling down Shoe Lane, passing the workhouse on the left, the building sombre but at least providing a roof for the poor unfortunates who had fallen on hard times. Blake insisted upon the diversion to avoid the crowds that were sure to be around Newgate as the markets began to open and, of course, the likely interest in the several carts that carried those arrested at O'Rourkes'. We travelled over the Fleet Bridge and through Ludgate, which Blake quite rightly reasoned would be less busy and allowed for easier passage towards St Paul's. Having successfully skirted around Newgate, we travelled along to Lombard Street before turning right into St Clement's Lane.

Blake checked his pistol as he guided the driver down to a row of houses nestling between a cloth merchant's and a coffee house, where he bid the driver pull up, just before the houses. He turned to me and grinned. 'End house on the right, ground floor. I will lead. Cummings is about to get a surprising early morning call,' he added, mischievously and with relish.

I could see a small row of brick houses, each four storeys high, with steps leading up to the door and railings to either side. We climbed down and Blake ordered the driver to wait, with the incentive of withholding the fare, promising instead a healthy addition to that owed when we concluded our business at Newgate. The driver protested, not at all happy regarding the promise, as he had heard it all before and indeed had previously lost fares as the passengers had run off leaving him out of pocket, but Blake ignored him.

The inside shutters were closed, the occupant apparently asleep. Blake marched up to the door and tried to gain entry. He pushed and tweaked the handle but it would not budge and then he sighed in frustration before pounding upon it.

'Is that wise?' I asked, as he knocked for the third time.

'There are four floors; we could be seeking any of the families here.'

'Then there must be a back way, a yard with a privy?'

'Yes, but it only leads to that alley there,' he said, pointing to a gap next to the coffee house. 'That is the only way out.'

I nodded. 'Then I'll take a look anyway. If you get in before, then wait.'

He raised his eyebrows as if surprised that I had given him an order. 'Very well, Hopgood. Though make haste, I will only wait a few moments.'

I walked swiftly away and stepped into the narrow alley, just wide enough for a handcart to get through, by which the night-soil men must get to the house of business. The alley led to another path, which ran along behind the row of houses and shops. I turned and followed the path down until I came to Cummings's house. The gate opened and I stepped into the yard, past the tub for washing the clothes and up to the back door of the house. As I reached for the door handle, I heard a loud report and instinctively I crouched; it sounded like the discharge of a pistol.

I gripped the handle of the door and pushed, the unlocked door swung open easily and I hastened through a scullery and then into the hall. Ahead of me, I could see the open front door and I ran forward. Just before the front door on my right, I saw another open door and I could see Blake lying on the floor inside the room, blood oozing onto the floor beneath him.

There was no sign of Cummings, just an odour of burning left hanging in the air. I now had two choices: help Blake or run after Cummings.

I looked at Blake, his eyes were open and his lips twisted in a grimace of pain as he writhed on the floor.

'Get him, Hopgood,' groaned Blake.

I nodded and ran out the front door to see the driver of the hackney still there, trying to pacify his startled horse; the noise of the discharged weapon having caused the animal to try to run.

'The man that just ran out, which way did he go?' I asked, urgently.

The driver, still struggling with the horse, pointed with a twitch of his head. 'Over there,' he yelled, indicating the narrow street opposite.

'There is an injured man in there,' I said, pointing to the front door. 'He needs help urgently. I will be back soon.'

I then ran off to the street hoping that the driver would attend upon Blake or at least rouse another person who would. I charged through the empty street at full speed, the path leading to The Nag's Head, just wide enough for a coach to pass and then I entered a court, which had two exits, and I hesitated, trying to decide which one to take. I decided to the right and ran down, passing The Three Tuns tavern before entering Gracechurch Street and there I had to stop. Traffic and pedestrians had already built up, most of it heading down to the Bridge and on into Southwark. I looked up and down but could not see Cummings, I asked people passing but they were all in a hurry and said they had seen nothing. Cummings had completely disappeared and I did not know which way to go.

I stood there for several seconds hoping that fortune would smile upon me but I knew it was a forlorn hope, so I turned and hurriedly retraced my steps, back to St Clement's Lane to see if

Blake still lived.

I arrived back to see the hackney still in attendance, though now a small boy stood by the horse's head, holding onto the traces. I could see the back of a woman standing in the door entrance and now a few people were stood on the doorsteps of the other houses, all looking to see what had occurred.

I pushed in through the door, the woman protesting in a most undignified manner that I was spoiling her view. Blake still lay there and movement suggested that he had not yet succumbed to his injuries. The carriage driver knelt by his head, pressing a wad of cloth to a wound beneath his shirt on the right shoulder, while two other men were standing there observing but not doing very much.

'How is he?' I asked, bending down by the driver.

Blake's eyes were closed, his breath coming in ragged gasps.

'You're asking me?' replied the driver, a look of panic upon his face. 'How would I know? I'm just a driver.'

'Yes, but you knew what to do.'

'He needs a doctor, that's what I do know,' he replied, vehemently.

I could not argue with that. If Blake had any chance of survival then he needed to be treated and soon. 'St Thomas's Hospital is not far,' I said. 'Would you take him?'

'Across the bridge?' He shook his head. 'Not at this time of day. It will be at a stand.'

'Then where? St Bartholomew's?'

He nodded. 'It will have to be.'

'Blake? Can you hear me?' I asked, leaning over.

Blake opened his eyes. 'Did you get him?' he asked, his voice small and caught with pain.

'No,' I replied. 'He got away. What happened?'

I heard him say an expletive. 'Cummings opened the door

when you went down the path. I rushed him but I tripped over the door ledge. He ran back in here and as I followed him in, he turned and raised a pistol and shot me. He must have had it ready.'

'Do you think he knew what happened at O'Rourkes'?'

'I do not know—'

A spasm of pain caught him and he screwed up his eyes, beads of sweat broke out on his brow and I knew we had to get him to a doctor quickly.

'Can you help us?' I asked the two men standing. They nodded and I addressed Blake again. 'We are going to move you, Blake. It might hurt.'

He gave a croaky laugh. 'A little more will make no difference.'

We managed to get him to his feet but then his pallor whitened further, his knees buckled and he all but passed out. I sent one of the men to Cummings's bedroom to fetch a blanket; when he returned, he lay it on the floor and we laid Blake down upon it. Each of us took a corner of the blanket and we stumbled out, pulling and lifting around the corner and then out to the hackney. By now, a crowd had gathered, all craning to get a better look at the injured man, all speculating on what had occurred. I suspected the two who had helped would be the centre of attention once we had departed.

With Blake now lying on the floor of the carriage and the driver about to climb up to his seat, a watchman appeared, somewhat belatedly but at least he had arrived. I told him whom I worked for and told him to prevent anyone from entering Cummings's rooms until either I or an official arrived. He seemed reluctant at first but Blake had come back to his senses and uttered dire threats if he did not do as I instructed.

The trip to St Bartholomew's seemed to take forever, the

jolting, rattling carriage seemingly hitting every bump and obstacle that lay on the roads, causing me to lurch around as I knelt above Blake, still pressing the wad to his shoulder. He would wince and flinch and once or twice grabbed my arm after a wheel had bounced quite brutally, causing me to press down with more force than I intended. Occasionally, I would look up and try to gauge where we were from the fleeting scene of rooftops in my vision, but the unfamiliar landscape escaped my knowledge, so I had no idea where we were. Eventually, we pulled up and the driver jumped down and hastened to get some assistance.

I furnished the hospital staff with the details of what had happened and that Blake held office with the Duke of Newcastle and left them to do what they had to do, promising them that someone from the duke's retinue would arrive shortly, which I hoped would be a good enough incentive to do their best for Blake.

The driver and I found somewhere to clean ourselves of Blake's blood and then returned to the carriage.

'All this won't come cheap, you know,' he announced, as he walked by my side.

I turned my head to look at him and saw a little light in his eyes, a twitch at the corner of his mouth and I suspected he quite enjoyed the little adventure.

'I am sure some recompense will come your way,' I replied, as I nodded and gave a knowing smile. 'But you are not yet finished. I have to go to Newgate and then I need to go back to that house. After that I do not know.'

'Be better if you hire me for the day, then.'

'I might well do, how much?'

'A pound,' he answered, quickly.

'A pound?' I exclaimed, knowing he would be hard-pressed

to earn even half that in a day.

We settled on fifteen shillings after a little haggling, which pleased him more than me.

'Right you are, sir. Newgate is it?'

I nodded and climbed on board, keeping my feet away from the blood Blake had left on the floor, which reminded me to mention it to him, so that he could swill a bucket of water over it when next we stopped.

Newgate was just around the corner but it seemed as if all the farmers around London had descended upon the market at once. Even as we left the hospital, herds of cattle, pigs and sheep roamed about, all heading for the pens, the noise of their bleating, their lowing and the grunts deafening the ears and the discharges from anuses and bladders covered the area in a wash of ordure. People you could move out of your way but animals would go exactly where they wanted to, blocking the street, the only solace being to know that they would all be carcasses very soon. It would have been quicker to walk.

Eventually we managed to force a path through the melee, and shortly after, turned into Newgate Street with the gate and prison just ahead of us.

We passed through the gate and stopped by the Lodge, where the prisoners were taken on their first acquaintance with the prison, I judged that I would most likely find Jarmin there, or at least someone who would find him for me. I stepped out of the carriage and walked quickly to the door and gained entry into the receiving room, where I found a confusing mass of people, most of whom were awaiting process. Evidently, the many prisoners arriving at once had caught the prison off-guard and the turnkeys shouted and yelled at the orderlies, sending them running hither and thither in searching out the fetters to attach to them all

The noise dulled my ears as the cacophony rendered my mind numb. I looked around for someone I would recognise and eventually I saw De Veil as the crush of people parted for a moment.

De Veil saw me as I pushed through and eagerly beckoned me over. 'You have that man you went after?' he asked, with suppressed excitement.

I shook my head. 'No, he managed to escape, but not before he shot Blake.'

He pursed his lips. 'Careless of you, Hopgood. I would have expected more from you.'

I squeezed my fists and felt my hackles rise but I managed to quench the outburst before it erupted. 'Where is Jarmin?' I asked instead, through gritted teeth.

He flapped a hand vaguely. 'Somewhere, though I doubt he will be pleased to hear of your failure.'

No, I thought, he will not, but he may be a little more understanding of the circumstances.

I turned away from De Veil and began to search for Jarmin, at least I now knew he was somewhere in the building. I spied him at last returning from a passageway that led towards the holding cells with the Keeper.

Jarmin saw me, excused himself from the Keeper and came over. I could tell he knew that I did not have good news to impart.

'What happened?' he asked, sombrely. 'Your face displays a certain reticence.'

'You're right: Cummings shot Blake. He's in the hospital, St Bartholomew's.'

Jarmin closed his eyes and sighed, passing his palm over his face. 'Dead?'

'No, well, not when I left him.'

'Then that is something. Tell me all,' he said, guiding me over to the door of the Lodge. We then stepped outside into the relative peace of the street.

We stood away from the crowds as I related events and he listened without interruption, just nodding sagely at the pertinent points. His main concern focussing on the welfare of Blake, rather than the loss of Cummings, though that undoubtedly grieved him.

'I cannot afford to lose good men,' he said, though I could hear anger in his voice. 'Despite what you may think, Blake is a good man.'

'I do not doubt you, Jarmin,' I said, raising my hand, my palm outwards, in order to stop him from making an excuse. 'I only hope the doctors are successful in saving his life.'

'As do I, Hopgood. I will send a man over to find out how he does; the Duke will be most aggrieved to learn of it.'

'And Cummings?' I asked, feeling that we should be addressing that problem now.

'Ah, yes, Cummings.' His face broke out in a smile, which did not go anywhere near his eyes. 'That man will rue the day he put on a Jacobite cloak.'

CHAPTER 21

The driver had done as I requested and had swilled out the floor of the carriage and now it was probably cleaner than it had been for many a month. Jarmin joined me in the carriage, as well as two of his men. We were on our way back to Cummings's rooms with the intention of searching every inch of it for any indication of where he might have gone. He also dispatched a man to the hospital to find out how Blake fared, hoping that the news would be good.

All of us in the carriage were determined to finish the job that had begun last night. So far, not counting those from the alehouse: Armitage, the press-workers, Musgrave and two other couriers now lodged at Newgate. The other men, those protecting the pamphlet distributors, were being rounded up at that very moment.

The haul taken from the O'Rourkes' included muskets, ammunition and powder, swords, knives and several pistols, a veritable arms cache but for an unknown destination.

We made steady progress through the streets with barely a hold-up of any sort, so we arrived reasonably quickly outside of Cummings's rooms, to find the place devoid of curious onlookers — it also seemed devoid of a watchman too.

The two men went around to the back of the house as Jarmin and I approached the front door. We thought it possible that Cummings might have returned and, if so, having spied us arriving, he may well try to make an escape; Jarmin did not believe the risk worth taking. In the event, we did not need to be cautious as we gained access through the unlocked front door, though Cummings's door was locked.

Jarmin and I looked at each other, puzzled for a few seconds, until the watchman returned in a rush, carrying a hunk of bread in one hand and a pie in the other.

'Sorry, sirs,' he apologised, as he saw me. 'Hungry business this standing around,' he added, as explanation to his absence.

Jarmin nodded and gave a wry smile. 'I take it you locked the door?'

'Oh, yes, sir. Take me responsibilities serious, sir, I do. Yes, yes, I have the very key hereabouts, somewhere. Hold that, sir, if you please,' he said, handing Jarmin the hunk of bread.

Jarmin and I exchanged glances as the watchman fumbled in his pockets for a few seconds and then with a triumphant grin, produced the key and unlocked the door.

'Has anyone been here enquiring at all?' asked Jarmin.

'Just the neighbours and those upstairs, sir. I told them to mind their own. They all know me around here, sir.'

'I am sure of your diligence,' replied Jarmin. 'So, we can say that no one, other than your acquaintances, made enquiry?'

'No, sir.'

'Very good. If you would care to stay out here then we can begin.'

'Thank you, sir. Um...If you would be so kind, sir. Could you tell me who you are?'

Jarmin grinned. 'Are you sure you wish to know?'

'Er...I think I should do, sir.'

Jarmin nodded and then turned to one of his colleagues. 'Would you?'

The man nodded and took the watchman outside. A few moments later I heard an expletive as the man explained

Jarmin's position.

'Let us get to work, Hopgood. See what secrets Cummings has hiding.'

There were two rooms to search, the front room in which we were standing, the distinguishing feature being the blood of Blake staining the floor and half of the painted floor cloth. There were two upholstered chairs either side of the fireplace; a small eating table with two other plain chairs; another small table with paper and writing implements upon it; a cupboard with shelves, upon which were several ornaments; a food cupboard upon the wall with more shelves next to it, upon which were drinking vessels. Sundry cooking items were next to the fireplace. A chest for storage held several books.

The bedroom had a curtained bed; a chest and a table for his toilet; a small cabinet and another chest containing neatly piled clothing.

Cummings appeared to be quite fastidious in his habits, as everything appeared neat and tidy and in its proper place.

Jarmin and one man searched the bedroom, leaving the other man and me to search the front room. We did it thoroughly, piece by piece and I found it quite distasteful going through another man's belongings, even with knowing what Cummings had done. I had searched other houses in the past but I had done that surreptitiously, in secret and mostly at night, but here we were doing it openly and for me it put a different slant on things; it felt like prying, which indeed we were. His books gave me a little insight into his personality, as amongst the standard pieces like Defoe and Fielding, there were short books and works of a more carnal nature and these were tucked away within compartments, hidden as it were and I suspected, supplied by Armitage. The table with the writing implements proved decidedly banal, I had hopes there but the correspondence pertained to his finances, bills and receipts and such. We put the documents to the side for later study.

'Nothing here that stands out,' I said loudly to Jarmin as we continued to search. 'Have you better luck?'

Jarmin walked in from the bedroom. 'No, not really. It would seem he is wary of keeping anything that could be construed as incriminating. Do not forget the floorboards, Bryant,' he said to the man with me. 'And any secret place that could have been made.'

'Doing that now, sir,' replied Bryant.

'What is that?' I asked, seeing something grasped in his hand.

'This?' he said, looking down. 'A picture of his lover, I presume. There are letters of a personal nature with it.'

I took the small miniature painting from his hand and received quite a shock as I studied it. 'Do you know who this is?' I enquired, excitedly.

He shook his head. 'Elizabeth, I believe, if she is the one to have written the letters.'

'It's a painting of Elizabeth Thompson. A very good likeness too. The daughter of Jonathon Thompson, his employer. I believe it had disappeared from the warehouse, supposedly at the same time as the items stolen by Joseph Morton but was not recovered.'

'The young man in Newgate that you told me of?'

I nodded. 'Yes, the one who has a relationship with Elizabeth.'

'Then how is it that Cummings has it in his possession?'

'Morton professed his innocence and I believed him. This may be the proof of that innocence. Where are the letters, let me see them.'

I walked into the bedroom with Jarmin and he showed me the letters that accompanied the painting. As I read them, I could hardly believe the content, to say that they were graphic would be an understatement and I would be hard-pressed to believe that Elizabeth Thompson would even know of some of the practices described, let alone had experience of them. Something then jarred me and it was not the slight smell of perfume that came from them.

'This is not Elizabeth Thompson's hand. I've seen her letters to Joseph Morton and am certain that she did not write these.'

'You are sure?'

'Yes, these were *not* written by her,' I said, relieved, considering the content.

'Then perhaps another Elizabeth?'

'Possibly, but why keep the letters with the picture, as if implying they were from her?'

'Why indeed.'

Then it hit me. 'Jarmin, I followed Cummings when he left Armitage's. His route took him to where Elizabeth Thompson lives and he manufactured a meeting with her; just happened to be passing but I had seen him wait just around the corner and he checked his watch before walking the last few steps when she came out of her house. The man might well be infatuated with her.'

'How did she appear?'

'She did not seem pleased to see him, I will say that.'

'If she did write these, then I suppose she might have some embarrassment?'

I shook my head. 'No, there was no embarrassment. To be certain, I'll go and speak to her and I will take a sample of a less descriptive letter, so I can compare.'

'Then do it now and then return to Newgate; it should be a bit quieter by now.'

I wondered briefly if Jarmin would regret me leaving in the

hackney but I reasoned he would find some transport easily enough.

As we traversed London's streets, I mulled over the picture and the letters; first, that it seemed that Cummings stole the picture and not Morton. Why would he do that and then keep it if not because he thought he loved her. Cummings must have learnt that Morton and Elizabeth were involved in a relationship and became jealous, wanting to stop it, so he had stolen the watch, the ring and the painting but had used the other items to remove Morton, get him arrested, probably to end up on the end of a noose, leaving him free to pursue her. But why the letters? For certain, Elizabeth did not write them, so who did and why? I also considered the books hidden in the chest, the books that in lurid detail described various encounters of a carnal nature that were not dissimilar to those of the letters. Could he be taking the fantasy of the books and making a fantasy of a more personal nature? Had he paid a woman to write them to him and imagine the correspondence had come from Elizabeth? I did not wish to dwell on what he would have gained from that, a thought that would send me to the very basement of human nature.

We pulled up outside the Thompson's residence and for some reason I felt a little nervous of the forthcoming encounter with Elizabeth. As ever, I had to bear in mind the fact that I could be wrong and that she could have instigated and contrived everything, she could be manipulating Cummings for her own purposes; I had to remember that people often do the strangest of things.

I walked up the path and knocked on the door, waiting for some moments before a servant opened it. I stated my name and enquired if Elizabeth was able to take callers. The servant bid me enter and showed me to a small comfortable room just off the hall where I waited for several minutes, admiring the pictures that hung upon the wall, until the door opened behind me and Elizabeth appeared in a state of anticipation.

'Mr Hopgood,' she began. 'You have news?' she asked, eyes bright with hope, her hands clasped tightly together.

'I will say that things have moved forward,' I replied, a little guardedly. 'But there are a couple of things I need to know from you.' My appearance must have seemed somewhat dishevelled and grimy, so I apologised for presenting myself such.

She waved away my apologies as if it were of no concern and offered me a seat, which I gladly took. 'May I get you some refreshment?' she asked, sitting down opposite me.

'No, but thank you,' I said, as I studied her face. 'I would like you to tell me of the miniature portrait that went missing, the one of yourself, if you please.'

'Oh, that. I cannot tell you very much except that it has not been seen since the constable took Joseph away. It was not found upon him and has not come to light in the interim.'

'This portrait stood originally on your father's desk in the warehouse and he thought he might have taken it home with him?'

'Yes, but it is not here, we have looked.'

'And it disappeared at the same time as the watch and ring?'

She nodded again. 'Yes.'

'So, if Joseph did not have it, and you have not found it here, then where do you think it could have gone?'

She shrugged her shoulders. 'The Magistrate believed that Joseph must have secreted it somewhere, but he could not have because he did not take those things in the first place. Besides, if it had been hidden in the warehouse, it would have been discovered by now.'

'One would have thought so,' I replied. 'Miss Thompson, can you state with absolute honesty that you have no idea of its whereabouts?' I looked at her keenly, trying to discern any sort of guile in her reply.

'I can, Mr Hopgood. Please tell me why you are so interested in it?'

'In a moment, if you'll please bear with me.' I put my hand in my pocket and brought out the page of the letter I had taken from Cummings's rooms. I looked at it again, just to make certain that it was presentable then passed it to her. 'Do you recognise the hand that wrote these lines?' I asked, handing her the page.

She accepted it but appeared confused as to why I asked her. She looked at it and then shook her head. 'No, Mr Hopgood. I do not. Who is Nicholas?'

'I had hoped you would tell me,' I said, taking the page back. 'You are certain though, that you do not recognise the hand?'

'Yes, of course.'

'It isn't one of your household?'

'No.'

'It isn't yours?'

'No!' This quite vehemently. 'Mr Hopgood, would you please explain yourself.'

I reached back into my pocket, pulled out the miniature portrait and handed it over. 'Is this the portrait that went missing?'

'But...but...Yes, it is. How?' She looked straight at me, eyes wide and I could see a slight trembling in her shoulders as she gripped the miniature tightly. 'How did you find it? Where? It could prove Joseph innocent.'

'It could, Miss Thompson,' I agreed, showing her a slight smile. 'Is that what you wish?'

'What? Of course I do, how could I not wish for anything other?' I sensed surprise, indignity and shock in her reply.

'What I'm enquiring into is whether you are still wholly given to the idea of a relationship with Joseph.'

'Of course I am, Mr Hopgood. How could you suggest anything else?'

'There is no one else that has come into your life whom you could envisage having a future with?'

She shook her head forcefully. 'No, Mr Hopgood.' I could see her eyes begin to glisten as tears formed. I did not feel proud of myself for probing, causing upset, but I had to do it, so I continued. 'I'm suggesting that you are looking fairly upon another and have given cause, or encouragement, that you may be amenable to the idea.'

'Never! Mr Hopgood, I do not like your implications, your questions.' She sat up straight, a blaze of anger in her eyes now, mixed with distress. 'I thought you had come here to give me welcome news but you have come with false accusations and innuendo and if you do not explain yourself, I will have to ask you to leave.' She stood up, challenging me.

'I apologise, Miss Thompson,' I said, holding up my hand in submission. 'My questions have not been without foundation. This morning, together with another man, I went to arrest someone of your acquaintance, who shot my companion and escaped. We found the portrait within his rooms when we searched them. I wish to know if you gave the portrait to him.'

'Who?' she asked, sitting back down with a thump. 'Who?'

'Cummings,' I replied. 'Nicholas Cummings.'

'Cummings?' she repeated. 'What has that man got to do with me? Wait a moment, you said he shot someone?'

'He did, though the man still lived when I delivered him to the hospital.'

'Cummings?' she said again, staring at the picture. 'He had this portrait in his rooms?' She raised her head to look at me, her confusion evident.

I nodded slowly. 'It was with letters, that being one of them,' I said, indicating the single sheet.

Her mouth opened and closed like a fish but no sound emerged. Her eyes were wide, staring, intense and the colour had drained from her face. 'Cummings?' she said again, quietly, when she did eventually find her voice. 'What were you arresting him for?'

I gave her a light smile. 'He is a Jacobite, an important member, involved in procuring arms for the cause.'

'Thomas was a Jacobite,' she said, looking sharply at me.

'Yes, as you told me. Cummings murdered Thomas; I heard him say so.'

'Cummings killed Thomas?' Her hand went to her breast and she stared at me, hardly believing the news I brought her.

'It is possible that Cummings not only killed Thomas but that he stole those items and put them in Joseph's pocket so that he would be arrested for the crime of theft.'

'So it proves Joseph innocent?' she said, and I could see that hope had returned to her, a joy and relief in her tone.

'So it would seem,' I replied, nodding.

Though only, I thought, if I can find Cummings.

CHAPTER 22

'He called him a murdering Jacobite bastard,' said Jarmin, as I sat with him inside the Keeper's office at Newgate. 'Blake apologises for it but thinks that was why Cummings shot him and ran.'

I sighed. 'At least he's honest enough to admit it,' I replied, thinking that for his outburst, we would have Cummings already here at Newgate. Jarmin, I supposed, probably thought the same thing. 'Will he survive?'

'Blake? That I do not know. The ball passed through him, so he has a better chance than if they had removed it. Only time will tell.'

I nodded. I liked Blake and hoped he would survive his injury but I could not help but feel annoyed at his impetuousness.

'Which leaves us with Cummings and having to discover his whereabouts,' said Jarmin, getting to the point. 'From what you have learnt, we can dismiss Elizabeth Thompson as she will never give aid to the man.'

'So, who would?' I asked, suspecting he may have an idea. He hesitated and I could tell he was weighing something up which lent credence to my suspicion. 'I believe I have the right to know, Jarmin,' I said, breaking the pause.

He sighed. 'You are right, Hopgood. The man to whom we suspect Cummings reports to and receives instruction from.'

'Who is he, then?'

Jarmin blew out his cheeks, his reluctance to name, evident.

'Morgan,' he said quietly in the end.

'Morgan who?'

'David Morgan, a lawyer from the Middle Temple. A Welshman. He left London for Wales some years ago but he still returns and spends time in London, especially when the Duke of Beaufort is here, which has been the case these last few weeks.'

'I have met Beaufort, only the other evening I saw him at the Foundling Hospital. He is a Governor there.'

'He is, but his philanthropy does not hide his politics; Morgan and he move in the same circles. They wish a Stuart on the throne.'

'Then Beaufort is involved too?'

'Yes, we think Beaufort controls Morgan who controls—'

'Cummings,' I finished for him.

'That is what we think.'

'And Morgan has chambers at the Middle Temple?'

Jarmin nodded. 'He does and Cummings has been known to go there.'

'Do you think he will go there now?'

'Possibly. As far as I know, Cummings has no one else to turn to. He will either visit or send a message. He needs help to leave London, that is for certain; he has nowhere to stay, no money and us after him. I doubt if he would go to his place of work, but I will send someone anyway.'

'Then I will go to the Middle Temple.'

'I may be wrong, Hopgood,' he warned.

'Yes, but we have nothing else and we cannot just chase blindly around London.'

'I will send a few men out looking for Cummings and I will send one with you, more will join you at the Temple as I can spare them.'

*

'We agreed Fifteen shillings, did we not?' I asked the driver as we stepped down in Fleet Street.

'Yes, sir, but the day is not yet done.'

'It will be once you do one more trip.' I gave him my address and told him to bring Mr Edward Tripp to the Middle Temple as quickly as he could. 'Be free in telling him what you've seen, but please, do not say to anyone else, not for a day or so at least. Here,' and I gave him a guinea, which I felt he had truly earned.

'Thank you, sir. I'll do as you ask and thank you again, the wife'll be well pleased with this day's work.'

I grinned as the driver flicked the reins and the carriage moved off to collect Ned, leaving me with Philip Monk. Monk had previously watched Morgan, so he knew both what he looked like and which chamber he occupied. Monk was an unassuming man just a few years younger than me; he had an open friendly face, topped by dark wavy hair; like me, he avoided wearing a wig.

The hackney had dropped us off a short way from the Middle Temple and we began to walk beneath the arch and down Middle Temple Lane; to the left of us was The Inner Temple with the Middle Temple to our right.

'The place has lost some of its lustre of years gone by, with alehouses and shops moving in along with some families of the lower class, taking up empty premises and turning them into homes. But I suppose you are already aware of this,' said Monk, as we walked.

'Yes, I am. The Inns authorities are also want to overlook some deficiencies in the scholars studying, for a consideration, that is,' I replied, adding my knowledge to the pool. 'As you say, the lustre has been polished off over the years.'

True to our expectations, as we stepped into the precincts of the Inns of Court, we were besieged by feral children running amok amongst the stalls of traders; there must have been twenty or more running and chasing, until one doughty stallholder picked up a stave and ran screaming after them, not caring which of them he hit.

'Which are Morgan's chambers?' I asked, taken up with the entertainment of the stallholder missing with a swing and landing flat on his back.

'Just there,' he said, indicating a hall of residence close by. 'Best we get a bottle and make friends with a wall. We'll blend in that way.'

'Show me the wall and you can get the bottle,' I replied. 'I trust you get reimbursed.'

'I wish,' said Monk, ruefully.

He left me near to the fountain against a wall with a step so that we could sit comfortably with a place to rest our backs.

The weather was mild with little wind, the afternoon sun still giving vent of its warming powers. The trees around the fountain rustled as a brief breath of air wafted through the precinct. I closed my eyes for a moment, realising just how tired I felt and knew how easily it would have been to succumb to the temptation of just a few minutes of sleep. I snapped my eyes open to find Monk sitting next to me, a bottle between us.

'I apologise,' I said, shifting my position. 'Sleep caught me unawares.'

He turned his head and grinned. 'Normally happens much further into the vigil,' he replied, without condemnation. 'I once slept for two whole hours and only awoke when the man I watched slammed his door as he left. If he hadn't done that, I would probably still be there, but as a beggar without employment.'

'I trust Jarmin does not know that?'

'No, neither must he, but it is something we all know can occur, even to the best of us.'

I thanked him for his understanding and then set to the task, resolving not to rest my eyes again, though those few minutes revived me and I felt equal to the wait ahead.

'What do you know of Morgan?' I asked, looking around.

Monk thought for a moment. 'He's about forty years of age, stout structure, has a wife and lands around Shoreditch. He thinks himself to be a poet too; Armitage has printed some in praise of a Stuart King. He is friendly with some Tories, most of whom lean towards the Jacobite cause.'

'Not Catholics?'

'No, only those who object to a Hanover monarch, they want an English one, or at least Scottish.'

'Primogeniture,' I said. 'The next in line, regardless of his talents or his religion.'

'Exactly. They hide their actions in rhetoric, so an openly supporting Jacobite is a difficult one to catch. Beaufort being a case in point. They are very careful in what they say and in what they do; hence Morgan as a conduit.'

'To Cummings?'

'And others. Look, there he is, standing on the step.'

I gazed at Morgan for the first time: well-dressed in expensive clothes, a full wig, a little overweight perhaps. He appeared to be searching for someone and then he hailed a young man and beckoned him over. They exchanged a few words and then Morgan gave the young man something, who then hurried off. Morgan stood for a few seconds watching him go, then turned around and went back in.

'What do you think that was about?' I asked.

Monk shrugged his shoulders. 'I don't know. I would like to

see where he goes but we cannot leave here unless we have Cummings in our sights or until we have more men.'

The young man disappeared as he turned a corner, which put paid to the idea of following.

Thankfully, our little bottle contained just small beer, which diminished in quantity as the afternoon progressed. Ned arrived a little later than I expected but he found us eventually. He said he had been wandering around for ages but did not think to look for two vagrants polishing the stone with their backsides. Ned and Monk exchanged pleasantries and then I sent him to fetch more beer and something to eat for his cheek.

Ned returned with the supplies, sat down and then listened as I detailed what had happened last night and so far today. He was not at all happy that he had not been there, though he did receive the note I had penned from Plumptre Street, but complained that I had failed to tell him that they all went to Newgate, if I had, he would have gone there earlier.

'No matter, nothing has been lost.'

'Only Cummings,' he replied, wryly.

I thought he might have had a point there but I decided not to say anything with Monk sitting next to me.

As dusk descended, the precinct stayed as busy as ever, we had spent a long time sitting and doing nothing and I felt stiffness in my joints. I wanted desperately to stretch my legs, as too did Monk, who also complained of aching limbs. We had picked a position where we could not be seen should Morgan look out of his window, so Monk and I discussed the need for movement, and in the end, Ned bid us both to go for a few minutes, if only to stop us whining. Monk and I took a walk around, keeping Ned and the chambers of Morgan in sight. Monk ambled towards Middle Temple Lane, hoping to spy some of his colleagues, while I just took a brisk walk around the court, easing the aches in my thighs and buttocks. As I began to return, I saw the young man from earlier come in from the direction of the Lane, I looked for Monk but I could not see him, so hoped that he too had spotted him and kept back a little. He headed for Morgan's chambers again, so I looked up at the window and saw a figure looking out and then turn and walk away; now I decided that I would be drunk, drunk enough to collapse but I had to make sure I got there first.

I staggered and nearly tripped, then began to swear as my wobbly legs carried me weaving towards Morgan's chambers and there I fell against the wall, retching, trying to heave up the contents of my stomach. Just as Morgan came out of the door, I fell to my knees; I desperately wanted to look but I continued to pretend misery, loudly, putting all my effort into it.

I heard the words "piss-maker" and "bingo-boy," aimed at me in my drunken stupor but then the voices lowered and I struggled to hear what they said. I groaned and tried to stand up but failed miserably and fell again; then I heard a Welsh voice spit contemptuously, "Make sure, I do not wish to hear from him again." I groaned and retched again and then I felt a boot connect to my side and then a laugh. A door shut beside me and I risked turning over, seeing the young man's back moving away from me, but not back towards the Lane; he went over by the fountain and off towards the New Court. Morgan had gone back inside. I turned my head and could see Ned watching me, wide-eyed in alarm. I gave the young man a few seconds to make sure he did not turn back and then waved Ned over.

'Help me up,' I said, as he knelt down.

'What? Did he hurt you?'

'No. That young man will lead us to Cummings, I am certain of it. Can you see Monk?'

Ned shook his head. 'No.'

'Then there is nothing we can do about it. We follow him, Monk or no Monk.'

The people around took no notice of a drunkard and his helper as we made serpentine steps away from where we sat towards the court the man had gone to. They also did not notice the rapidity of my sobering as we moved further away, until by the time we turned into Deveraux Court, it seemed as if I had never touched a drop of alcohol in my life.

Ahead of us, the man continued to walk, oblivious to our presence, the fading light helping to obscure us but as the light diminished, his form diminished too, so that we had to close the gap in order to keep him in sight.

'Still no Monk?' I asked Ned.

'No, I kept looking for him as we moved away but it is just down to you and me.'

'Oh, well. We are used to that, are we not? I will not like to be in Monk's shoes when Jarmin finds out we had to leave him.'

'He should have stayed within the Court.'

'There is that, though I may be wrong and we're just going to a tavern. Cummings still might come to Morgan's'

'But you don't think so.'

'No, I think that young man will lead us to him.'

We walked by the Grecian Coffee House in which I had spent many a happy hour drinking the brew and indulging in the latest news and gossip, and opposite, Mr Twining's shop, where Mary purchases our tea, both places I frequent and both brews I enjoy, but not now, despite feeling I wished the time to indulge. We crossed into Little Essex Street and walked its length to The Cheshire Cheese at the junction with Milford Lane and then across into a narrow pathway with unsavoury tenements, eventually emerging into Water Lane. All the time I thought he would turn and discover us but the young man seemed sure of his safety and did not cast an eye over his shoulder. Shortly we entered Arundel Street and I then began to doubt my wisdom in following him. He turned right and followed the road to its conclusion then walked through the alleyway into Strand Lane opposite Somerset House, the palatial former palace that had begun to decline, the garden wall of which abutted Strand Lane. A little brook meandered down the lane from The Strand to empty into the river under a small bridge by the landing stage.

By now, the darkness had come upon us and I could smell the river in my nostrils. From where we stood, we could see the night-lights of boats still working as they plied their night trade. The Strand Inn, down on our left, spewed out raucous noise, full of the local inhabitants, boatmen and those from Somerset House, seeking a respite for a few hours.

'Did you see which door he took?' asked Ned, close to my ear.

'I did but let us wait a moment to see if he comes out again. Morgan told him to "Make sure," as he did not wish to hear from him again.'

'It sounds a bit as if he wishes him dead.'

'No, I don't think so. The timbre of his voice did not indicate violence. I think he wishes him away from London.'

'How will he do that, then?'

'We are by a landing stage on the river. My guess is that there will be a waterman. I have not been down this way for a while but I think that building is for storage.'

The young man did not reappear, so we began to move down the lane towards the river. We had to take care of our footing because of the slight incline and because the cobbles were slick with mud and slime. I looked into the window of the Inn as we passed by and found it crammed with people with a noise to match, they were singing a shanty and it seemed as if the whole

Inn joined in. A few more steps and we were past and adjacent to the building next to the storehouse. I looked ahead, anticipating the young man coming back out but I had no need to worry. I looked at Ned, who nodded towards the door. I shook my head and pointed forward, towards the river. I wished to see what lay in front before venturing inside. We carried on past the door to the small bridge, which crossed the brook, the path leading to a gate in the wall of the old palace. Beyond the bridge, I saw the landing stage, by the steps, which had four boats tied to the posts. I could see that the tide was on the ebb, the flow heading downstream towards the sea. We moved over to our left so we could view the front of the storehouse, which faced the river.

In front, a small deck area jutted into the river, the water lapping beneath, presumably a place to load and unload, with double doors leading into the building; from the gaps between the planks of wood, a little light illuminated and I grinned to Ned who grinned back.

Ned pointed to the front, eased himself down onto the deck and then crept towards the doors, and I watched as he tried to angle his head, trying to look inside. He tried a few places but turned to me and shook his head, then returned, just as quietly.

'The overlap of the panels, allows light but I can't see a thing.'

'Then I think it's time to find out if Cummings is inside. There are two of us, maybe just two of them. You happy to try?'

'Good odds,' said Ned, patting his pocket, which hid his cudgel.

We turned and walked back to the door, resolving to get this over with and Cummings put safely away. It had been a long day with little food and sleep and I wanted my chair and my pipe and a bottle of wine.

I turned the handle and pushed but the door would not

budge, even with gentle pressure, so I pushed a bit harder and put my shoulder to it. It still would not move.

I turned to Ned. 'Time for your skills, I think.'

'Let me see,' he said, as we swopped places. He tested the door and then the frame, picking small lumps out with his fingers. 'Rotten,' he announced, and then he pulled out his knife and began to dig around where the lock fitted into the frame.

It took just a minute or so to chisel the wood down to the receiving bolt, which he then forced back by levering with his knife.

'Push it now,' I said, readying myself.

He pushed and the door swung open but then it smacked against something, causing things to crash to the ground — so much for stealth and secrecy. Ned pushed again and we scrambled in, over empty boxes and crates, which had been stacked up behind the door, and we had just tipped them all over, giving advance warning of our arrival.

I heard a shout as we gained entrance and then another crash and bang from the front of the storehouse and then calls to make haste.

Ned and I kicked some more boxes out of the way but some had fallen into the narrow corridor, which hampered us. At the end of the corridor, another door blocked our way, but this one looked flimsy. Ned forced his way through the boxes and came up to the door, lifted the latch and put his shoulder to it straight away. It did not move.

'Let me,' I said, as I raised my leg and kicked the door by the latch; then Ned joined me and we both kicked, now no longer worrying about making a noise. We aimed for the weak spots and continued kicking until the wood began to splinter, then as the door finally opened, we heard a clatter as the bars, which they had placed as props, fell away. We entered the storage area and ahead of us, I could see the double doors of the river entrance wide open. We ran over and as we got to the opening, I could see the grey outline of a wherry moving away from the landing stage; it passed at an angle away from us, heading down river and I could see one man rowing hard, putting his back into it but two more figures sat in the stern, one with a hand upon the other. A head turned and I locked eyes with Nicholas Cummings.

CHAPTER 23

I stared at the wherry for perhaps two seconds before my mind found the solution.

'Quick Ned. The Inn. Find a waterman, either sober or drunk, and I'll pay him a guinea if he comes now.'

Ned ran, leaving me to watch the wherry as the oars plunged into the slate grey waters, slowly drawing away. Cummings turned his head back to the oarsman, his hand still on the huddled form beside him and I wondered as to the identity of yet another Jacobite who needed to get away; for beyond any doubt, Cummings now knew what had befallen the O'Rourkes and Armitage last night.

I heard footsteps behind me and Ned came running up with a rough looking man of about thirty years, behind them, a group poured out of the Inn and into the lane, to view the madmen who would pay a guinea for a trip on the Thames.

The waterman caught up a mooring rope and stepped in, inviting us to do the same but in the foul-mouthed common discourse normal for one in that particular trade.

'Where to?' asked the waterman, as he settled his oars.

'Down, a wherry just left from here and we would wish to catch up with it,' I replied, sitting down in the seat. 'So, the sooner you catch up with it, the quicker you'll have your money.'

'Then light that lamp there, 'cause I ain't running on this river at night wivout it. There be a flint in that locker there,' and he indicated a small compartment beside me. 'Why you want to catch up wiv it anyway?' he asked.

'The man on board is a murderer,' I replied, giving Ned the flint.

'You ain't constables, so who is yer?'

'Crown Officers,' replied Ned. 'That is all you need to know.'

I looked at Ned and raised an eyebrow but he just gave a grin.

'Crown Officers, eh? Well, as long as the crown pays me a guinea, it don't worry me much.'

The man quickly set to a rhythm, sculling at a pace that I suspected he could keep up for hours. The river was choppy with little wavelets that slapped against the side of the boat as we moved through the water, surging with the oarsman's pull, gliding with the recover. The oars cut into the surface with a splash, a grunt on the pull and the oars lifted out, water dripping from the blades before plunging back in again as the stroke began anew.

Being low on the surface of the river at night made for an interesting experience, the barges and boats this side of the bridge lay scattered upon the surface as they rested for the night, there were no ships, as they could not pass between the starlings, but even so, there were still a large number of obstacles to avoid. Our waterman seemed to know his business, keeping on a steady course and changing direction in plenty of time.

Though nighttime, the grey light gave enough illumination to see reasonably well, the night lanterns indicating the positions of the boats at anchor, the larger vessels that travelled inland to Richmond and beyond, with most of the smaller vessels moored up along the shore.

I looked hard, trying to spy the boat that carried Cummings, watching for a wake that would indicate the passing of a boat, looking for a shadow moving sleekly across the water.

The lights from the shore glowed a yellow-orange but all

sense of identification, all sense of landmarks were lost from our vantage point on the water and I had difficulty in judging our progress. I hoped our waterman knew his place on the river better than we did and that he knew its moods, as often I had heard tell that the Thames was a living breathing entity, ill-used by those who worked upon its surface.

The river gave off a pungent odour: I could smell the salt of the sea, of vegetation, of decomposition, the refuse of people and beasts. Occasionally the smell became rank as if passing through a miasma and I held my breath not daring to inhale the foul discharges that assailed my nostrils. We passed carcasses of dead animals, bloated from putrefaction, rolling on the waves, the prow of the boat nudging them aside as we passed by. The unearthly silence, apart from the rhythmic slap of the oars, seemed strange as if the night had sucked up all forms of sound, storing it, ready to release it at the coming of the day. The river seemed to sense our urgency, seemed to know the tension in our bodies, in our souls, as it gave hissing noises from the cut of the boat as it knifed through, pushing the water to the side, calling out its protest at being disturbed by those who yearned to tame it.

The flow of the river and the muscled arms of our oarsman, carried us along on the ebb tide and the outgoing water made it easy to journey, but Cummings's boat had the same advantage.

'Where do you think he'll land?' asked Ned, gazing at the Southwark bank.

'I wish I knew,' I replied, looking towards the northern side. 'If I were he, I'd be looking to leave the country as I would be doubly damned as a murderer and a rebel.'

'He could cross to Southwark and make his way to the Kent ports.'

'He could, but he could have done that earlier. Why take

refuge in that storehouse all day when he could have crossed the river and taken refuge over there, or be halfway to the Kent ports by now?'

'He wanted to be close to Morgan?'

'No, messages could have been passed just as easily and he would have been safer. There's some reason to stay this side.'

'He worked in shipping,' said Ned. 'He knows ships, he knows the itineraries.'

'True, you're thinking that he has arranged passage in one?'

'Possibly, but nothing is moving now, the tide is right but it's night and nothing of the size of a sea-going vessel will leave now. It would be too dangerous.'

'No but the next tide will be in daylight. Do not forget that we have disturbed him. I'll wager that he would have stayed there until morning but we forced his hand and made him flee precipitously.'

'That makes sense; so if we don't catch up with him, we just have to discover which ships are leaving tomorrow.'

'Ships, boats, barges, wherries, any number of vessels in truth. He could even go further down the river to Wapping or beyond, to some ship moored closer to the sea.'

'Then we have to catch up with him.'

'We do,' I said, and it sounded a finality.

The boat ploughed on, the pace steady but fast, the oars rising and falling, the slaps of water more noticeable now as our tension grew. Our eyes tried hard to pierce the gloom, still looking for that elusive shadow to indicate a boat on the move.

We must have travelled over a mile by now and still no sign of Cummings and I began to feel that we had lost him, that he had already gained access to the shore somewhere behind us and that he now stood there, laughing, as he watched us pull by but then Ned grabbed my arm and pointed.

'Look! There!'

I snapped my head around to where he pointed, just ahead of us on our left side, closer to the shore. I could see a shadow moving low in the water about fifty yards ahead of us, with tiny ripples of reflected light as something disturbed the surface and as I watched it began to angle in towards the shore and the Old Swann Stairs.

Until now, I had not really noticed what loomed large in front of us, but now I did. Hundreds of small lights seemed to be winking at us from houses that lined the side of the bridge, about two hundred yards ahead of us with the distance diminishing rapidly.

I signalled to our oarsman to show that we had found our boat and he turned his head to look.

'I'll get you to the stairs ahead of 'im, don't you worry,' he said, turning inshore and pulling hard.

I could immediately sense that we were moving faster, as if we were in a sprint race and we were stretching to reach the finishing line. We closed rapidly with the boat ahead, cutting across his wake and then moving up alongside.

'Cummings,' I yelled, my hands cupping my mouth to direct my voice. 'Give way now and come with us. It is all over.'

I could see Cummings as he looked venomously towards us, then he raised his arm and pointed. I saw a spark and then heard the report of a pistol firing, its barrel spouting flame and lead, a puff of smoke expanding into the night air. The shot went wide, the movement of the boats thankfully making aiming difficult.

Our oarsman had immediately stopped rowing, ducked his head and protected himself with his arms. Cummings boat surged ahead and then straightened away from the shore and towards the bridge. Ned swore loudly and shook his fist.

'Do not worry, Ned, we'll have him soon enough.'

'Soon enough may not be soon enough; he's going for the bridge.'

I leant forward to our rower. 'After them,' I yelled.

The waterman shook his head. 'Dangerous by day, suicide by night,' he called back. 'And you never mentioned that I might be shot!'

'Remiss of me, I apologise. Now, another guinea if you just follow them.'

'You realise what it's like?'

'No, I've never done it, have you?'

'Yes, several times but each time I was lucky.'

'Then you can be lucky again. An extra guinea to do something you have already done.'

'Not at night, I ain't.'

I waited a moment. 'An extra guinea,' I repeated.

'Oh, hell!' he said, as he picked up the oars. 'Just don't blame me if you end up dead.'

Ned turned to look at me as if I were mad but then he grinned, anticipating the excitement and the ale he would be bought on the back of the story of shooting the bridge at night.

Shooting the Bridge was a sport loved by river watchers as the watermen tried to ride the racing waters that flowed between the starlings, the drop between the two levels being anything up to six or seven feet at times and I just prayed that I only had to worry about a mere few inches, for many had perished in the tumult that resulted from such discrepancies.

We gathered speed, following in the wake of Cummings's boat. Now I could hear the rumble beneath the bridge as the waters failed to run true. There came a low rushing noise the closer we got, like the crashing of a waterfall, but many of them as each span of the bridge had its own singular one, which resulted in a cacophony of noise. I had stood upon the bridge and had watched from the bank but the noise I heard then did not resemble the noise I heard now.

Our oarsman angled our boat away from Cummings in order to take a separate span of arch as two boats going through the same arch could only end up with the death of us all. The thought of going over the edge frightened me, for to capsize meant certain death as no one would be able to come to our rescue, our bodies would just drift on the current into the Pool to lay amongst the ships there, to be found floating in the morning as daylight breaches the horizon.

Suddenly the flow of the water increased in pace, pulling us inexorably towards the bridge, as if we were in a millrace with no hope of breaking free. Ned and I were helpless, we could only hold on and give ourselves to the expertise of our waterman, his skill and knowledge our only salvation. With deft touches of the oars, he kept the boat straight within the current, just a few yards to the right of Cummings, whose oarsman had noticeably less skill than ours and seemed to be struggling to remain on a true course.

Cummings's boat twisted and gyrated against the forces of nature, the oar strokes haphazard and panicked. I watched as the aft end slewed around, the pressure of the water flow not now on the stern but against the side, the rower needed to make the adjustments instantly, otherwise the boat would be lost in the maelstrom on the far side of the bridge.

The adjustment required did not occur and I gripped the side of our boat with my hand until the knuckles turned white, my grip strong and unbreakable as I watched Cummings's boat, slowly at first, turn and twist and buck before the roll began, against which, there was no hope of retrieval. The collision with the stone base now inevitable, the starling that supported the pillars of the bridge. The narrowness of the gap allowed for no deviation from the straight and true and Cummings's boat now hit it sideways and despite the noise of the water rushing over the edge, I could hear the timbers of the boat crack and split under the impact. The boat twisted again as the flow of the river pushed the bow end up onto the starling and then it began to turn, the aft end dipping below the surface, then the whole boat suddenly jerked and flipped, casting the occupants into the unforgiving depths, just on the edge where the water plunged into tumults and eddies and whirlpools on the far side.

We were helpless as we watched just a few yards behind and to the side and my mouth suddenly became dry, feeling a nausea in my stomach, knowing that what we had just witnessed could happen to us too. I braced myself for the inevitable disaster and I stole a quick look at Ned who sat transfixed and wide-eyed in excitement; I, on the other hand, was transfixed by terror. I closed my eyes as the flow of the water took us in its grip, my heart bounding in my chest as if it were ready to burst asunder. I did that thing that any mortal would do and I prayed to any god to protect me from death and destruction. I felt my ears buffeted from the sound reflected against the stone and I sensed the narrowness of the passage that we were trying to pass through. I opened my eyes and ahead of me, I could see the waterman wearing an expression of exhilaration and wonder. Straight and true, our boat ploughed between the starlings, racing at a speed I could hardly believe possible. The prow hit the edge of the drop and sailed over, bringing the rest of our boat with it, so that for a brief half-second it seemed as if we were flying like a bird on the air, wings outstretched, gliding and free of the constraints of the earth.

We crashed into the maelstrom with a bone-jarring crack as the hull met the water, the spray soaking us, our boat awash with river water but we were alive and floating and our oarsman gave a whoop of glee, then he screamed success in an outburst of unrestrained emotion.

Ned grabbed my hand, gripped it tightly and then threw his head back, yelling defiance and relief into the night air. I joined him and all three of us poured out a passion that went against our normal restraint.

For those few seconds I had no reason to think of Cummings and dwell on his fate, being so immersed in my own experience, but now my mind switched and I looked to the span of the bridge that he had traversed and saw the silhouetted wreckage of the boat, upturned and floating silently away. Of its occupants, I could see no sign at all.

I congratulated our waterman for his success, at that moment not realising how great that success was, in shooting London Bridge in the dark of night, and bid him to regain his senses so that we could search for Cummings.

Still grinning from his escape, he picked up the oars and began to turn the boat, his vigour renewed, his excitement undiminished.

We came before the span and he backed his oars to remain static in the flow as all three of us leant our eyes to the task. I scanned what I could of the surface, seeking a denser shadow, which might indicate a person. Slowly the waterman allowed our boat to drift with the current, allowing that anything would float in the same direction and that we should eventually come upon them.

Following this tactic, I first spied the anomaly on the river's surface, just ahead of us to my left-hand side. The boat eased towards it until we came alongside and I could reach out and grab hold. The body drifted face down and I managed to roll it slightly, and saw the features of Cummings looking back at me. I heard him splutter and gasp and so I held on tightly and together with Ned, we managed to drag him aboard, laying him down, groaning, on the wooden boards at our feet.

'There,' cried Ned. 'There's the other.'

I turned to the opposite side and there too floated a form just a few feet away, rolling in the current, the flow taking it steadily away. Our rower cast his eyes over his shoulder and then guided us, bringing us alongside. Ned leant over the side and managed to grab hold of the sodden lump and pull it towards us. I could see that the body was face down too but the weight of the clothes appeared to be dragging it under. Both Ned and I wrestled the body from the grip of the river just in time, I believe, as we hauled it in without grace and then dragged it over the side and dumped it besides Cummings in the bottom of the boat.

Then I stared. Shocked. Uncomprehending, at the gentle face of Elizabeth Thompson.

Her eyes were open, unblinking; her face, pale as ivory; her lips, blue as if bruised. She was not breathing. She lay there, unmoving in death.

'Get the water out of 'er.' yelled the waterman. 'Turn 'er an' press 'er back.'

She lay at my feet so I leant forward, put my arm beneath her neck and my other I slipped beneath her waist and pulled her up onto my bent legs. I turned her over so that her face dipped below my legs.

'Push on her back, Ned,' I yelled. 'Push hard; get the river out of her.'

I held her face with my left hand as Ned pressed down hard, compressing her chest against my thighs.

'Harder, Ned,' I said, as I felt a little dribble go onto my hand.

I felt the pressure on my legs as he gave a particularly firm compression, which forced a large cupful of water to spew out of her. I shook her, turned her back over and willed her to breathe. I began to rub her arms, her face, I even ignored her modesty and rubbed hard on her chest, but she still did not draw breath. Then quite suddenly, I remembered something I had read only a few weeks ago, an experiment in France, which achieved a remarkable result. I had nothing to lose.

I cradled her head with my arm, lifted it up towards my face and pressed my lips to hers, a kiss without passion. Drawing in a breath, I covered her mouth with mine and blew my own breath into her, feeling a puff of air on my cheek as it escaped from her nose.

'Pinch her nose, Ned,' I ordered, as I bent to the task again.

This time, with Ned squeezing her nose, I breathed into her once more and out of the corner of my eye, I could see her chest rise, just slightly, but enough to know that the breath went into her lungs. Three more times I sent my breath into her and as I inhaled to begin the fourth, she gasped, her eyes blinked and then she gasped again and then lurched to the side, her head away from me and vomited a stream of water and bile into the well of the boat.

'Make for the shore, man, as quickly as possible,' I said, desperate to get Elizabeth Thompson back on dry land.

'What about the other rower?' asked Ned, now returned to casting his eyes upon the surface.

'Later, we will look for him later.'

*

I carried Elizabeth up Billingsgate stairs onto the wharf, her head nestling against my shoulder, her arm languid about my neck. Ned followed with Cummings; his hands restrained with a short length of rope. A crowd had gathered, all of them

278

watchmen, guarding the warehouses for their respective owners, all concerned as to the welfare of the young lady I carried and curious as to the reason why a man came with her, bound about the wrists.

Instead of seeking the closest place to lay Elizabeth down, I hurried along the wharf to her father's warehouse, thinking that she would be more at ease in a familiar environment. Cummings might not find the familiarity conducive but Ned marched him along behind. The waterman, keen not to lose his money, followed closely on our heels.

I could see a watchman standing on the wharf watching our progress, and as we closed, I realised I recognised him; Loxley looked bemused until I quickly appraised him of the situation, allowing him a few moments contemplating Cummings in all his ignominy, before he hastily opened the door to allow us entry.

'Mr Gutteridge is still here,' said Loxley, as he guided us inside. 'He'll want to know what's going on.'

'Then please fetch him,' I replied. 'But first, find dry blankets for Miss Thompson,' I said, putting her down, leaning her back against a crate.

'What is all that noise, Loxley?' came a voice from the offices above.

'It's Miss Thompson,' cried Loxley. 'She's fair drowned, she is, sir.'

'What? What the devil do you mean?'

A tall thin man of around fifty years of age, dressed in just a waistcoat and breeches came hurrying down the steps. He wore no wig, his head bald apart from a halo of grey running from ear to ear. He took in the tableau before him, light coming from Loxley's lantern.

'Elizabeth! What has happened?' he said, hurrying towards her. 'And Cummings? What is this?' he added, seeing his bedraggled chief clerk with his wrists tied.

Gutteridge returned his attention to Elizabeth. 'Blankets, damn you, Loxley. The poor lass is freezing.'

Loxley and another of their watchman ran off to get the blankets as Gutteridge knelt down and began to help Elizabeth out of her sodden outer garments. I refrained from assisting when I caught sight of Gutteridge's dangerous eyes.

'My name is Richard Hopgood, Mr Gutteridge,' I said. 'I have spent the last few days trying to speak with you. This is Mr Edward Tripp who is working with me.'

'Ah, Hopgood,' he said, depositing Elizabeth's cape and jacket onto the floor. He returned his attention to her gown but then hesitated. 'I believe I may have to leave things here,' he added, withdrawing his hands.

Loxley and the watchman appeared with blankets, maybe even horse blankets but at least they were dry. Gutteridge wrapped Elizabeth quickly but Cummings trembled and shivered without the luxury of a blanket.

'I think you may have to explain yourself, Hopgood. I believe you were seeking Thomas's murderer.'

I looked at him sharply. He did not say Sorley's, but Thomas's murderer.

Elizabeth stirred and pulled the blankets tight about her. 'It was Cummings,' she answered, sniffing.

'What?' exclaimed Gutteridge.

'Mr Hopgood will tell you,' she replied. 'He knows it all.'

Gutteridge snapped his head around. 'Tell me,' he said, almost an order.

I quickly explained what I knew and watched as Gutteridge's face changed from one of bemusement to become hard and fierce as he stared at Cummings and I wondered what emotion was running through his body, and what that might signify. I decided not to press for an answer to that, as I needed to hear what Elizabeth had to say, so turned my attention straight back to her. 'But I do not quite know all,' I said, placing my hand on her shoulder. 'How did you come to be with Cummings on that boat?'

She looked up at me and then sneaked a hand from out of the blanket and placed it on mine. She shivered a little and then became still once more. 'Thank you, Mr Hopgood. You have saved my life in more ways than one. Cummings deceived me. A note came purporting to be from my father, bidding me to meet with him at St Mary Le Strand. I went but did not meet with my father. Instead, Cummings waited there.'

She looked at me and then over towards Cummings.

'He took hold of me, grabbed me; I tried to run but he prevented me and then he showed a pistol he had upon him, warning me to do as he said.'

Cummings avoided her look and stared at the floor as if he had no wish to hear what she said.

'He took me down a lane to a small warehouse, pushed me inside and then he lay siege, apologising and professing his love and devotion for me; said he intended to take me away so that we could be together, for always.'

I felt her hand grip me tightly as she related the events.

'He kept apologising, even though he still had that pistol, said that I would come to thank him in the end and that I would learn to love him as he loves me.' She turned directly to look into my eyes. 'Mr Hopgood, I never gave him any encouragement at all. I only ever treated him with the respect due to him. I tried to be friendly but gave no encouragement for anything else. He said we were going to Spain first and then we would go to live in France and raise our children together.'

She shivered again and tried to make herself small as she

finished her shocking discourse and I saw her eyes water and she subdued a sob. I turned my head to look at Cummings who steadfastly refused to meet my gaze. I felt nothing but contempt for him.

Gutteridge kept shaking his head, hardly able to bear what Elizabeth described. He stood up and took a step towards Cummings who still stared at the floor. Ned quickly appraised the situation and stepped to intercept Gutteridge.

'No, sir.' said Ned, shaking his head. 'If you have a go at him then there might not be much left for the judges. You would regret it anyway, he's not worth it.'

Gutteridge nodded, took a deep breath and unclenched his fists. 'Maybe you are right,' he said, stepping back.

Ned relaxed a little and then stood back just as Gutteridge took another step forward and bunching his fist, punched Cummings hard on the side of his face, toppling him to the side with the force of the blow.

'I had second thoughts,' explained Gutteridge. 'I decided I would not regret it.'

Ned grinned. 'No, I wouldn't have either, in truth,' he said, agreeing.

'He began by killing Thomas and putting him into the river,' added Gutteridge, 'and it ended with the river turning Cummings out of that boat. The Thames has always been a river of retribution but I wanted mine.'

I could see our waterman waiting, listening and I suspect, he had not had a night like this for many a long year.

'Ned, will you go with our friend to look for the rower of Cummings's boat?'

'Of course, sir. If you're sure that is?'

I nodded. 'Yes, please find him.'

'Wot about my fee?' said the waterman.

'You are up to two guineas, I believe, go with Ned and find the missing man and I will make it three.'

He could not turn down the prospect of earning three guineas, a rare opportunity for a waterman and he dragged Ned out of the warehouse and onto the wharf in short order, in a hurry to fetch the body and receive his money.

I turned my attention back to Gutteridge. 'You did everything you could to avoid my questions,' I said, still kneeling by Elizabeth. 'Why?' I asked.' I thought for a time that you might have killed Thomas. You were the last to see him that night.'

'Yes, but I only saw him as I left. He said he wished to talk to me but I said to leave it until the next day. I had a meeting to attend at The Salutation. I wish now that I had delayed and allowed him to talk, if I had, he may still be alive. I would never wish harm on Thomas, Hopgood, never.'

'Then why?'

'In truth, I mourned for him. I had no wish to discuss him with anyone.'

'In mourning? For a clerk?'

'Not only my clerk, Hopgood. It is a long story but Thomas was more a son to me, a son I never had. His mother and I know each other well.'

I held up a hand. 'His mother? I can recall Elizabeth telling me a little.'

'Maybe, but she does not know it all. Thomas came from Scotland, like his mother. Years ago, I had a commission as a junior officer on a ship sent north, in seventeen nineteen, in fact, to the castle of Eilean Donan on Loch Alsh. There was a Jacobean revolt and we were sent to put it down. I had to take a party of men ashore and one of them shot Thomas's father against my orders. I feared what would happen to his mother, being a pretty thing, should the crew and more soldiers come ashore. She would have been a spoil of war. I helped her and Thomas come south, to Devon, to settle and start a new life. There is more, obviously but that is the gist of it. It does not need me to tell you that I have been a frequent visitor to Devon ever since. When Thomas wanted to come to London, I offered him a place here, though we decided to keep our relationship secret. I believe he even kept that secret from his closest friends,' he said, looking at Elizabeth sadly. 'I now have to travel to Devon to break the news to his mother, a task I am not looking forward to.'

Elizabeth looked at him with eyes wide. 'He never said anything, William. I... we, did not know. I just wished we did.'

'He chose to keep our relationship secret, Elizabeth, and I went along with it. He may not have been my son, nor his mother my wife, but I loved them both and they would have been both had they wanted it.'

'I am so sorry, William,' said Elizabeth, from her cocoon of blankets.

I creased up my brow. 'So you knew he was a Jacobite?'

'I did,' confessed Gutteridge, 'but I did not know he was involved with them here in London and I certainly did not know he was involved with scum like him,' he added, pointing his finger at Cummings. 'And the man who killed him has been working for me. Why, Cummings? Why did you do it?'

Cummings now sat with his back against a box. He looked at Gutteridge and then spat on the floor. He looked up at that point and then jabbed his hands towards Elizabeth. 'She belongs to me and no one else!'

I heard a sharp intake of breath come from Gutteridge and I turned my head and shook it briefly.

'You are mad,' said Gutteridge to Cummings.

I could not but agree with him.

*

Ned returned after perhaps an hour with the news that the body had been found hard up against the hull of a ship in the Pool. They had left him in a cart at the end of the wharf, awaiting identification before someone decides what to do with him.

'Anatomists,' reckoned Ned with a grin. 'Just what he deserves.'

Gutteridge had taken Elizabeth home to the safety of her father and then had graciously sent his carriage back for us to convey Cummings to Newgate.

The waterman stood before me with his hand outstretched waiting for payment. 'You know,' he said. 'No one will ever believe that I took the bridge at night. No one. It ain't thought possible but I dun it, didn't I?'

'You did,' I replied, handing the money over. 'And if ever you need proof, then I will gladly vouch for you.'

'I may hold you to that, sir; but promise me something.'

I raised my eyebrows in question.

'Never ask me to do it again,' he said, clamping his hand shut on the coins.

EPILOGUE

Jarmin and I sat nursing a pot of ale each in The Swan, Newgate Street, just opposite the prison. It would have been impossible to squeeze another man into the confines of the tavern and we were lucky to get a table. The pot-boys and girls were hard-pressed to keep up with the demand, hurrying with jugs in both hands between the tables. Outside, the crowds were gathering to witness the final journey of the condemned. St Sepulchre's bell had been ringing out its mournful toll since six o'clock that morning, it's slow cumbersome sound giving voice to the gravity of the proceedings to come, and only rang its last at ten, just a short while ago, drawing the crowds from across London. Two horse-drawn open carts were waiting to carry the burden assigned. Soldiers from the militia stood formally, in effect, cordoning off the door through which the prisoners would come, giving some protection from the crowd — at least to begin with. The Cavalry had yet to get into position.

Within the tavern and without, it seemed as if a fair had come to the city. Londoners were giving voice to high levels of excitement and anticipation in respect to the forthcoming entertainment. Street hawkers peddled food, gin and trinkets, making the most of the situation, as were the pickpockets: I had already witnessed several of these at their trade but more fool the men and women who came to this type of gathering and did not take appropriate precaution of their person.

'You will give the proposal serious consideration?' asked

Jarmin, as he returned the pot to the table.

I adopted a relaxed posture whilst sitting on the bench, my back to the wall. 'I will,' I replied. 'There is much to think upon, though Newcastle was most persuasive.'

'Then I will not burden you with more entreaties as I know you will not look kindly on me should I try to convince you.'

The proposal happened to be the one I most feared and the one that I would have the most difficulty in refusing, especially now, after I had gone to Jarmin to seek his assistance following my visit to O'Rourkes'. Newcastle would have me be a man under him, to undertake duties much like Jarmin, with access to information and resources. I had convinced myself that I had no wish to become an intelligencer, but now, having dipped my toe into the intrigues involved, I was not quite so sure that I wished to remain apart.

'Cummings shot Blake,' I said, adding a negative to the conversation.

'He did but Blake survives and will make a full recovery. It is the nature of our work that these things happen but so it is with yours. There are very little differences between the dangers we both face.'

'And Monk?'

Jarmin laughed. 'That young man has a lot to make up for. I am yet to decide what sanction I will employ. Though I'll not dismiss him, not yet anyways.'

I smiled. 'You cannot place all the blame on Monk; some of it you can put on me. Tell me truly, Jarmin,' I asked, changing the subject. 'Are you satisfied with the outcome?'

'I am and I am not,' he said, after a brief period of thought. 'We have nullified one part of the threat against us, though there are more dangers out there to be discovered. The fact that we have removed Cummings and his group is satisfying, but I am still not satisfied. I strive to remove all threats.'

'That is an impossible hope.'

'I know but it is what drives me. We remove pieces bit by bit. We have now removed an important element: Cummings used his position at the shipping company to smuggle in arms for distribution to sympathisers up and down the country, he falsified manifests and he arranged and re-routed ships to call at appropriate ports to take on these arms in innocent importation. The O'Rourkes then took those arms and stored them until Cummings again arranged for them to be moved on.'

'What about David Morgan?'

'Ah, yes. Morgan. Unfortunately, with his contacts, he is untouchable at the moment.'

'Which is why you are not satisfied?'

'Partly. The thing is, we put our finger in one hole to stop the leak only for another to open up elsewhere. The likes of Beaufort, Sir John Hynde Cotton and Sir Watkin Williams-Wynn will use Morgan to open other avenues, so we must always be on our guard.'

I took a mouthful of ale and looked through the window, seeing some movement, which indicated that the procession was soon to begin. Jarmin saw it too but grabbed the arm of a passing pot-girl and ordered two more. 'Plenty of time yet, Hopgood,' he explained. 'Another half an hour at least before we need to take our positions.'

Our positions were at the rear of the procession as part of the protective screen behind the foot soldiers, along with the duke's men, ostensibly, not part of the procession, although involved in the procession.

Nine were to be hanged today: two men, guilty of burglary; one woman, guilty of killing her husband, although I believe the man had grievously abused her; the two O'Rourke brothers, guilty of treason, murder and extortion; Evans, guilty of killing Fulton's brother as well as treason; a man guilty of stealing lead; Abe Gordon, who somehow avoided the gaol fever and Nicholas Cummings, guilty of treason, murder, attempted murder and the abduction of Elizabeth Thompson.

Armitage turned King's evidence, pouring out his soul in an attempt to preserve his life, which in his case, he succeeded, but he had been sentenced to transportation to America for seven years; the printers in his employ were given time in Bridewell with hard labour, the same with Musgrave and the other couriers and protectors.

I never enjoyed seeing anyone on the hanging tree even though their crimes sometimes warranted it, but in Cummings's case, I felt no sympathy. Liam O'Rourke and Cummings had attacked Thomas Sorley as he left the warehouse on the evening he died, as Liam had beaten him, Cummings watched with malicious glee, and from the account given by O'Rourke, Cummings then plunged a knife into the defenceless young man's back. They then put him on a handcart and took him to a boat, then rowed him out into the Pool and tipped him into the river. The O'Rourkes had murdered other men, as detailed by the gang members desperate to save their own lives, most of them relating to war between the competing gangs in the slums. The O'Rourkes were hard men living hard lives and acknowledged that they risked being caught and what the likely outcome would be, but Cummings had prospects, he had employment, he had a comfortable life, yet he wanted the unobtainable and he would do anything he could to get it. If his crime had been solely that of a political nature, then I could understand and even sympathise; however, his obsession with Elizabeth and what he did to her, and Joseph, and Thomas, made sympathy impossible. He decided he would do anything to possess her, and to that purpose, he stole the items found on Joseph Morton, placed them in the coat pocket and then brought Gutteridge's attention to the theft, keeping the miniature portrait in his possession. He killed Thomas Sorley because Thomas saw the portrait and he did not want to risk being suspected of taking it, as he thought Sorely would tell Gutteridge that he had it in his possession, so he used Liam O'Rourke, saying to him that Thomas was about to betray them to the authorities. He had purchased a cabin in a ship leaving the Pool for Spain that day, negotiated by the man who died in the river. No one mentioned Morgan's name, though Jarmin suspected that he arranged it all. He forged the note from Jonathan Thompson, which drew Elizabeth to St Mary Le Strand, enabling him to take her captive and force her to go with him, and she would undoubtedly have suffered a serious assault upon her person. Cummings's confession had taken several days, though I had not taken part in it.

Jarmin and I finished our drinks and then squeezed through the crowd towards our horses. Most of the prisoners were already on the carts, their hands bound at the wrists and a binding wrapped around the upper arms and body leaving movement from just the elbows and below. Their nooses were loose about their necks, the end of the ropes wound about their bodies. Their coffins, their eternal home, were stacked beside them. I mounted my horse and watched as the final prisoners came out: the O'Rourkes and Cummings. Cummings wept and did not mount the cart willingly, crying out his protest and denying his guilt. The O'Rourke brothers found it amusing, as did the crowd, as they jeered and laughed at Cummings's antics.

Cavalry now surrounded the carts with the Ordinary of Newgate reciting prayers for the condemned, riding with the prisoners in the rearmost cart. The Marshall took up his position upon his horse behind the mounted troops, along with other dignitaries and then behind them, foot soldiers. Jarmin and I mounted our horses and waited with the other men from the duke's retinue as the procession set off.

The crowds were thick along the pavement of Newgate Street and vocal in either their condemnation or support of the prisoners. The woman, Margaret Tinal, seemed to be garnering the most support, the crowd calling and yelling, citing the injustice of her sentence, hoping to save her from the gallows.

As we approached the Church of St Sepulchre, the bell began to toll once again and the churchman stood with a bible in his hands, reading the scripture as the two carts passed by; whether the condemned heard or took succour from it, I did not know but his voice rose above that of the crowd.

Slowly, oh so slowly, we moved forward and it seemed as if we were moving inch by inch, many of the crowd walking with us, not daring to miss a moment of the entertainment.

Up Snow Hill and the toll of the church bell rang out just once more and then silenced but here the crowds thinned a little, allowing us to move more quickly but we slowed again as we entered Holborn. By now, the crowd had started to throw things at the prisoners, most of it aimed at Cummings, as all those in the street would be aware of his crimes, how he kidnapped a young lady for his own immoral purposes; he would be the main target for their venom. Rotting fruit, excrement, stones and putrefying meat, he had it all hurled at him and his predicament prevented him from avoiding the deluge. The O'Rourke brothers tried to move away and hurled their own abuses at him, making his last hours as uncomfortable as could be. Evans did likewise and Cummings could only wallow in misery and self-loathing.

The familiar sights of Holborn disappeared behind us and we

came to St Giles and Broad Street, where the crowds began to thicken again and became raucous as the slums' inhabitants came out to give their farewells to the O'Rourkes, Evans, Abe Gordon and the two burglars, who had made their homes there. The people supported those felons vociferously but I doubt they would have wanted them back in their midst.

Traditionally, just before we entered Oxford Street, the procession stopped, it had taken something over an hour to get to this point and the time for refreshment had arrived, a brief interlude at The Crown, sometimes called The Bowl Inn. Each prisoner received a bowl of wine to drink, the aim being to nullify the senses, so they would be more pliable as they approached journey's end. The hiatus took perhaps ten minutes as the prisoners emptied the bowls, however, Cummings just stood there, not drinking, as if to partake would be to acknowledge his fate. Liam soon relieved him of it and drunk it down in just a few short gulps. The crowd cheered and Liam acknowledged them by dropping the bowl over the side of the cart: a lucky charm for the fortunate person who claimed it.

The procession lurched down Oxford Street, the houses crammed full of spectators, some of whom had paid a shilling or two to hang out of the windows to watch from a vantage point. With the throng now well lubricated, the singing began and for most of them it was an occasion to celebrate, a show put on just for them and they were determined to enjoy every minute of the spectacle.

Cummings continually received the ire of the crowd and I still could not find any sympathy for his treatment. He began to goad the crowd, spitting expletives at them, cursing them, spewing his hatred for them into their faces and they retaliated and it did occur to me that he did it in the hope that they would find a way to exact their revenge before the King did, thus saving him the ignominy of hanging.

We finally managed to travel the length of Oxford Street and now entered Tyburn Road, the last stage of the journey before reaching our destination. We were now coming into the countryside as to our right were the green fields and market gardens, so far it had taken well over two hours and it had not ended yet.

Just one more stop, one more chance for a final drink before the end arrived at Tyburn; a last chance for fortification, a last chance to dull the senses and addle the mind with alcohol. Up ahead, I could see the crowd amassing as we stopped, and this time, I noticed that Cummings drank his down and then proffered his bowl for a second, needless to say, this was denied as he had denied Thomas Sorley his life and Joseph Morton and Elizabeth Thompson their Liberty.

The procession moved on relentlessly towards the Tyburn Tree, now just a few minutes away and the crowd now began to quieten down, not so much for respect to the condemned but so that they might not miss the reactions of the prisoners as they saw what awaited them.

The Tree came into view, the three-sided gallows had room for eight victims along each side, twenty-four in all, should that number be required but today it would support just nine, five on one side, four on another.

Behind the gallows, temporary seating in a gallery had been erected, called Mother Procter's Pews, and for two shillings you could take a seat but the best seats could cost as much as a few pounds, depending on who was to be turned off; the more infamous the victims, the higher the cost and the seats were always full.

Already the printers had been at work, as last night the prisoners were making their peace with God. The clerk of the ordinary took their last statements and these were quickly printed and were now for sale for a few pennies each. A memento of the day that people read and showed until, like the lives of its speakers, they faded and disintegrated, turning to dust.

The carts rolled forward and then turned beneath the gallows and finally the crowd became silent as the official began to read out the names of the condemned and to relate their crimes, asking each if they wished to confess to God at this last opportunity for redemption. The first four men answered, confessing their guilt and asking for forgiveness and sending farewells to family and friends, then the official read the fifth name out, Margaret Tinal and then the Marshall held up his hand and pulled out a document. He read the document out loud, saying simply and without emotion that her sentence of death had been commuted and that instead, she would be transported to America, on the next ship available.

Margaret closed her eyes in a silent prayer of thanks and then she sunk to her knees as the crowd cheered and screamed and waved. The hangman climbed onto the cart and removed the noose from her neck and then helped her down to await her journey back to Newgate and the next ship out of the country; a late reprieve in order to show how merciful the authorities could be, but also to show its cruelty, in allowing her to think that her time had come — the Marshall had had that document on his person since before leaving Newgate.

Evans and the O'Rourke brothers refused to confess their guilt, instead spewing vitriol at all the dignitaries in attendance, which went down well with the common people watching on.

The official called Nicholas Cummings last and as he moved his head to look at everyone around him, he said not a word. He just stared maliciously until his eyes met mine and then he spat and sneered and then he turned his head away.

The hangman then produced the hoods and calmly covered the heads of the condemned but the O'Rourke brothers refused, shaking their heads and saying that they wished to see the world out.

'Proceed,' shouted the Marshall, delaying no more.

The hangman unwound the ropes of the nooses from around their torsos and handed them up to his assistant to tie to the beam. When he had tied all eight firmly, the hangman locked eyes with the Marshall, who nodded, and then the carts drove slowly away, leaving the prisoners to fall off the cart, their only support now, the hempen rope about their necks, which tightened and squeezed as their bodies dropped.

I kept my eye on Cummings whose feet jerked violently as the rope reached its extension. The crowd's noise rose until the shouts were deafening: they cheered, shouted calls of derision, cries of anguish, screeches of anger, all manner of emotion poured out as though released from an enforced containment.

Cummings's body spun around under his gyrations and I could see him sucking the hood into his mouth as he fought to take a breath. His movements were panicked, a last final attempt to cling onto life as the rope tightened further. I looked at the O'Rourkes, the only ones unhooded and I saw their faces appear to puff out, the colour taking on a purplish tinge, the eyes staring and bulging, their mouths hanging open as if in a scream; already their feet were beginning to slow as the futile attempts to find the ground failed.

So far, the soldiers had kept the crowd away from the gallows, but now at a signal, the friends, the families, the loved ones rushed forward, to grab the legs of the hanging men, dragging them down further, adding their weight to that of the condemned to hasten their departure. Cries of anguish, tears of sorrow fell as the extra weight squeezed the neck harder, cutting out any hope of taking air. I saw Poll Gordon's massive weight on the end of Abe's legs and I knew that his end had already come.

One by one the hanging men ceased any form of movement and with wails of grief, those who had aided their departure released their holds, allowing the bodies to swing free, all life extinct, all pain over: all that is except for Cummings who had no loved ones, no family, no friends to help him on his way. He still moved, his feet still danced, his body still twisted against the rope at his neck. He had a light frame, so where a heavy man would die quickly, a lighter man would take longer, and Cummings was taking far longer. Several minutes had now passed since the cart drove away and the crowd watched and shouted and gesticulated and poked fun at Cummings, especially now as they saw that his member had become stiff beneath his breeches, his feet still kicking out in jerks, his body swinging and spinning under the movement.

I did not count the minutes as I watched the end of Cummings's life but the time seemed inordinately long, as though the minutes and seconds were protracted, but slowly, so slowly, the body became less mobile, the feet losing the urge to kick and then finally they stilled, as life was extinguished with the voiding of both bladder and bowels.

I looked at Jarmin and he looked at me and we both gave a nod to each other, acknowledgement that the job had been well done.

Already the melee had begun around the hanged men as relatives and friends fought for control of the bodies, trying to prevent the men from the anatomists from claiming their dues, as they waited for the ropes to be cut and the bodies lowered to the ground. I had no wish to witness the scene any further so I turned my horse away.

'Come to see me, Hopgood,' said Jarmin. 'Once you have made your decision, that is.'

I nodded. 'I will, Jarmin. I promise,' I said, as I forced my way through the crowd.

I knew Ned would be here somewhere, as he had indicated his intent to see Cummings draw his last breath, and Kitty, who wished to see Abe Gordon pay his dues for killing Peggy. They must have seen me on the horse as I could see them coming towards me.

'A bad end but no less than he deserved,' said Ned, looking up at me.

'I wonder if any man deserves to die like that,' I replied. 'But if anyone did, it would be the likes of Cummings. I switched my gaze to Kitty and saw her soft eyes looking back, a warm smile creasing her lips and I knew that we were both remembering the night of Cummings's arrest when I came to her lodgings, arriving after midnight and staying until the afternoon of the day. I had not seen her since but she did not seem to hold that against me. 'Abe Gordon has paid and let us hope that Peggy now lies easier.'

She looked up at me. 'He has and I am satisfied, Richard; though I wish it had never come to this.'

'No, I neither, but this is the way of the world we live in.'

'There are better ways.'

'There are indeed.' I hesitated a little. 'Speaking of which; do you happen to be at leisure this evening, Miss Marham?' I asked, hopefully.

'I am, sir,' she replied, with a shy downward look.

'Then may I call upon you around eight?'

'You may, sir,' she replied, now looking up, her eyes shining brightly. 'I will get in some provisions to sustain us.'

I felt my eyebrows go up and I could not help but smile back. 'Make sure she arrives home safe, Ned,' I said, as I kicked my horse forward. 'I feel I may be very hungry come this evening.'

I still had a smile with me as I trotted along the streets. Kitty had shifted my mood and I felt content with the world again.

I tied my horse to the post outside the house in Red Lyon Square and walked up the steps to the door. I had hardly knocked when the door opened and a servant ushered me inside.

Jonathon Thompson rose from his chair as I entered the room, his face a picture of eager anticipation. I nodded at the unspoken question, the reason for me being there.

I knew William Gutteridge had gone to Tyburn, though I did not see him there; he had indicated his desire to see the end of Cummings and I did not think him one to change his mind. Jonathan Thompson admitted that he had no stomach for such scenes and had stated that he would not attend; imploring me instead to come to him once the sentence had been carried out.

'Is it over then?' asked Thompson, needing verbal confirmation.

'Yes, Mr Thompson,' I replied. 'Cummings has paid his dues.'

Thompson nodded and then stepped over to a cabinet and poured four glasses of brandy. He then moved his hand to the bell-pull and tugged it. He picked up a glass, handed it to me and then raised his own in a salute.

The door opened and in walked Elizabeth and Joseph Morton, holding each other's hand.

I smiled at them, and they smiled back, as Jonathon Thompson handed them a glass each. Joseph still bore the scars of Newgate on his face and on his body. He looked thin, his features drawn and he had a weakness about him. I knew he would recover in time and more quickly under the ministrations of this house. His release came only after Cummings had been

298

found guilty, just a few days ago and he had been taken immediately into the Thompsons' care.

'Joseph and I wish to thank you, Mr Hopgood, for all that you have done. I dare not think what would have happened, if not for you,' said Elizabeth, with tears in her eyes; and I suspect not for the first time since Joseph's release.

'Miss Thompson,' I said, bowing my head in acknowledgement of her sentiment. 'Your ordeal is now at an end and I am grateful to have been of service.'

'I wish to add my thanks too, Mr Hopgood,' said Joseph, his hand still tightly holding on to Elizabeth's. 'I am only sorry that Cummings was not discovered before he murdered Thomas but we will always remember him as a friend to both of us.' He turned to Elizabeth and smiled at her. 'We are to be married, Mr Hopgood. Elizabeth and I. Something good has come out of all this in the end.'

'Then I wish you joy in your marriage,' I said, raising my glass. 'It has been hard won and I believe you both deserve it.'

Neither of them wished to know the details of Cummings's demise and I had no wish to relate what I witnessed anyway, so as soon as I finished my glass of brandy, I took my leave.

I mounted my horse and rode off: I had done what I set out to do, I had found the murderer of Thomas Sorley; but I did not ever think where that would take me and to what machinations I would be exposed. I take no pleasure in seeing a man suffer the ultimate sanction but with some men, like Cummings, there is an inevitability that at some point, they will take the long road to Tyburn.

A short dictionary of St Giles' canting language.

Backdoor games — Homosexual practices.

Barking Iron — Pistol

Bene-cove — A good man.

Bingo-boy — Drunkard.

Chink — Money, specifically coins.

Clowes — Ruffians.

Cove — Man

Cull — A whore's customer.

Diver — Pickpocket.

Doxy/Doxies — Cheap whore/s.

Drab — A sluttish whore.

Fogus — Tobacco.

Gage — A pipe and tobacco.

Glaziers — Eyes.

Heavers — Women's breasts.

Hush/Hushed — To kill/killed.

Jade — Whore.

Jenny — A small iron bar used to force open a chest or door etc.

Libken — A house to lie in. (A whore's room)

Madge — A male prostitute. A homosexual.

Making a cull easy — To kill a man.

Man-trap — A vagina.

Mumpers Hall — A drinking den for ruffians and vagabonds.

Nutmegs — Testicles.

Phyz — Face.

Piss-maker — Drunkard. A great drinker.

Rum-duke — A well set up gentleman. A handsome fellow.

Seraglio — A brothel, a house for Gentleman to get their pleasure.

Shabbaroon — A poor untidy, unkempt man. A mean spirited fellow.

Tib — A young girl.

Trull — A whore.

ABOUT THE AUTHOR

Clive Ridgway spent a number of years as a paramedic, until deciding that there must be another way of making a living. He lives in Bedfordshire in the UK with his wife, son, and dogs.

He also writes humorous fantasy under the name of Clive Mullis. The following are available in both ebook and paperback.

Banker's Draft
Scooters Yard
Under Gornstock

A River of Retribution is a work of fiction. It is set in London in 1741 and some of the characters within this novel were real people; their roles and personalities within this story are entirely fictitious. Any resemblance to actual persons, living or dead, of the other characters, or actual events, is purely coincidental. In order to write this historical novel, I have poured over numerous books and used many online resources. I apologise for any mistakes or errors, which are entirely my own.

The following is a list of the main resources I used.

Locating London's Past- John Rocque's 1746 online map of London.
Blackguardiana: or a dictionary of rogues-HathiTrust digital library.
The Gentleman's Magazine v11 1741- HathiTrust digital library.
The Chronicles of Newgate by Arthur Griffiths (Project Gutenberg)
The Old Bailey online
British History online
London in the Eighteenth Century by Jerry White
London, the Biography by Peter Ackroyd
Georgian London, into the streets by Lucy Inglis

Printed in Great Britain
by Amazon